The

Brigadier

and the

Golf Widow

Books by John Cheever

⊷§⧽⊷

THE BRIGADIER AND THE GOLF WIDOW

THE WAPSHOT SCANDAL

SOME PEOPLE, PLACES, AND THINGS THAT WILL NOT APPEAR IN
   MY NEXT NOVEL

THE HOUSEBREAKER OF SHADY HILL

THE WAPSHOT CHRONICLE

THE ENORMOUS RADIO

THE WAY SOME PEOPLE LIVE

JOHN CHEEVER

The Brigadier and the Golf Widow

HARPER & ROW, PUBLISHERS
NEW YORK, EVANSTON, AND LONDON

The stories in this collection first appeared in
The New Yorker, and the author is grateful to
the editors for their permission to reprint.

LIBRARY OF CONGRESS CATALOG CARD NUMBER: 64:20543

K-O

To Alwyn Lee

Contents

The

Brigadier

and the

Golf Widow

The Brigadier and the Golf Widow

❧❧

I WOULD NOT WANT TO BE ONE OF THOSE WRITERS WHO
begin each morning by exclaiming, "O Gogol, O Chekhov, O
Thackeray and Dickens, what would you have made of a
bomb shelter ornamented with four plaster-of-Paris ducks, a
birdbath, and three composition gnomes with long beards
and red mobcaps?" As I say, I wouldn't want to begin a day
like this, but I often wonder what the dead would have done.
But the shelter is as much a part of my landscape as the
beech and horse-chestnut trees that grow on the ridge. I can
see it from this window where I write. It was built by the
Pasterns, and stands on the acre of ground that adjoins our
property. It bulks under a veil of thin, new grass, like some
embarrassing fact of physicalness, and I think Mrs. Pastern
set out the statuary to soften its meaning. It would have been
like her. She was a pale woman. Sitting on her terrace, sitting
in her parlor, sitting anywhere, she ground an axe of self-
esteem. Offer her a cup of tea and she would say, "Why,
these cups look just like a set I gave to the Salvation Army

last year." Show her the new swimming pool and she would
say, slapping her ankle, "I suppose this must be where you
breed your gigantic mosquitoes." Hand her a chair and she
would say, "Why, it's a nice imitation of those Queen Anne
chairs I inherited from Grandmother Delancy." These trumps
were more touching than they were anything else, and seemed
to imply that the nights were long, her children ungrateful,
and her marriage bewilderingly threadbare. Twenty years
ago, she would have been known as a golf widow, and the
sum of her manner was perhaps one of bereavement. She
usually wore weeds, and a stranger watching her board a train
might have guessed that Mr. Pastern was dead, but Mr.
Pastern was far from dead. He was marching up and down
the locker room of the Grassy Brae Golf Club shouting,
"Bomb Cuba! Bomb Berlin! Let's throw a little nuclear hardware at them and show them who's boss." He was brigadier
of the club's locker-room light infantry, and at one time or
another declared war on Russia, Czechoslovakia, Yugoslavia,
and China.

It all began on an autumn afternoon—and who, after all
these centuries, can describe the fineness of an autumn day?
One might pretend never to have seen one before, or, to
more purpose, that there would never be another like it. The
clear and searching sweep of sun on the lawns was like a
climax of the year's lights. Leaves were burning somewhere
and the smoke smelled, for all its ammoniac acidity, of beginnings. The boundless blue air was stretched over the
zenith like the skin of a drum. Leaving her house one late
afternoon, Mrs. Pastern stopped to admire the October light.
It was the day to canvass for infectious hepatitis. Mrs. Pastern
had been given sixteen names, a bundle of literature, and a

printed books of receipts. It was her work to go among her neighbors and collect their checks. Her house stood on a rise of ground, and before she got into her car she looked at the houses below. Charity as she knew it was complex and reciprocal, and almost every roof she saw signified charity. Mrs. Balcolm worked for the brain. Mrs. Ten Eyke did mental health. Mrs. Trenchard worked for the blind. Mrs. Horowitz was in charge of diseases of the nose and throat. Mrs. Trempler was tuberculosis, Mrs. Surcliffe was Mothers' March of Dimes, Mrs. Craven was cancer, and Mrs. Gilkson did the kidney. Mrs. Hewlitt led the birth-control league, Mrs. Ryerson was arthritis, and way in the distance could be seen the slate roof of Ethel Littleton's house, a roof that signified gout.

Mrs. Pastern undertook the work of going from house to house with the thoughtless resignation of an honest and traditional laborer. It was her destiny; it was her life. Her mother had done it before her, and even her old grandmother had collected money for smallpox and unwed mothers. Mrs. Pastern had telephoned most of her neighbors in advance, and most of them were ready for her. She experienced none of the suspense of some poor stranger selling encyclopedias. Here and there she stayed to visit and drink a glass of sherry. The contributions were ahead of what she had got the previous year, and while the money, of course, was not hers, it excited her to stuff her kit with big checks. She stopped at the Surcliffes' after dusk, and had a Scotch-and-soda. She stayed too late, and when she left it was dark and time to go home and cook supper for her husband. "I got a hundred and sixty dollars for the hepatitis fund," she said excitedly when he walked in. "I did everybody on my list but the Blevins and the Flannagans. I want to get my kit in tomorrow morning—would you mind doing them while I cook the dinner?"

"But I don't know the Flannagans," Charlie Pastern said.

"Nobody does, but they gave me ten last year."

He was tired, he had his business worries, and the sight of his wife arranging pork chops in the broiler only seemed like an extension of a boring day. He was happy enough to take the convertible and race up the hill to the Blevins', thinking that they might give him a drink. But the Blevins were away; their maid gave him an envelope with a check in it and shut the door. Turning in at the Flannagans' driveway, he tried to remember if he had ever met them. The name encouraged him, because he always felt that he could *handle* the Irish. There was a glass pane in the front door, and through this he could see into a hallway where a plump woman with red hair was arranging flowers.

"Infectious hepatitis," he shouted heartily.

She took a good look at herself in the mirror before she turned and, walking with very small steps, started toward the door. "Oh, please come in," she said. The girlish voice was nearly a whisper. She was not a girl, he could see. Her hair was dyed, and her bloom was fading, and she must have been crowding forty, but she seemed to be one of those women who cling to the manners and graces of a pretty child of eight. "Your wife just called," she said, separating one word from another, exactly like a child. "And I am not sure that I have any cash—any *money*, that is—but if you will wait just a minute I will write you out a check if I can find my checkbook. Won't you step into the living room, where it's cozier?"

A fire had just been lighted, he saw, and things had been set out for drinks, and, like any stray, his response to these comforts was instantaneous. Where was *Mr.* Flannagan, he wondered. Traveling home on a late train? Changing his clothes upstairs? Taking a shower? At the end of the room there was a desk heaped with papers, and she began to riffle these, making sighs and noises of girlish exasperation. "I am terribly sorry to keep you waiting," she said, "but won't you make yourself a little drink while you wait? Everything's on the table."

"What train does Mr. Flannagan come out on?"

"Mr. Flannagan is away," she said. Her voice dropped. "Mr. Flannagan has been away for six weeks. . . ."

"I'll have a drink, then, if you'll have one with me."

"If you will promise to make it weak."

"Sit down," he said, "and enjoy your drink and look for your checkbook later. The only way to find things is to relax."

All in all, they had six drinks. She described herself and her circumstances unhesitatingly. Mr. Flannagan manufactured plastic tongue depressors. He traveled all over the world. She didn't like to travel. Planes made her feel faint, and in Tokyo, where she had gone that summer, she had been given raw fish for breakfast and so she had come straight home. She and her husband had formerly lived in New York, where she had many friends, but Mr. Flannagan thought the country would be safer in case of war. She would rather live in danger than die of loneliness and boredom. She had no children; she had made no friends. "I've seen you, though, before," she said with enormous coyness, patting his knee. "I've seen you walking your dogs on Sunday and driving by in the convertible. . . ."

The thought of this lonely woman sitting at her window touched him, although he was even more touched by her plumpness. Sheer plumpness, he knew, is not a vital part of the body and has no procreative functions. It serves merely as an excess cushion for the rest of the carcass. And knowing its humble place in the scale of things, why did he, at this time of life, seem almost ready to sell his soul for plumpness? The remarks she made about the sufferings of a lonely woman seemed so broad at first that he didn't know what to make of them, but after the sixth drink he put his arm around her and suggested that they go upstairs and look for her checkbook there.

"I've never done this before," she said later, when he was arranging himself to leave. Her voice shook with feeling, and he thought it lovely. He didn't doubt her truthfulness, although he had heard the words a hundred times. "I've never done this before," they always said, shaking their dresses down over their white shoulders. "I've never done this before," they always said, waiting for the elevator in the hotel corridor. "I've never done this before," they always said, pouring another whiskey. "I've never done this before," they always said, putting on their stockings. On ships at sea, on railroad trains, in summer hotels with mountain views, they always said, "I've never done this before."

"Where have you been?" Mrs. Pastern asked sadly, when he came in. "It's after eleven."

"I had a drink with the Flannagans."

"She told me he was in Germany."

"He came home unexpectedly."

Charlie ate some supper in the kitchen and went into the

TV room to hear the news. "Bomb them!" he shouted. "Throw a little nuclear hardware at them! Show them who's boss!" But in bed he had trouble sleeping. He thought first of his son and daughter, away at college. He loved them. It was the only meaning of the word that he had ever known. Then he played nine imaginary holes of golf, choosing his handicap, his irons, his stance, his opponents, and his weather in detail, but the green of the links seemed faded in the light of his business worries. His money was tied up in a Nassau hotel, an Ohio pottery works, and a detergent for window washing, and luck had been running against him. His worries harried him up out of bed, and he lighted a cigarette and went to the window. In the starlight he could see the trees stripped of their leaves. During the summer he had tried to repair some of his losses at the track, and the bare trees reminded him that his pari-mutuel tickets would still be lying, like leaves, in the gutters near Belmont and Saratoga. Maple and ash, beech and elm, one hundred to win on Three in the fourth, fifty to win on Six in the third, one hundred to win on Two in the eighth. Children walking home from school would scuff through what seemed to be his foliage. Then, getting back into bed, he thought unashamedly of Mrs. Flannagan, planning where they would next meet and what they would do. There are, he thought, so few true means of forgetfulness in this life that why should he shun the medicine even when the medicine seemed, as it did, a little crude?

A new conquest always had a wonderful effect on Charlie. He became overnight generous, understanding, inexhaustibly good-humored, relaxed, kind to cats, dogs, and strangers,

expansive, and compassionate. There was, of course, the re-
proachful figure of Mrs. Pastern waiting for him in the evenings, but he had served her well, he thought, for twenty-five
years, and if he were to touch her tenderly these days she
would likely say, "Ouch. That's where I bruised myself in
the garden." On the evenings that they spent together, she
seemed to choose to display the roughest angles of her personality; to grind her axe. "You know," she said, "Mary
Quested cheats at cards." Her remarks fell a good deal short
of where he sat. If these were indirect expressions of disappointment, it was a disappointment that no longer touched
him.

He met Mrs. Flannagan for lunch in the city, and they
spent the afternoon together. Leaving the hotel, Mrs. Flannagan stopped at a display of perfume. She said that she liked
perfume, worked her shoulders, and called him "Monkey."
Considering her girlishness and her claims to fidelity, there
was, he thought, a distinct atmosphere of practice about her
request, but he bought her a bottle of perfume. The second
time they met, she admired a peignoir in a store window
and he bought this. On their third meeting, she got a silk
umbrella. Waiting for her in the restaurant for their fourth
meeting, he hoped that she wasn't going to ask for jewelry,
because his reserves of cash were low. She had promised to
meet him at one, and he basked in his circumstances and the
smells of sauce, gin, and red floor carpets. She was always
late, and at half past one he ordered a second drink. At
a quarter to two, he saw his waiter whispering to another
waiter—whispering, laughing, and nodding his head in
Charlie's direction. It was his first intimation of the chance
that she might stand him up. But who was she—who did she

think she was that she could do this to him? She was nothing but a lonely housewife; she was nothing but that. At two, he ordered his lunch. He was crushed. What had his emotional life been these last years but a series of sometimes shabby one-night stands, but without them his life would be unendurable.

There is something universal about being stood up in a city restaurant between one and two—a spiritual no man's land, whose blasted trees, entrenchments, and ratholes we all share, disarmed by the gullibility of our hearts. The waiter knew, and the laughter and lighthearted conversations at the tables around Charlie honed his feelings. He seemed to be helplessly elevated on his disappointment like a flagpole sitter, his aloneness looming larger and larger in the crowded room. Then he saw his own swollen image in a mirror, his gray hair clinging to his pate like the remains of a romantic landscape, his heavy body shaped a little like a firehouse Santa Claus, the paunch enlarged by one or two of Mrs. Kelly's second-best sofa cushions. He pushed his table away and started for a telephone booth in the hall.

"Is there anything wrong with your lunch, Monsieur?" the waiter asked.

She answered the phone, and in her most girlish voice said, "We cannot go on like this. I have thought it over, and we cannot go on. It is not because I do not want to, because you are a very virile man, but my conscience will not let me."

"Can I stop by tonight and talk it over?"

"Well . . ." she said.

"I'll come straight up from the station."

"If you'll do me a favor."

"What?"

"I will tell you when I see you tonight. But please park your car behind the house and come in the back door. I do not want to give these old gossips here anything to talk about. You must remember that I have never done this before."

Of course she was right, he thought. She had her self-esteem to maintain. Her pride, he thought, was so childish, so sterling! Sometimes, driving through a New Hampshire mill town late in the day, he thought, you will see in some alley or driveway, down by the river, a child dressed in a tablecloth, sitting on a broken stool, waving her sceptre over a kingdom of weeds and cinders and a few skinny chickens. It is the purity and the irony of their pride that touches one; and he felt that way about Mrs. Flannagan.

She let him in at the back door that night, but in the living room the scene was the same. The fire was burning, she made him a drink, and in her company he felt as if he had just worked his shoulders free of a heavy pack. But she was coy, in and out of his arms, tickling him and then tripping across the room to look at herself in the mirror. "I want my favor first," she said.

"What is it?"

"Guess."

"I can't give you money. I'm not rich, you know."

"Oh, I wouldn't think of taking money." She was indignant.

"Then what is it?"

"Something you wear."

"But my watch is worthless, my cufflinks are brass."

"Something else."

"But what?"

"I won't tell you unless you promise to give it to me."

He pushed her away from him then, knowing that he could easily be made a fool of. "I can't make a promise unless I know what it is you want."

"It's something very small."

"How small?"

"Tiny. Weeny."

"Please tell me what it is." Then he seized her in his arms, and this was the moment he felt most like himself: solemn, virile, wise, and imperturbable.

"I won't tell you unless you promise."

"But I can't promise."

"Then go away," she said. "Go away and never, never come back."

She was too childish to give the command much force, and yet it was not wasted on him. Could he go back to his own house, empty but for his wife, who would be grinding her axe? Go there and wait until time and chance turned up another friend?

"Please tell me."

"Promise."

"I promise."

"I want," she said, "a key to your bomb shelter."

The demand struck at him like a sledge-hammer blow, and suddenly he felt in all his parts the enormous weight of chagrin. All his gentle speculations on her person—the milltown girl ruling her chickens—backfired bitterly. This must have been on her mind from the beginning, when she first lit the fire, lost her checkbook, and gave him a drink. The demand abraded his lust, but only for a moment, for now she was back in his arms, marching her fingers up and down his rib cage, saying, "Creepy, creepy, creepy mouse, come to live in Charlie's house." His need for her was crippling; it seemed like a cruel blow at the back of his knees. And yet in some chamber of his thick head he could see the foolishness and the obsolescence of his hankering skin. But how could he reform his bone and muscle to suit this new world; instruct his meandering and greedy flesh in politics, geography, holocausts, and cataclysms? Her front was round, fragrant, and soft, and he took the key off its ring—a piece of metal one and one-half inches long, warmed by the warmth of his hands, a genuine talisman of salvation, a defense against the end of the world—and dropped it into the neck of her dress.

The Pasterns' bomb shelter had been completed that spring. They would have liked to keep it a secret; would have liked at least to soft-pedal its existence; but the trucks and bulldozers going in and out of their driveway had informed everyone. It had cost thirty-two thousand dollars, and it had two chemical toilets, an oxygen supply, and a library, compiled by a Columbia professor, consisting of books meant to inspire hopefulness, humor, and tranquillity. There were stores of survival food to last three months, and several cases of hard liquor. Mrs. Pastern had bought the plaster-of-Paris ducks, the birdbath, and the gnomes in an attempt to give the lump in her garden a look of innocence; to make it acceptable—at least to herself. For, bulking as it did in so pretty and domestic a scene and signifying as it must the death of at least half the world's population, she had found it, with its grassy cover, impossible to reconcile with the blue sky and the white clouds. She liked to keep the curtains drawn at that side of the house, and they were drawn the next afternoon, when she served gin to the bishop.

The bishop had come unexpectedly. Her minister had telephoned and said that the bishop was in the neighborhood and would like to thank her for her services to the church, and could he bring the bishop over now? She threw together some things for tea, changed her dress, and came down into the hall just as they rang the bell.

"How do you do, Your Grace," she said. "Won't you come in, Your Grace? Would you like some tea, Your Grace—or would you sooner have a drink, Your Grace?"

"I would like a Martini," said the bishop.

He had the gift of a clear and carrying voice. He was a well-built man, with hair as black as dye, firm and sallow skin deeply creased around a wide mouth, and eyes as glittering and haggard, she thought, as someone drugged. "If you'll excuse me, Your Grace . . ."

This request for a cocktail confused her; Charlie always mixed the drinks. She dropped ice on the pantry floor, poured a pint or so of gin into the shaker, and tried to correct what appeared to her to be a lethal drink with more vermouth.

"Mr. Ludgate here has been telling me how indispensable you are to the life of the parish," the bishop said, taking his drink.

"I do try," said Mrs. Pastern.

"You have two children."

"Yes. Sally's at Smith. Carkie's at Colgate. The house seems so empty now. They were confirmed by the old bishop. Bishop Tomlinson."

"Ah, yes," the bishop said. "Ah, yes."

The presence of the bishop made her nervous. She wished

she could give the call a more natural air; she wished at least to make her presence in her own parlor seem real. She was suffering from an intense discomfort that sometimes attacked her during committee meetings, when the parliamentary atmosphere had a disintegrating effect on her personality. She would, sitting in her folding chair, seem to go around the room on her hands and knees, gathering the fragments of herself and cementing them together with some virtue, such as, I am a Good Mother, or, I am a Patient Wife.

"Are you two old friends?" she asked the bishop.

"No!" the bishop exclaimed.

"The bishop was just driving through," the minister said weakly.

"Could I see your garden?" the bishop asked.

Taking his Martini glass with him, he followed her out the side door onto the terrace. Mrs. Pastern was an ardent gardener, but the scene was disappointing. The abundant cycle of bloom was nearly over; there was nothing to see but chrysanthemums. "I wish you could see it in the spring, especially in the *late* spring," she said. "The star magnolia is the first to bloom. Then we have the flowering cherries and plums. Just as they finish, we have the azalea, the laurel, and the hybrid rhododendron. I have bronze tulips under the wisteria. The lilac is white."

"I see that you have a shelter," the bishop said.

"Yes." She had been betrayed by her ducks and gnomes. "Yes, we have, but it's really nothing to see. This bed is all lily of the valley, all this bed. I feel that roses make a better cutting than an ornamental garden, so I keep the roses behind the house. The border is *fraises des bois*. So sweet, so winy."

"Have you had the shelter long?"

"We had it built in the spring," said Mrs. Pastern. "That hedge is flowering quince. Over there is our little salad garden. Lettuce and herbs. That sort of thing."

"I would like to see the shelter," the bishop said.

She was hurt—a hurt that seemed to reverberate all the way back to her childhood, when she had been wounded by the discovery that the friends who came to call on rainy days had not come because they liked her but to eat her cookies and hog her toys. She had never been able to put a good countenance on selfishness, and she scowled as they passed the birdbath and the painted ducks. The gnomes with their mobcaps looked down on the three of them as she unlocked the fire door with a key that she wore around her neck.

"Charming," the bishop said. "Charming. Why, I see you even have a library."

"Yes," she said. "The books were chosen for their humor, tranquillity, and hopefulness."

"It is an unfortunate characteristic of ecclesiastical architecture," said the bishop, "that the basement or cellar is confined to a small space under the chancel. This gives us very little room for the salvation of the faithful—a characteristic, I should perhaps add, of our denomination. Some churches have commodious basements. But I shan't take up any more of your time." He strode back across the lawn toward the house, put his cocktail glass on the terrace wall, and gave her his blessing.

She sat down heavily on her terrace steps and watched the car drive off. He had not come to praise her, she knew that. Was it impious of her to suspect that he was traveling around his domain picking and choosing sanctuaries? Was it possible that he meant to exploit his holiness in this way? The burden of modern life, even if it smelled of plastics—as it seemed to—bore down cruelly on the supports of God, the Family, and the Nation. The burden was top-heavy, and she seemed to hear the foundations give. She had believed all her life in the holiness of the priesthood, and if this belief was genuine, why hadn't she offered the bishop the safety of her shelter at once? But if he believed in the resurrection of the dead and the life of the world to come, why was a shelter anything that he might need?

The telephone rang, and she answered its ringing with a forced lightheartedness. It was a woman named Beatrice, who came to clean Mrs. Pastern's house two days a week.

"This is Beatrice, Mrs. Pastern," she said, "and there is something I think you ought to know. As you know, I'm not a gossip. I'm not like that Adele, who goes around from lady to lady telling that the So-and-Sos aren't sleeping together, and that So-and-So had six empty whiskey bottles in his wastebaskets, and that nobody came to So-and-So's cocktail party. I'm not like that Adele. I'm not a gossip, and you know that, Mrs. Pastern. But there is something I think you ought to know. I worked for Mrs. Flannagan today, and she showed me a key, and she said it was a key to your bomb shelter, and that your husband gave it to her. I don't know whether it was the truth or not, but I thought you ought to know."

"Thank you, Beatrice."

He had dragged her good name through a hundred escapades, debauched her excellence, and thrown away her love, but she had never imagined that he would betray her in their plans for the end of the world. She poured what was left of the bishop's cocktail into a glass. She hated the taste of gin, but her accumulated troubles had grown to seem like the pain of an illness, and gin dimmed this, although it inflamed her indignation. Outside, the sky darkened, the wind changed, it began to rain. What could she do? She couldn't go back to Mother. Mother didn't have a shelter. She couldn't pray for guidance. The bishop's apparent worldliness had reduced the comforts of Heaven. She couldn't contemplate her husband's foolish profligacy without drinking more gin. And then she remembered the night—the night of judgment— when they had agreed to let Aunt Ida and Uncle Ralph burn, when she had sacrificed her three-year-old niece and he his five-year-old nephew; when they had conspired like murderers and had decided to deny mercy even to his old mother.

She was quite drunk by the time Charlie came in. "I couldn't spend two weeks in any hole in the ground with that Mrs. Flannagan," she said.

"What are you talking about?"

"I took the bishop down to show him the shelter and he—"

"What bishop? What was a bishop doing here?"

"Stop interrupting me and listen to what I have to say. Mrs. Flannagan has a key to our shelter, and you gave it to her."

"Who told you this?"

"Mrs. Flannagan," she said, "has a key to our shelter, and you gave it to her."

He went back out through the rain to the garage and jammed his fingers in the door. In haste and rage he stalled the car, and, waiting for the carburetor to drain, was faced, in the headlights, with the backstage of his wasteful domestic life which had accumulated in the garage. Here was a fortune in broken garden furniture and power tools. When the car started, he slammed out of his driveway and passed a red light at the first intersection, where, for a moment, his life hung by a thread. He didn't care. Slamming up the hill, he clutched the wheel as if he already had his hands on her plump and silly neck. It was his children's honor and peace of mind that she had damaged. It was his children, his beloved children, that she had harmed.

He stopped the car at the door. The house was lighted, and he could smell wood smoke, but the place was quiet and, peering through the glass pane, he couldn't see any signs of life or hear anything but the rain. He tried the door. It was locked. Then he pounded on the frame with his fist. It was a long time before she appeared, from the living room, and he guessed she must have been asleep. She was wearing the peignoir he had bought her. She straightened her hair. As soon as she opened the door, he pushed his way into the hall and shouted, "Why did you do it? Why did you do such a damn fool thing?"

"I do not know what you are talking about."

"Why did you tell my wife you had the key?"

"I did not tell your wife."

"Then who did you tell?"

"I did not tell anyone."

She worked her shoulders and looked down at the tip of her slipper. Like most incurable fibbers, she had an extravagant regard for the truth, which she expressed by sending up signals meant to indicate that she was lying. He saw then that he could not get the truth out of her, that he could not shake it out of her with all the strength in his arms, and that her confession, if he had it, would have done him no good.

"Get me something to drink," he said.

"I think you had better go away and come back later, when you are feeling better," she said.

"I'm tired," he said. "I'm tired. Oh God, I'm tired. I haven't sat down all day."

He went into the living room and poured himself a whiskey. He saw his hands, blackened by the trains and the bannisters, the doorknobs and the papers, of a long day, and in the mirror he saw that his hair was soaked with rain. He went out of the living room and through the library to the downstairs bathroom. She made a little noise, scarcely a cry. When he opened the bathroom door, he found himself face to face with an absolutely naked stranger.

He shut the door, and then there was that nearly metronomic stillness that precedes a howling confrontation. It was she who broke the silence. "I do not know who he is, and I have been trying to make him go away. . . . I know what you are thinking, and I do not care. It is my house, after all, and I did not invite you into it, and I do not have to explain everything that goes on to you."

"Get away from me," he said. "Get away from me or I'll break your neck."

He drove home through the rain. When he let himself in, he noticed the noise and the smell of cooking from the kitchen. He supposed that these sounds and odors must have been one of the first signs of life on the planet, and might be one of the last. The evening paper was in the living room, and, giving it a shake, he shouted, "Throw a little nuclear hardware at them! Show them who's boss!" And then, falling into a chair, he asked softly, "Dear Jesus, when will it ever end?"

"I've been waiting for you to say that," said Mrs. Pastern quietly, coming in from the pantry. "I've been waiting nearly three months now to hear just that. I first began to worry when I saw that you'd sold your cufflinks and your studs. I wondered what was the matter then. Then, when you signed the contract for the shelter without a penny to pay for it, I began to see your plan. You *want* the world to end, don't you? Don't you, Charlie, don't you? I've known it all along, but I couldn't admit it to myself, it seemed so ruthless—but then one learns something new every day." She walked past him into the hallway and started up the stairs. "There's a hamburger in the frying pan," she said, "and some potatoes in the oven. If you want a green vegetable, you can heat up the leftover broccoli. I'm going to telephone the children."

We travel with such velocity these days that the most we can do is to remember a few place names. The freight of metaphysical speculation will have to catch up with us by slow train, if it catches up with us at all. The rest of the story was recounted by my mother, whose letter caught up with me in Kitzbühel, where I sometimes stay. "There have been so many changes in the last six weeks," she wrote, "that I hardly know where to begin. First, the Pasterns are gone and I mean gone. He's in the county jail serving a two-year sentence for grand larceny. Sally's left college and is working at Macy's, and the boy's still looking for a job, I hear. He's living with his mother somewhere in the Bronx. Someone said they were on home relief. It seems that Charlie ran through all of that money his mother left him about a year ago and they were just living on credit. The bank took everything and they moved to a motel in Tansford. Then they moved from motel to motel, traveling in a rented car and never paying their bills. The motel and the car-rental people were the first ones to catch up with them. Some nice people named Willoughby bought the house from the bank. And the Flannagans have divorced. Remember her? She used to walk around her garden with a silk parasol. He didn't have to give her a settlement or anything and someone saw her on Central Park West in a thin coat on a cold night. But she did come back. It was very strange. She came back last Thursday. It had just begun to snow. It was a little while after lunch. What an old fool your mother is but as old as I am I never cease to thrill at the miracle of a snowstorm. I had a lot of work to do but I decided to let it go and stand by the window awhile and watch it snow. The sky was very dark. It was a fine, dry snow and covered everything quickly like a spread of light. Then I saw Mrs. Flannagan walking up the street. She must have come out on the two-thirty-three and walked up from the station. I don't suppose she can have very much money if she can't afford a cab, do you? She was not very warmly dressed and she had on high heels and no rubbers. Well, she walked up the street and she walked right across the Pasterns' lawn, I mean what used to be the Pasterns' lawn, to their bomb shelter and just stood there looking at it. I don't know what in the world she was thinking of but the shelter looks a little like a tomb, you know, and she looked like a mourner standing there with the snow falling on her head and shoulders and it made me sad to think she hardly knew the Pasterns. Then Mrs. Willoughby telephoned me and said there was this strange woman standing in front of her bomb shelter and did I know who it was and I said that

I did, that it was Mrs. Flannagan who used to live up on the hill, and then she asked what I thought she should do and I said the only thing to do I guessed was to send her away. So then Mrs. Willoughby sent her maid down and I saw the maid telling Mrs. Flannagan to go away and then in a little while Mrs. Flannagan walked back through the snow to the station."

The Angel of the Bridge

☙❧

You may have seen my mother waltzing on ice
skates in Rockefeller Center. She's seventy-eight years old
now but very wiry, and she wears a red velvet costume with
a short skirt. Her tights are flesh-colored, and she wears
spectacles and a red ribbon in her white hair, and she waltzes
with one of the rink attendants. I don't know why I should
find the fact that she waltzes on ice skates so disconcerting, but
I do. I avoid that neighborhood whenever I can during the
winter months, and I never lunch in the restaurants on the
rink. Once when I was passing that way, a total stranger took
me by the arm and, pointing to Mother, said, "Look at that
crazy old dame." I was very embarrassed. I suppose I should
be grateful for the fact that she amuses herself and is not a
burden to me, but I sincerely wish she had hit on some less
conspicuous recreation. Whenever I see gracious old ladies
arranging chrysanthemums and pouring tea, I think of my
own mother, dressed like a hat-check girl, pushing some paid

rink attendant around the ice, in the middle of the third-biggest city of the world.

My mother learned to figure-skate in the little New England village of St. Botolphs, where we come from, and her waltzing is an expression of her attachment to the past. The older she grows, the more she longs for the vanishing and provincial world of her youth. She is a hardy woman, as you can imagine, but she does not relish change. I arranged one summer for her to fly to Toledo and visit friends. I drove her to the Newark airport. She seemed troubled by the airport waiting room, with its illuminated advertisements, vaulted ceiling, and touching and painful scenes of separation played out to an uproar of continuous tango music. She did not seem to find it in any way interesting or beautiful, and compared to the railroad station in St. Botolphs it was indeed a strange background against which to take one's departure. The flight was delayed for an hour, and we sat in the waiting room. Mother looked tired and old. When we had been waiting half an hour, she began to have some noticeable difficulty in breathing. She spread a hand over the front of her dress and began to gasp deeply, as if she was in pain. Her face got mottled and red. I pretended not to notice this. When the plane was announced, she got to her feet and exclaimed, "I want to go home! If I have to die suddenly, I don't want to die in a flying machine." I cashed in her ticket and drove her back to her apartment, and I have never mentioned this seizure to her or to anyone, but her capricious, or perhaps neurotic, fear of dying in a plane crash was the first insight I had into how, as she grew older, her way was strewn with invisible rocks and lions and how eccentric were the paths she took, as the world seemed to change its boundaries and become less and less comprehensible.

At the time of which I'm writing, I flew a great deal myself. My business was in Rome, New York, San Francisco, and Los Angeles, and I sometimes traveled as often as once a month between these cities. I liked the flying. I liked the incandescence of the sky at high altitudes. I liked all eastward flights where you can see from the ports the edge of night move over the continent and where, when it is four o'clock by your California watch, the housewives of Garden City are washing up the supper dishes and the stewardess in the plane is passing a second round of drinks. Toward the end of the flight, the air is stale. You are tired. The gold thread in the upholstery scratches your cheek, and there is a momentary feeling of forlornness, a sulky and childish sense of estrangement. You find good companions, of course, and bores, but most of the errands we run at such high altitudes are humble and terrestrial. That old lady, flying over the North Pole, is taking a jar of calf's-foot jelly to her sister in Paris, and the man beside her sells imitation-leather inner soles. Flying westward one dark night—we had crossed the Continental Divide, but we were still an hour out of Los Angeles and had not begun our descent, and were at such an altitude that the sense of houses, cities, and people below us was lost—I saw a formation, a trace of light, like the lights that burn along a shore. There was no shore in that part of the world, and I knew I would never know if the edge of the desert or some bluff or mountain accounted for this hoop of light, but it seemed, in its obscurity—and at that velocity and height— like the emergence of a new world, a gentle hint at my own obsolescence, the lateness of my time of life, and my inability to understand the things I often see. It was a pleasant feeling, completely free of regret, of being caught in some observable mid-passage, the farther reaches of which might be understood by my sons.

I liked to fly, as I say, and had none of my mother's anxieties. It was my older brother—her darling—who was to inherit her resoluteness, her stubbornness, her table silver, and some of her eccentricities. One evening, my brother—I had not seen him for a year or so—called and asked if he could come for dinner. I was happy to invite him. We live on the eleventh floor of an apartment house, and at seven-thirty he telephoned from the lobby and asked me to come down. I thought he must have something to tell me privately, but when we met in the lobby he got into the automatic elevator with me and we started up. As soon as the doors closed, he showed the same symptoms of fear I had seen in my mother. Sweat stood out on his forehead, and he gasped like a runner.

"What in the world is the matter?" I asked.

"I'm afraid of elevators," he said miserably.

"But what are you afraid of?"

"I'm afraid the building will fall down."

I laughed—cruelly, I guess. For it all seemed terribly funny, his vision of the buildings of New York banging against one another like ninepins as they fell to the earth. There has always been a strain of jealousy in our feelings about one another, and I am aware, at some obscure level, that he makes more money and has more of everything than I, and to see him humiliated—crushed—saddened me but at the same time and in spite of myself made me feel that I had taken a stunning lead in the race for honors that is at the bottom of our relationship. He is the oldest, he is the favorite, but watching his misery in the elevator I felt that he was merely my poor old brother, overtaken by his worries. He stopped in the hallway to recover his composure, and explained that he had been suffering from this phobia for over a year. He was going to a psychiatrist, he said. I couldn't see that it had done him any good. He was all right once he got out of the elevator, but I noticed that he stayed away from the windows. When it was time to go, I walked him out to the corridor. I was curious. When the elevator reached our floor, he turned to me and said, "I'm afraid I'll have to take the stairs." I led him to the stairway, and we climbed slowly down the eleven flights. He clung to the railing. We said goodbye in the lobby, and I went up in the elevator, and told my wife about his fear that the building might fall down. It seemed strange and sad to her, and it did to me, too, but it also seemed terribly funny.

It wasn't terribly funny when, a month later, the firm he worked for moved to the fifty-second floor of a new office building and he had to resign. I don't know what reasons he gave. It was another six months before he could find a job in a third-floor office. I once saw him on a winter dusk at the corner of Madison Avenue and Fifty-ninth Street, waiting for the light to change. He appeared to be an intelligent, civilized, and well-dressed man, and I wondered how many of the men waiting with him to cross the street made their way as he did through a ruin of absurd delusions, in which the street might appear to be a torrent and the approaching cab driven by the angel of death.

He was quite all right on the ground. My wife and I went to his house in New Jersey, with the children, for a weekend, and he looked healthy and well. I didn't ask about his phobia. We drove back to New York on Sunday afternoon. As we approached the George Washington Bridge, I saw a thunderstorm over the city. A strong wind struck the car the moment we were on the bridge, and nearly took the wheel out of my hand. It seemed to me that I could feel the huge structure swing. Halfway across the bridge, I thought I felt the roadway begin to give. I could see no signs of a collapse, and yet I was convinced that in another minute the bridge would split in two and hurl the long lines of Sunday traffic into the dark water below us. This imagined disaster was terrifying. My legs got so weak that I was not sure I could brake the car if I needed to. Then it became difficult for me to breathe. Only by opening my mouth and gasping did I seem able to take in any air. My blood pressure was affected and I began to feel a darkening of my vision. Fear has always seemed to me to run a course, and at its climax the body and perhaps the spirit defend themselves by drawing on some new and fresh source of strength. Once over the center of the bridge, my pain and terror began to diminish. My wife and the children were admiring the storm, and they did not seem to have noticed my spasm. I was afraid both that the bridge would fall down and that they might observe my panic.

I thought back over the weekend for some incident that might account for my preposterous fear that the George Washington Bridge would blow away in a thunderstorm, but it had been a pleasant weekend, and even under the most exaggerated scrutiny I couldn't uncover any source of morbid nervousness or anxiety. Later in the week, I had to drive to Albany, and, although the day was clear and windless, the memory of my first attack was too keen; I hugged the east bank of the river as far north as Troy, where I found a small, old-fashioned bridge that I could cross comfortably. This meant going fifteen or twenty miles out of my way, and it is humiliating to have your travels obstructed by barriers that are senseless and invisible. I drove back from Albany by the same route, and next morning I went to the family doctor and told him I was afraid of bridges.

He laughed. "You, of all people," he said scornfully. "You'd better take hold of yourself."

"But Mother is afraid of airplanes," I said. "And Brother hates elevators."

"Your mother is past seventy," he said, "and one of the most remarkable women I've ever known. I wouldn't bring *her* into this. What *you* need is a little more backbone."

This was all he had to say, and I asked him to recommend an analyst. He does not include psychoanalysis in medical science, and told me I would be wasting my time and money, but, yielding to his obligation to be helpful, he gave me the name and address of a psychiatrist, who told me that my fear of bridges was the surface manifestation of a deep-seated anxiety and that I would have to have a full analysis. I didn't have the time, or the money, or, above all, the confidence in the doctor's methods to put myself in his hands, and I said I would try and muddle through.

There are obviously areas of true and false pain, and my pain was meretricious, but how could I convince my lights and vitals of this? My youth and childhood had their deeply troubled and their jubilant years, and could some repercussions from this past account for my fear of heights? The thought of a life determined by hidden obstacles was unacceptable, and I decided to take the advice of the family doctor and ask more of myself. I had to go to Idlewild later in the week, and, rather than take a bus or a taxi, I drove the car myself. I nearly lost consciousness on the Triborough Bridge. When I got to the airport I ordered a cup of coffee, but my hand was shaking so I spilled the coffee on the counter. The man beside me was amused and said that I must have put in quite a night. How could I tell him that I had gone to bed early and sober but that I was afraid of bridges?

I flew to Los Angeles late that afternoon. It was one o'clock by my watch when we landed. It was only ten o'clock in California. I was tired and took a taxi to the hotel where I always stay, but I couldn't sleep. Outside my hotel window was a monumental statue of a young woman, advertising a Las Vegas night club. She revolves slowly in a beam of light. At 2 A.M. the light is extinguished, but she goes on restlessly turning all through the night. I have never seen her cease her turning, and I wondered, that night, when they greased her axle and washed her shoulders. I felt some affection for her, since neither of us could rest, and I wondered if she had a family—a stage mother, perhaps, and a compromised and broken-spirited father who drove a municipal bus on the West Pico line? There was a restaurant across the street, and I watched a drunken woman in a sable cape being led out to a car. She twice nearly fell. The crosslights from the open door, the lateness, her drunkenness, and the solicitude of the man with her made the scene, I thought, worried and lonely. Then two cars that seemed to be racing down Sunset Boulevard pulled up at a traffic light under my window. Three men piled out of each car and began to slug one another. You could hear the blows land on bone and cartilage. When the light changed, they got back into their cars and raced off.

The fight, like the hoop of light I had seen from the plane, seemed like the signs of a new world, but in this case an emergence of brutality and chaos. Then I remembered that I was to go to San Francisco on Thursday, and was expected in Berkeley for lunch. This meant crossing the San Francisco–Oakland Bay Bridge, and I reminded myself to take a cab both ways and leave the car I rented in San Francisco in the hotel garage. I tried again to reason out my fear that the bridge would fall. Was I the victim of some sexual dislocation? My life has been promiscuous, carefree, and a source of immense pleasure, but was there some secret here that would have to be mined by a professional? Were all my pleasures impostures and evasions, and was I really in love with my old mother in her skating costume?

Looking at Sunset Boulevard at three in the morning, I felt that my terror of bridges was an expression of my clumsily concealed horror of what is becoming of the world. I can drive with composure through the outskirts of Cleveland and Toledo—past the birthplace of the Polish Hot Dog, the Buffalo Burger stands, the used-car lots, and the architectural monotony. I claim to enjoy walking down Hollywood Boulevard on a Sunday afternoon. I have cheerfully praised the evening sky hanging beyond the disheveled and expatriated palm trees on Doheny Boulevard, stuck up against the incandescence, like rank upon rank of wet mops. Duluth and East Seneca are charming, and if they aren't, just look away. The hideousness of the road between San Francisco and Palo Alto is nothing more than the search of honest men and women for a decent place to live. The same thing goes for San Pedro and all that coast. But the height of bridges seemed to be one link I could not forge or fasten in this hypocritical chain of acceptances. The truth is, I hate freeways and Buffalo Burgers. Expatriated palm trees and monotonous housing developments depress me. The continuous music on special-fare trains exacerbates my feelings. I detest the destruction of familiar landmarks, I am deeply troubled by the misery and drunkenness I find among my friends, I abhor the dishonest practices I see. And it was at the highest point in the arc of a bridge that I became aware suddenly of the depth and bitterness of my feelings about modern life, and of the profoundness of my yearning for a more vivid, simple, and peaceable world.

But I couldn't reform Sunset Boulevard, and until I could, I couldn't drive across the San Francisco–Oakland Bay Bridge. What *could* I do? Go back to St. Botolphs, wear a Norfolk jacket, and play cribbage in the firehouse? There was only one bridge in the village, and you could throw a stone across the river there.

I got home from San Francisco on Saturday, and found my daughter back from school for the weekend. On Sunday morning, she asked me to drive her to the convent school in Jersey where she is a student. She had to be back in time for nine-o'clock Mass, and we left our apartment in the city a little after seven. We were talking and laughing, and I had approached and was in fact on the George Washington Bridge without having remembered my weakness. There were no preliminaries this time. The seizure came with a rush. The strength went out of my legs, I gasped for breath, and felt the terrifying loss of sight. I was, at the same time, determined to conceal these symptoms from my daughter. I made the other side of the bridge, but I was violently shaken. My daughter didn't seem to have noticed. I got her to school in time, kissed her goodbye, and started home. There was no question of my crossing the George Washington Bridge again, and I decided to drive north to Nyack and cross on the Tappan Zee Bridge. It seemed, in my memory, more gradual and more securely anchored to its shores. Driving up the parkway on the west shore, I decided that oxygen was what I needed, and I opened all the windows of the car. The fresh air seemed to help, but only momentarily. I could feel my sense of reality ebbing. The roadside and the car itself seemed to have less substance than a dream. I had some friends in the neighborhood, and I thought of stopping and asking them for a drink, but it was only a little after nine in the morning, and I could not face the embarrassment of asking for a drink so early in the day, and of explaining that I was afraid of bridges. I thought I might feel better if I talked to someone, and I stopped at a gas station and bought some gas, but the attendant was laconic and sleepy, and I couldn't explain to him that his conversation might make the difference between life and death. I had got onto the Thruway by then, and I wondered what alternatives I had if I couldn't cross the bridge. I could call my wife and ask her to make some arrangements for removing me, but our relationship involves so much self-esteem and face that to admit openly to this foolishness might damage our married happiness. I could call the garage we use and ask them to send up a man to chauffeur me home. I could park the car and wait until one o'clock, when the bars opened, and fill up on whiskey, but I had spent the last of my money for gasoline. I decided to take a chance, and turned onto the approach to the bridge.

All the symptoms returned, and this time they were **much**

worse than ever. The wind was knocked out of my lungs as by a blow. My equilibrium was so shaken that the car swerved from one lane into another. I drove to the side and pulled on the hand brake. The loneliness of my predicament was harrowing. If I had been miserable with romantic love, racked with sickness, or beastly drunk, it would have seemed more dignified. I remembered my brother's face, sallow and greasy with sweat in the elevator, and my mother in her red skirt, one leg held gracefully aloft as she coasted backward in the arms of a rink attendant, and it seemed to me that we were all three characters in some bitter and sordid tragedy, carrying impossible burdens and separated from the rest of mankind by our misfortunes. My life was over, and it would never come back, everything that I loved—blue-sky courage, lustiness, the natural grasp of things. It would never come back. I would end up in the psychiatric ward of the county hospital, screaming that the bridges, all the bridges in the world, were falling down.

Then a young girl opened the door of the car and got in. "I didn't think anyone would pick me up on the bridge," she said. She carried a cardboard suitcase and—believe me—a small harp in a cracked waterproof. Her straight light-brown hair was brushed and brushed and grained with blondness and spread in a kind of cape over her shoulders. Her face seemed full and merry.

"Are you hitchhiking?" I asked.

"Yes."

"But isn't it dangerous for a girl your age?"

"Not at all."

"Do you travel much?"

"All the time. I sing a little. I play the coffeehouses."

"What do you sing?"

"Oh, folk music, mostly. And some old things—Purcell and Dowland. But mostly folk music. . . . 'I gave my love a cherry that had no stone,'" she sang in a true and pretty voice. "'I gave my love a chicken that had no bone/I told my love a story that had no end/I gave my love a baby with no cryin'.'"

She sang me across a bridge that seemed to be an astonishingly sensible, durable, and even beautiful construction designed by intelligent men to simplify my travels, and the water of the Hudson below us was charming and tranquil. It all came back—blue-sky courage, the high spirits of lustiness, an ecstatic sereneness. Her song ended as we got to the toll station on the east bank, and she thanked me, said goodbye, and got out of the car. I offered to take her wherever she wanted to go, but she shook her head and walked away, and I drove on toward the city through a world that, having been restored to me, seemed marvelous and fair. When I got home, I thought of calling my brother and telling him what had happened, on the chance that there was also an angel of the elevator banks, but the harp—that single detail—threatened to make me seem ridiculous or mad, and I didn't call.

I wish I could say that I am convinced that there will always be some merciful intercession to help me with my worries, but I don't believe in rushing my luck, so I will stay off the George Washington Bridge, although I can cross the Triborough and the Tappan Zee with ease. My brother is still afraid of elevators, and my mother, although she's grown quite stiff, still goes around and around and around on the ice.

An Educated American Woman

Item: "I remain joined in holy matrimony to my unintellectual 190-pound halfback, and keep myself busy chauffeuring my son Bibber to and from a local private school that I helped organize. I seem, at one time or another, to have had the presidency of every civic organization in the community, and last year I ran the local travel agency for nine months. A New York publisher (knock on wood) is interested in my critical biography of Gustave Flaubert, and last year I ran for town supervisor on the Democratic ticket and got the largest Democratic plurality in the history of the village. Polly *Coulter* Mellowes ('42) stayed with us for a week on her way home from Paris to Minneapolis and we talked, ate, drank, and thought in French during her visit. Shades of Mlle. de Grasse! I still find time to band birds and knit Argyle socks."

This report, for her college alumnae magazine, might have suggested an aggressive woman, but she was not that at all. Jill *Chidchester* Madison held her many offices through competence, charm, and intellect, and she was actually quite shy. Her light-brown hair, at the time of which I'm writing, was dressed simply and in a way that recalled precisely how she had looked in boarding school twenty years before. Boarding school may have shaded her taste in clothing; that and the fact that she had a small front and was one of those women who took this deprivation as if it was something more than the loss of a leg. Considering her comprehensive view of life, it seemed strange that such a thing should have bothered her, but it bothered her terribly. She had pretty legs. Her coloring was fresh and high. Her eyes were brown and set much too close together, so that when she was less than vivacious she had a mousy look.

Her mother, Amelia Faxon Chidchester, was a vigorous, stocky woman with splendid white hair, a red face, and an emphatic accent whose roots seemed more temperamental than regional. Mrs. Chidchester's words were shaped to express her untiring vigor, her triumph over pain, her cultural enthusiasm, and her trust in mankind. She was the author of seventeen unpublished books. Jill's father died when she was six days old. She was born in San Francisco, where her father had run a small publishing house and administered a small estate. He left his wife and daughter with enough money to protect them from any sort of hardship and any sort of financial anxiety, but they were a good deal less rich than their relatives. Jill appeared to be precocious, and when she was three her mother took her to Munich, where she was entered in the Gymnasium für Kinder, run by Dr. Stock for the purpose of observing gifted children. The competition was fierce, and her reaction tests were only middling, but she was an amiable and a brilliant girl. When she was five, they shifted to the Scuola Pantola in Florence, a similar institution. They moved from there to England, to the famous Tower Hill School, in Kent. Then Amelia, or Melee, as she was called, decided that the girl should put down some roots, and so she rented a house in Nantucket, where Jill was entered in the public school.

I don't know why it is that expatriate children should seem underfed, but they often do, and Jill, with her mixed clothing, her mixed languages, her bare legs and sandals, gave the impression that the advantages of her education had worked out in her as a kind of pathos. She was the sort of child who skipped a lot. She skipped to school. She skipped home. She was shy. She was not very practical, and her mother encouraged her in this. "*You* shall not wash the dishes, my dear," she said. "A girl of your intelligence is not expected to waste her time washing dishes." They had a devoted servant —all of Melee's servants worshiped the ground she walked on—and Jill's only idea about housework was that it was work she was not expected to do. She did, when she was about ten, learn to knit Argyle socks and was allowed this recreation. She was romantic. Entered in her copybook was the following: "Mrs. Amelia Faxon Chidchester requests the honor of your company at the wedding of her daughter Jill to Viscount Ludley-Huntington, Earl of Ashmead, in Westminster Abbey. White tie. Decorations." The house in Nantucket was pleasant, and Jill learned to sail. It was in Nantucket that her mother spoke to her once about that subject for which we have no vocabulary in English—about love. It was late afternoon. A fire was burning and there were flowers on a table. Jill was reading and her mother was writing. She stopped writing and said, over her shoulder, "I think I should tell you, my dear, that during the war I was in charge of a canteen at the Embarcadero, and I gave myself to many lonely soldiers."

The remark was crushing. It seemed to the girl emotionally and intellectually incomprehensible. She wanted to cry. She could not imagine her mother giving herself, as she put it, to a string of lonely soldiers. Her mother's manner firmly and authoritatively declared her indifference to this side of things. There seemed to be no way of getting around what had been said. It stuck up in the girl's consciousness like a fallen meteor. Perhaps it was all a lie, but her mother had never lied. Then, for once, she faced up to the limitations of her only parent. Her mother was not a liar, but she was a fraud. Her accent was a fraud, her tastes were fraudulent, and the seraphic look she assumed when she listened to music was the look of someone trying to recall an old telephone number. With her indomitable good cheer, her continual aches and pains, her implacable snobbism, her cultural squatter's rights, her lofty friends, and her forceful and meaningless utterances, she seemed, for a moment, to illustrate a supreme lack of discernment in nature. But was Jill meant to fabricate, single-handed, some cord of love and wisdom between this stranger who had given her life and life itself as she could see it, spread out in terms of fields and woods, wondrous and fair, beyond the windows? Could she not instead— But she felt too young, too thin, too undefended to make a life without a parent, and so she decided that her mother had not said what she said, and sealed the denial with a light kiss.

Jill went away to boarding school when she was twelve, and took all the prizes. Her scholastic, social, and athletic record was unprecedented. During her second year in college, she visited her relatives in San Francisco, and met and fell in love with Georgie Madison. He was not, considering her intelligence, the sort of man she would have been expected to choose, but it may have been sensible of her to pick a man whose interests were so different. He was a quiet, large-boned man with black hair and those gentle looks that break the hearts of the fatherless of all ages; and she was, after all, fatherless. He worked as a junior executive in a San Francisco shipyard. He had graduated from Yale, but when Melee once asked him if he liked Thackeray he said sincerely and politely that he had never tasted any. This simmered down to a family joke. They got engaged in her junior year, and were married a week after she graduated from college, where she again took all the prizes. He was transferred to a Brooklyn shipyard, and they moved to New York, where she got a public-relations job in a department store.

In the second or third year of their marriage, she had a son, whom they called Bibber. The birth was difficult, and she would not be able to have more children. When the boy was still young, they moved to Gordenville. She was happier in the country than she had been in town, since the country seemed to present more opportunities for her talents. The presidencies of the civic organizations followed one after the other, and when the widow who ran the local travel agency got sick, Jill took over and ran this successfully. Their only problem in the country was to find someone to stay with Bibber. A stream of unsatisfactory old women drifted through the house, augmented by high-school girls and cleaning women. Georgie loved his son intemperately. The boy was bright enough, but his father found this brightness blinding. He walked with the boy, played with him, gave him his bath at bedtime, and told him his story. Georgie did everything for his son when he was at home, and this was just as well, since Jill often came in later than he.

When Jill put down the reins of the travel agency, she decided to organize a European tour. She had not been abroad since their marriage, and if she wrote her own ticket she could make the trip at a profit. This, at least, was what she claimed. Georgie's shipyard was doing well, and there was no real reason for her to angle for a free trip, but he could see that the idea of conducting a tour stimulated and challenged her, and in the end he gave her his approval and his encouragement. Twenty-eight customers signed up, and early in July Georgie saw Jill and her lambs, as she called them, take off in a jet for Copenhagen. Their itinerary was to take them as far south as Naples, where Jill would put her dependents aboard a home-bound plane. Then Georgie would meet her in Venice, where they would spend a week. Jill sent her husband postcards each day, and several of her customers were so enthusiastic about her leadership that they wrote Georgie themselves to tell him what a charming, competent, and knowledgeable wife he possessed. His neighbors were friendly, and he mostly dined with them. Bibber, who was not quite four, had been put into a summer camp.

Before Georgie left for Europe, he drove to New Hampshire to check on Bibber. He had missed the little boy painfully and had seen him much oftener in his reveries than he had seen his wife's vivacious face. To put himself to sleep, he imagined some implausible climbing tour through the Dolomites with Bibber when the boy was older. Night after night, he helped his son up from ledge to ledge. Overhead, the thin snow on the peaks sparkled in the summer sunlight. Carrying packs and ropes, they came down into Cortina a little after dark. The bare facts of his trip north contrasted sharply with this Alpine reverie.

The drive took him most of a day. He spent a restless night in a motel and scouted out the camp in the morning. The weather was mixed, and he was in the mountains. There were showers and then pale clearings—an atmosphere not so much of gloom as of bleakness. Most of the farms that he passed were abandoned. As he approached the camp, he felt that it and the surrounding countryside had the authority of a remote creation; or perhaps this was a reprise of his own experience of summers and camps as interludes unconnected with the rest of time. Then, from a rise of ground, he saw the place below him. There was a small lake—a pond, really: one of those round ponds whose tea-colored waters and pine groves leave with you an impression of geological fatigue. His own recollections of camp were sunny and brilliant, and this rueful water hole, with its huddle of rotting matchboard shanties, collided violently with his robust memories. He guessed—he insisted to himself—that things would look very different when the sun shone. Arrows pointed the way to the administration building, where the directress was waiting for him. She was a blue-eyed young woman whose efficiency had not quite eclipsed her good looks. "We've had a bit of trouble with your son," she said. "He's not gotten along terribly well. It's quite unusual. We seldom if ever have cases of homesickness. The exception is when we take children from divided families, and we try never to do this. We can cope with normal problems, but we cannot cope with a child who brings more than his share of misery with him. As a rule, we turn down applications from children of divorce."

"But Mrs. Madison and I are not divorced," Georgie said.

"Oh, I didn't know. You are separated?"

"No," Georgie said, "we are not. Mrs. Madison is traveling in Europe, but I am going to join her tomorrow."

"Oh, I see. Well, in that case, I don't understand why Bibber has been so slow to adjust. But here is Bibber to tell us all about it himself!"

The boy threw off the hand of the woman with him and ran to his father. He was crying.

"There, there," said the directress. "Daddy hasn't come all this way to see a weeper, has he, Bibber?"

Georgie felt his heart heave in love and confusion. He kissed the tears from the boy's face and held him against his chest.

"Perhaps you'd like to take a little walk with Bibber," the directress suggested. "Perhaps Bibber would like to show you the sights."

Georgie, with the boy clinging to his hand, had to face certain responsibilities that transcended the love he felt for his son. His instinct was to take the boy away. His responsibility was to hearten and encourage him to shoulder the burdens of life. "What is your favorite place, Bibber?" he asked enthusiastically, keenly aware of the fatuity in his tone, and convinced of the necessity for it. "I want you to show me your favorite place in the whole camp."

"I don't have any favorite place," Bibber said. He was trying successfully to keep from crying. "That's the mess hall," he said, pointing to a long, ugly shed. Fresh pieces of yellow lumber had replaced those that had rotted.

"Is that where you have your plays?" Georgie asked.

"We don't have any plays," Bibber said. "The lady in charge of plays got sick and she had to go home."

"Is that where you sing?"

"Please take me home, Daddy," Bibber said.

"But I can't, Bibber. Mummy's in Europe, and I'm flying over tomorrow afternoon to join her."

"When *can* I go home?"

"Not until camp closes." Georgie felt some of the weight of this sentence himself. He heard the boy's breathing quicken with pain. Somewhere a bugle sounded. Georgie, struggling to mix his responsibilities with his instincts, knelt and took the boy in his arms. "You see, I can't very well cable Mummy and tell her I'm not coming. She's expecting me there. And anyhow, we don't really have a home when Mummy isn't with us. I have my dinners out, and I'm away all day. There won't be anyone there to take care of you."

"I've participated in everything," the boy said hopefully. It was his last appeal for clemency, and when he saw it fail he said, "I have to go now. It's my third period." He went up a worn path under the pines.

Georgie returned to the administration building reflecting on the fact that he had loved camp, that he had been one of the most popular boys in camp, and that he had never wanted to go home.

"I think things are bound to improve," the directress said. "As soon as he gets over the hump, he'll enjoy himself much more than the others. I would suggest, however, that you don't stay too long. He has a riding period now. Why don't you watch him ride, and leave before the period's ended? He takes pride in his riding, and in that way you'll avoid a painful farewell. This evening we're going to have a big campfire and a good long sing. I'm sure that he's suffering from nothing that won't be cured by a good sing with his mates around a roaring fire."

It all sounded plausible to Georgie, who liked a good camp-fire sing himself. Were there any sorrows of early life that couldn't be cured by a rousing performance of "The Battle Hymn of the Republic"? He walked over to the riding ring singing, "They have builded him an altar in the evening dews and damps. . . ." It had begun to rain again, and Georgie couldn't tell whether the boy's face was wet with tears or drops of rain. He was on horseback and being led around the ring by a groom. Bibber waved once to his father and nearly lost his seat, and when the boy's back was turned Georgie went away.

He flew to Treviso and took a train into Venice, where Jill waited for him in a Swiss hotel on one of the back canals. Their reunion was ardent, and he loved her no less for noticing that she was tired and thin. Getting her lambs across Europe had been a rigorous and exhausting task. What he wanted to do then was to move from their third-rate hotel to Cipriani's, get a cabaña at the Lido, and spend a week on the beach. Jill refused to move to Cipriani's—it would be full of tourists—and on their second day in Venice she got up at seven, made instant coffee in a toothbrush glass, and rushed him off to eight-o'clock Mass at St. Mark's. Georgie knew Venice, and Jill knew—or should have known—that he was not interested in painting or mosaics, but she led him by the nose, so to speak, from monument to monument. He guessed that she had got into the habit of tireless sight-seeing, and that the tactful thing to do would be to wait until the habit spent itself. He suggested that they go to Harry's for lunch, and she said, "What in the world are you *thinking* of, Georgie?" They had lunch in a *trattoria*, and toured churches and museums until closing time. In the morning, he suggested that they go to the Lido, but she had already made arrangements to go to Maser and see the villas.

Jill brought all her competence as a tour director to their days in Venice, although Georgie didn't see why. Most of us enjoy displaying our familiarity with the world, but he could not detect a trace of enjoyment in her assault. Some people love painting and architecture, but there was nothing loving in her approach to the treasures of Venice. The worship of beauty was mysterious to Georgie, but was beauty meant to crush one's sense of humor? She stood, one hot afternoon, before the façade of a church, lecturing him from her guidebook. She recited dates, naval engagements, and so on, and sketched the history of the Republic as if she were preparing him for an examination. The light in which she stood was bright and unflattering, and the generally festive air of Venice made her erudition, the sternness of her enthusiasm, seem ungainly. She was trying to impress him with the fact that Venice was to be taken seriously. And was this, he wondered, the meaning, the sum, of these brilliant marbles, this labyrinthine and dilapidated place, suffused with the rank and ancient smell of bilge? He put an arm around her and said, "Come off it, darling." She put him away from her and said, "I have no idea what you're talking about."

Had she lost an address, a child, a pocketbook, a string of beads, or any other valuable, her canvass of Venice couldn't have been more grueling and exhaustive. He spent the rest of their time in Venice accompanying her on this mysterious search. Now and then he thought of Bibber and his camp. They flew home from Treviso, and in the gentler and more familiar light of Gordenville she seemed herself again. They

took up their happiness, and welcomed Bibber when he was
released from camp.

"Isn't it divine, isn't it the most divine period in domestic
American architecture?" Jill always asked, showing guests
through their large frame house. The house had been built
in the eighteen-seventies, and had long windows, an oval
dining room, and a stable with a cupola. It must have been
difficult to maintain, but these difficulties—at parties, anyhow—were never felt. The high-ceilinged rooms were filled
with light and had a special grace—austere, gloomy, and
finely balanced. The obvious social responsibilities were all
hers; his conversation was confined to the shipbuilding in-
dustry, but he mixed the drinks, carved the roast, and poured
the wine. There was a fire in the fireplace, there were flowers,
the furniture and the silver shone, and no one knew and
no one would have guessed that it was he who polished the
furniture and forks.

"Housework simply isn't my style," she had said, and he
was intelligent enough to see the truth in her remark; intelligent enough not to expect her to recast this image of herself
as an educated woman. It was the source of much of her
vitality and joy.

One stormy winter, they weren't able to get any servants
at all. A fly-by-night cook came in when they had guests, but
the rest of the work fell to Georgie. That was the year Jill
was studying French literature at Columbia and trying to
finish her book on Flaubert. On a typical domestic evening,
Jill would be sitting at her desk in their bedroom, working
on her book. Bibber would be asleep. Georgie might be in

the kitchen, polishing the brass and silver. He wore an apron. He drank whiskey. He was surrounded by cigarette boxes, andirons, bowls, ewers, and a large chest of table silver. He did not like to polish silver, but if he did not do this the silver would turn black. As she had said, it was not her style. It was not his style, either, nor was it any part of his education, but if he was, as she said, unintellectual, he was not so unintellectual as to accept any of the vulgarities and commonplaces associated with the struggle for sexual equality. The struggle was recent, he knew; it was real; it was inexorable; and while she sidestepped her domestic tasks, he could sense that she might do this unwillingly. She had been raised as an intellectual, her emancipation was still challenged in many quarters, and since he seemed to possess more latitude, to hold a stronger traditional position, it was his place to yield on matters like housework. It was not her choice, he knew, that she was raised as an intellectual, but the choice, having been made by others, seemed irrevocable. His restless sexual nature attributed to her softness, warmth, and the utter darkness of love; but why, he wondered as he polished the forks, did there seem to be some contradiction between these attributes and the possession of a clear mind? Intellect, he knew, was not a masculine attribute, although the bulk of tradition had put decisive powers into the hands of men for so many centuries that their ancient supremacy would take some unlearning. But why should his instincts lead him to expect that the woman in whose arms he lay each night would at least conceal her literacy? Why should there seem to be some rub between the enormous love he felt for her and her ability to understand the quantum theory?

She wandered downstairs and stood in the kitchen doorway, watching him at his work. Her feeling was tender. What a kind, gentle, purposeful, and handsome man she had married. What pride he took in their house. But then, as she went on watching him, she suffered a spiritual chill, a paroxysm of doubt. Was he, bent over the kitchen table at a woman's work, really a man? Had she married some half male, some aberration? Did he like to wear an apron? Was he a transvestite? And was she aberrant herself? But this was inadmissible, and equally inadmissible was the reasoning that would bring her to see that he polished silver because he was forced to. Suddenly some vague, brutish stray appeared in the corner of her imagination, some hairy and drunken sailor who would beat her on Saturday nights, debauch her with his gross appetites, and make her scrub the floor on her hands and knees. That was the kind of man she should have married. That had been her destiny. He looked up, smiled gently, and asked her how her work was coming. "*Ça marche, ça marche,*" she said wearily, and went back upstairs to her desk. "Little Gustave didn't get along at all well with his school chums," she wrote. "He was frightfully unpopular . . ."

He came into their room when his work was done. He ran a hand lightly through her hair. "Just let me finish this paragraph," she said. She heard him take a shower, heard his bare feet on the carpet as he crossed the room and bounded happily into bed. Moved equally by duty and desire but still thinking of the glories of Flaubert, she washed, scented herself with perfume, and joined him in their wide bed, which, with its clean and fragrant linen and equal pools of light, seemed indeed a bower. *Bosquet,* she thought, *brume, bruit.* And then, sitting up in his arms, she exclaimed,

"Elle avait lu 'Paul et Virgine' et elle avait rêvé la maison-nette de bambous, le nègre Domingo, le chien Fidèle, mais surtout l'amitié douce de quelque bon petit frère, qui va chercher pour vous des fruits rouges dans des grands arbres plus hauts que des clochers, ou qui court pieds nus sur le sable, vous apportant un nid d'oiseau . . ."

"God damn it to hell!" he said. He spoke in utter bitter-ness. He got out of bed, got a blanket from the closet, and made his bed in the living room.

She cried. He was jealous of her intelligence—she saw that. But was she meant to pose as a cretin in order to be attrac-tive? Why should he rage because she had said a few words in French? To assume that intelligence, knowledge, the very benefits of education were male attributes was an attitude that had been obsolete for a century. Then she felt as if the strain put on her heart by this cruelty was too much. She seemed to feel one of its fastenings give, as if this organ was a cask and so heavily laden with sorrow that, like some ruptured treasure chest of childhood, its sides had burst. "Intelligence" was the word she returned to—intelligence was at stake. And yet the word should ring free and clear of the pain she was suffering. Intelligence was the subject up for discussion, but it had the sentience, at that hour, of flesh and blood. What she faced was the bare bones of pain, cleansed in the stewpot and polished by the hound's tooth; this intelligence had the taste of death. She cried herself to sleep.

Later she was awakened by a crash. She was afraid. Might he harm her? Had something gone wrong with the compli-cated machinery of the old house? Burglars? Fire? The noise had come from their bathroom. She found him naked on his

hands and knees on the bathroom floor. His head was under
the washbasin. She went to him quickly and helped him to
his feet. "I'm all right," he said. "I'm just terribly drunk."
She helped him back to their bed, where he fell asleep at
once.

They had a dinner party a few nights later, and all the
silver he had polished was used. The party went off without a
hitch. One of their guests, a lawyer, described a local scandal.
A four-mile link of highway, connecting two parkways in
the neighborhood, had been approved by the state and the
local governments. The cost was three million dollars, on a
bid given by a contractor named Felici. The road was to
destroy a large formal garden and park that had been main-
tained and open to the public for half a century. The owner,
an octogenarian, lived in San Francisco and was either help-
less, indifferent, or immobilized by indignation. The connecting road was of no use; no study of traffic patterns had
proved that there was any need for such a road. A beautiful
park and a large slice of tax money were to be handed over
to an unscrupulous and avaricious contractor.

It was the kind of story Jill liked. Her eyes were bright,
her color was high. Georgie watched her with a mixture of
pride and dismay. Her civic zeal had been provoked, and
he knew she would pursue the scandal to some conclusion.
She was very happy with this challenge, but it was, on that
evening, a happiness that embraced her house, her husband,
her way of life. On Monday morning she stormed the various
commissions that controlled highway construction, and veri-
fied the scandal. Then she organized a committee and circu-
lated a petition. An old woman named Mrs. Haney was

found to take care of Bibber, and a high-school girl came in to read to him in the afternoons. Jill was absorbed in her work, bright-eyed and excited.

This was in December. Late one afternoon, Georgie left his office in Brooklyn and went into New York to do some shopping. All the high buildings in midtown were hidden in rain clouds, but he felt their presence overhead like the presence of a familiar mountain range. His feet were wet and his throat felt sore. The streets were crowded, and the decorations on the store fronts were mostly at such an angle that their meaning escaped him. While he could see the canopy of light at Lord & Taylor's, he could only see the chins and vestments of the choir plastered across the front of Saks. Blasts of holy music wavered through the rain. He stepped into a puddle. It was as dark as night; it seemed, because of the many lights, the darkest of nights. He went into Saks. Inside, the scene of well-dressed and brightly lighted pillage stopped him. He stood to one side to avoid being savaged by the crowds that were pushing their way in and out. He distinctly felt the symptoms of a cold. A woman standing beside him dropped some parcels. He picked them up. She had a pleasant face, wore a black mink coat, and her feet, he noticed, were wetter than his. She thanked him, and he asked if she was going to storm the counters. "I thought I would," she said, "but now I think I won't. My feet are wet, and I have a terrible feeling that I'm coming down with a cold."

"I feel the same way," he said. "Let's find some quiet place and have a drink."

"Oh, but I couldn't do that," she said.

"Why not?" he asked. "It's a festival, isn't it?"

The dark afternoon seemed to turn on that word. It was meant to be festive. That was the meaning of the singing and the lights.

"I had never thought of it that way," she said.

"Come on," he said. He took her arm and led her down the avenue to a quiet bar. He ordered drinks and sneezed. "You ought to have a hot bath and go to bed," she said. Her concern seemed purely maternal. He introduced himself. Her name was Betty Landers. Her husband was a doctor. Her daughter was married and her son was in his last year at Cornell. She was alone a good deal of the time, but she had recently taken up painting. She went to the Art Students League three times a week, and had a studio in the Village. They had three or four drinks and then took a cab downtown to see her studio.

It was not his idea of a studio. It was a two-room apartment in one of the new buildings near Washington Square and looked a little like the lair of a spinster. She pointed out her treasures. That's what she called them. The desk she had bought in England, the chair she had bought in France, the signed Matisse lithograph. Her hair and her eyebrows were dark, her face was thin, and she might have been a spinster. She made him a drink, and when he asked to see her paintings she modestly refused, although he was to see them later, stacked up in the bathroom, where her easel and her other equipment were neatly stored. Why they became lovers, why in the presence of this stranger he should suddenly find himself divested of all his inhibitions and all his clothing, he never understood. She was not young. Her elbows and knees were lightly gnarled, as if she were some distant cousin of Daphne and would presently be transformed, not into a flowering shrub but into some hardy and common tree.

They met after this two or three times a week. He never discovered much about her beyond the fact that she lived on Park Avenue and was often alone. She was interested in his clothes and kept him posted on department-store sales. It was a large part of her conversation. Sitting in his lap, she told him that there was a sale of neckties at Saks, a sale of shoes at Brooks, a sale of shirts at Altman's. Jill, by this time, was so absorbed in her campaign that she hardly noticed his arrivals and departures, but, sitting one evening in the living room while Jill was busy on the upstairs telephone, he felt that he had behaved shabbily. He felt that it was time that the affair, begun on that dark afternoon before Christmas, was over. He took some notepaper and wrote to Betty: "Darling, I'm leaving for San Francisco this evening and will be gone six weeks. I think it will be better, and I'm sure you'll agree with me, if we don't meet again." He wrote the letter a second time, changing San Francisco to Rome, and addressed the note to her studio in the Village.

Jill was campaigning on the telephone the next night when he returned home. Mathilde, the high-school girl, was reading to Bibber. He spoke to his son and then went down to the pantry to make a drink. While he was there, he heard Jill's heels on the stairs. They seemed to strike a swift and vengeful note, and when she came into the pantry her face was pale and drawn. Her hands were shaking, and in one of them she held the first of the two notes he had written.

"What is the meaning of this?" she asked.

"Where did you find it?"

"In the wastepaper basket."

"Then I will explain," he said. "Please sit down. Sit down

for a minute, and I'll explain the whole thing."

"Do I *have* to sit down? I'm terribly busy."

"No, you don't have to sit down, but would you close the door? Mathilde can hear us."

"I can't believe you have anything to say that would necessitate closing a door."

"I have this to say," he said. He closed the door. "In December, just before Christmas, I took a mistress, a lonely woman. I can't explain my choice. It may have been because she had an apartment of her own. She was not young; she was not beautiful. Her children are grown. Her husband is a doctor. They live on Park Avenue."

"Oh, my God," she said. "Park Avenue!" and she laughed. "I adore that part of it. I could have guessed that if you invented a mistress she would live on Park Avenue. You've always been such a hick."

"Do you think this is all an invention?"

"Yes, I do. I think you've made the whole thing up to try and hurt me. You've never had much of an imagination. You might have done better if you'd tasted some Thackeray. Really. A Park Avenue matron. Couldn't you have invented something more delectable? A Vassar senior with blazing red hair? A colored night-club singer? An Italian princess?"

"Do you really think I've made this all up?"

"I do, I do. I think it's all a fabrication and a loathsome one, but tell me more, tell me more about your Park Avenue matron."

"I have nothing more to tell you."

"You have nothing more to tell me because your powers of invention have collapsed. Isn't that it? My advice to you, old chap, is never to embark on anything that counts on a powerful imagination. It isn't your forte."

"You don't believe me."

"I do not, and if I did I wouldn't be jealous. My sort of woman is never jealous. I have more important things to do."

At this point in their marriage, Jill's assault on the highway commission served as a sort of suspension bridge over which they could travel, meet, converse, and dine together, elevated safely above the turbulence of their feelings. She was working to have the issue brought to a public hearing, and was to appear before the commission with petitions and documents that would prove the gravity of her case and the number of influential supporters she had been able to enlist. Unluckily, at this time Bibber came down with a bad cold and it was difficult to find anyone to stay with him. Now and then, Mrs. Haney would come to sit beside his bed, and in the afternoons Mathilde read to him. When it was necessary for Jill to go to Albany, George stayed home from his office for a day so that she could make this trip. He stayed home on another day when she had an important appointment and Mrs. Haney couldn't come. She was sincerely grateful to him for these sacrifices, and he had nothing but admiration for her intelligence and tenacity. She was far superior to him as an advocate and as an organizer. She was to appear before the commission on a Friday, and he looked forward to having this much of their struggle behind them. He came home on Friday at around six. He called out, "Jill? Mathilde? Mrs. Haney?" but there was no answer. He threw off his hat and coat and bounded up the stairs to Bibber's room. The room was lighted, but the boy was alone and seemed to be asleep.

Pinned to his pillow was this note: "Dear Mrs. Madison my aunt and uncle came to visit with us and I have to go home and help my mother. Bibber's asleep so he won't know the difference. I am sorry. Mathilde." On the pillow next to the note was a dark stain of blood. He touched the boy lightly and felt the searing heat of fever. Then he tried to rouse the child, but Bibber was not sleeping; he was unconscious.

Georgie moistened the boy's lips with some water, and Bibber regained consciousness long enough to throw his arms around his father. The pathos of seeing the burden of grave illness on someone so innocent and so young made Georgie cry. There was a tumultuous power of love in that small room, and he had to subdue his feelings lest he harm the boy with the force of his embrace. They clung to one another. Then Georgie called the doctor. He called ten times, and each time he heard the idiotic and frustrating busy signal. Then he called the hospital and asked for an ambulance. He wrapped the boy in a blanket and carried him down the stairs, enormously grateful to have this much to do. The ambulance was there in a few minutes.

Jill had stopped long enough to have a drink with one of her assistants, and came in a half hour later. "Hail the conquering hero!" she called as she stepped into the empty house. "We shall have our hearing, and the scurvy rascals are on the run. Even Felici appeared to be moved by my eloquence, and Carter said that I should have been an advocate. I was simply stupendous."

Item: "intl pd florence via rca 22 23 9:35 amelia faxon chidchester care amexco: bibber died of pneumonia on thursday. can you return or may i come to you love jill"

Amelia Faxon Chidchester was staying with her old friend Louisa Trefaldi, in Fiesole. She bicycled down into Florence late in the afternoon of the twenty-third of January. Her bicycle was an old, high-seated Dutheil, and it elevated her a little above the small cars. She bumped imperturbably through some of the worst traffic in the world. Her life was threatened every few minutes by a Vespa or a trolley, but she yielded to no one, and the look on her ruddy face was serene. Elevated, moving with that somnambulistic pace of a cyclist, smiling gently at the death that menaced her at every intersection, she looked a little supernatural, and it may have been that she thought she was. Her smile was sweet, inscrutable, and adamantine, and you felt that, had she been knocked off her bicycle, this expression, as she sailed through the air, would not lose its patience. She pumped over a bridge, dismounted gracefully, and walked along the river to the American Express office. Here she barked out her greetings in Italian, anxious to disassociate herself from the horseless American cowboys and above all from her own kind, the truly lost and unwanted, who move like leaves around the edges of the world, gathering only long enough to wait in line and see if there is any mail. The place was crowded, and she read her tragic cable in the middle of the crowd. You could not, from her expression, have guessed its content. She sighed deeply and raised her face. She seemed ennobled. She wrote her reply at once: "NON POSSO TORNARE TANTI BACI FERVIDI. MELEE."

"Dearest darling," she wrote that evening. "I was frightfully sorry to have your tragic news. I can only thank God that I didn't know him better, but my experience in these matters is rather extensive, and I have come to a time of

life when I do not especially like to dwell upon the subject
of passing away. There is no street I walk on, no building
or painting I see here that doesn't remind me of Berenson,
dear Berenson. The last time I saw him, I sat at his feet and
asked if he had a magic carpet what picture in the whole wide
world would he ask to be transported to. Without a moment's
hesitation he chose the Raphael Madonna in The Hermitage.
It is not possible for me to return. The truth will out, and
the truth is that I don't like my own countrymen. As for
your coming over, I am now staying with dear Louisa and, as
you know, with her two is company, three is a crowd. Perhaps
in the autumn, when your loss is not so painful, we might
meet in Paris for a few days and revisit some of our old
haunts."

Georgie was crushed by the death of his son. He blamed
Jill, which was cruel and unreasonable and it seemed, in the
end, that he could be both. Jill went to Reno at his request
and got a consent decree. It was all made by Georgie to seem
like a punishment. Later on she got a job with a textbook
publishing firm in Cleveland. Her acumen and her charm
were swiftly recognized and she was very successful, but she
didn't marry again, or hadn't married when I last had any
news. The last I heard was from Georgie, who telephoned
one night and said that we *must* get together for lunch. It was
about eleven. I think he was drunk. He hadn't married again
either, and from the bitterness with which he spoke of
women that night I guessed that he never would. He told
me about Jill's job in Cleveland and said that Mrs. Chidchester was bicycling across Scotland. I thought then how
inferior he was to Jill, how immature. When I agreed to

call him about lunch he gave me his telephone number at the shipyard, his extension there, the telephone number of his apartment, the telephone number of a cottage he had in Connecticut and the telephone number of the club where he lunched and played cards. I wrote all these numbers on a piece of paper and when we said good-bye I dropped the paper into a wastebasket.

The Swimmer

❦

It was one of those midsummer Sundays when everyone sits around saying: "I *drank* too much last night." You might have heard it whispered by the parishioners leaving church, heard it from the lips of the priest himself, struggling with his cassock in the *vestiarium,* heard it from the golf links and the tennis courts, heard it from the wild-life preserve where the leader of the Audubon group was suffering from a terrible hangover. "I *drank* too much," said Donald Westerhazy. "We all *drank* too much," said Lucinda Merrill. "It must have been the wine," said Helen Westerhazy. "I *drank* too much of that claret."

This was at the edge of the Westerhazys' pool. The pool, fed by an artesian well with a high iron content, was a pale shade of green. It was a fine day. In the west there was a massive stand of cumulus cloud so like a city seen from a distance—from the bow of an approaching ship—that it might have had a name. Lisbon. Hackensack. The sun was hot. Neddy Merrill sat by the green water, one hand in it,

61

one around a glass of gin. He was a slender man—he seemed
to have the especial slenderness of youth—and while he
was far from young he had slid down his banister that morning and given the bronze backside of Aphrodite on the hall
table a smack, as he jogged toward the smell of coffee in
his dining room. He might have been compared to a summer's day, particularly the last hours of one, and while he
lacked a tennis racket or a sail bag the impression was definitely one of youth, sport, and clement weather. He had
been swimming and now he was breathing deeply, stertor-
ously as if he could gulp into his lungs the components of
that moment, the heat of the sun, the intenseness of his
pleasure. It all seemed to flow into his chest. His own house
stood in Bullet Park, eight miles to the south, where his four
beautiful daughters would have had their lunch and might
be playing tennis. Then it occurred to him that by taking a
dogleg to the southwest he could reach his home by water.

His life was not confining and the delight he took in this
observation could not be explained by its suggestion of escape. He seemed to see, with a cartographer's eye, that string
of swimming pools, that quasi-subterranean stream that
curved across the county. He had made a discovery, a contri-
bution to modern geography; he would name the stream
Lucinda after his wife. He was not a practical joker nor was
he a fool but he was determinedly original and had a vague
and modest idea of himself as a legendary figure. The day
was beautiful and it seemed to him that a long swim might
enlarge and celebrate its beauty.

He took off a sweater that was hung over his shoulders
and dove in. He had an inexplicable contempt for men who
did not hurl themselves into pools. He swam a choppy crawl,

breathing either with every stroke or every fourth stroke and counting somewhere well in the back of his mind the one-two one-two of a flutter kick. It was not a serviceable stroke for long distances but the domestication of swimming had saddled the sport with some customs and in his part of the world a crawl was customary. To be embraced and sustained by the light green water was less a pleasure, it seemed, than the resumption of a natural condition, and he would have liked to swim without trunks, but this was not possible, considering his project. He hoisted himself up on the far curb—he never used the ladder—and started across the lawn. When Lucinda asked where he was going he said he was going to swim home.

The only maps and charts he had to go by were remembered or imaginary but these were clear enough. First there were the Grahams, the Hammers, the Lears, the Howlands, and the Crosscups. He would cross Ditmar Street to the Bunkers and come, after a short portage, to the Levys, the Welchers, and the public pool in Lancaster. Then there were the Hallorans, the Sachses, the Biswangers, Shirley Adams, the Gilmartins, and the Clydes. The day was lovely, and that he lived in a world so generously supplied with water seemed like a clemency, a beneficence. His heart was high and he ran across the grass. Making his way home by an uncommon route gave him the feeling that he was a pilgrim, an explorer, a man with a destiny, and he knew that he would find friends all along the way; friends would line the banks of the Lucinda River.

He went through a hedge that separated the Westerhazys' land from the Grahams', walked under some flowering apple trees, passed the shed that housed their pump and filter, and came out at the Grahams' pool. "Why, Neddy," Mrs. Graham said, "what a marvelous surprise. I've been trying to get you on the phone all morning. Here, let me get you a drink." He saw then, like any explorer, that the hospitable customs and traditions of the natives would have to be handled with diplomacy if he was ever going to reach his destination. He did not want to mystify or seem rude to the Grahams nor did he have the time to linger there. He swam the length of their pool and joined them in the sun and was rescued, a few minutes later, by the arrival of two carloads of friends from Connecticut. During the uproarious reunions he was able to slip away. He went down by the front of the Grahams' house, stepped over a thorny hedge, and crossed a vacant lot to the Hammers'. Mrs. Hammer, looking up from her roses, saw him swim by although she wasn't quite sure who it was. The Lears heard him splashing past the open windows of their living room. The Howlands and the Crosscups were away. After leaving the Howlands' he crossed Ditmar Street and started for the Bunkers', where he could hear, even at that distance, the noise of a party.

The water refracted the sound of voices and laughter and seemed to suspend it in midair. The Bunkers' pool was on a rise and he climbed some stairs to a terrace where twenty-five or thirty men and women were drinking. The only person in the water was Rusty Towers, who floated there on a rubber raft. Oh how bonny and lush were the banks of the Lucinda River! Prosperous men and women gathered by the sapphire-colored waters while caterer's men in white coats passed them cold gin. Overhead a red de Haviland trainer was circling around and around and around in the sky with something like the glee of a child in a swing. Ned felt a passing affection for the scene, a tenderness for the gather-

ing, as if it was something he might touch. In the distance
he heard thunder. As soon as Enid Bunker saw him she
began to scream: "Oh look who's here! What a marvelous
surprise! When Lucinda said that you couldn't come I
thought I'd *die*." She made her way to him through the
crowd, and when they had finished kissing she led him to the
bar, a progress that was slowed by the fact that he stopped
to kiss eight or ten other women and shake the hands of as
many men. A smiling bartender he had seen at a hundred
parties gave him a gin and tonic and he stood by the bar for
a moment, anxious not to get stuck in any conversation that
would delay his voyage. When he seemed about to be surrounded he dove in and swam close to the side to avoid
colliding with Rusty's raft. At the far end of the pool he
bypassed the Tomlinsons with a broad smile and jogged up
the garden path. The gravel cut his feet but this was the
only unpleasantness. The party was confined to the pool, and
as he went toward the house he heard the brilliant, watery
sound of voices fade, heard the noise of a radio from the
Bunkers' kitchen, where someone was listening to a ballgame.
Sunday afternoon. He made his way through the parked cars
and down the grassy border of their driveway to Alewives'
Lane. He did not want to be seen on the road in his bathing
trunks but there was no traffic and he made the short distance
to the Levys' driveway, marked with a private property sign
and a green tube for the *New York Times*. All the doors and
windows of the big house were open but there were no signs
of life; not even a dog barked. He went around the side of
the house to the pool and saw that the Levys had only
recently left. Glasses and bottles and dishes of nuts were on
a table at the deep end, where there was a bathhouse or

gazebo, hung with Japanese lanterns. After swimming the pool he got himself a glass and poured a drink. It was his fourth or fifth drink and he had swum nearly half the length of the Lucinda River. He felt tired, clean, and pleased at that moment to be alone; pleased with everything.

It would storm. The stand of cumulus cloud—that city— had risen and darkened, and while he sat there he heard the percussiveness of thunder again. The de Haviland trainer was still circling overhead and it seemed to Ned that he could almost hear the pilot laugh with pleasure in the afternoon; but when there was another peal of thunder he took off for home. A train whistle blew and he wondered what time it had gotten to be. Four? Five? He thought of the provincial station at that hour, where a waiter, his tuxedo concealed by a raincoat, a dwarf with some flowers wrapped in newspaper, and a woman who had been crying would be waiting for the local. It was suddenly growing dark; it was that moment when the pin-headed birds seem to organize their song into some acute and knowledgeable recognition of the storm's approach. Then there was a fine noise of rushing water from the crown of an oak at his back, as if a spigot there had been turned. Then the noise of fountains came from the crowns of all the tall trees. Why did he love storms, what was the meaning of his excitement when the door sprang open and the rain wind fled rudely up the stairs, why had the simple task of shutting the windows of an old house seemed fitting and urgent, why did the first watery notes of a storm wind have for him the unmistakable sound of good news, cheer, glad tidings? Then there was an explosion, a smell of cordite, and rain lashed the Japanese lanterns that Mrs. Levy had bought in Kyoto the year before last, or was it the year before that?

He stayed in the Levys' gazebo until the storm had passed. The rain had cooled the air and he shivered. The force of the wind had stripped a maple of its red and yellow leaves and scattered them over the grass and the water. Since it was mid-summer the tree must be blighted, and yet he felt a peculiar sadness at this sign of autumn. He braced his shoulders, emptied his glass, and started for the Welchers' pool. This meant crossing the Lindleys' riding ring and he was surprised to find it overgrown with grass and all the jumps dismantled. He wondered if the Lindleys had sold their horses or gone away for the summer and put them out to board. He seemed to remember having heard something about the Lindleys and their horses but the memory was unclear. On he went, barefoot through the wet grass, to the Welchers', where he found their pool was dry.

This breach in his chain of water disappointed him absurdly, and he felt like some explorer who seeks a torrential headwater and finds a dead stream. He was disappointed and mystified. It was common enough to go away for the summer but no one ever drained his pool. The Welchers had definitely gone away. The pool furniture was folded, stacked, and covered with a tarpaulin. The bathhouse was locked. All the windows of the house were shut, and when he went around to the driveway in front he saw a for-sale sign nailed to a tree. When had he last heard from the Welchers—when, that is, had he and Lucinda last regretted an invitation to dine with them. It seemed only a week or so ago. Was his memory failing or had he so disciplined it in the repression

of unpleasant facts that he had damaged his sense of the truth?
Then in the distance he heard the sound of a tennis game.
This cheered him, cleared away all his apprehensions and let
him regard the overcast sky and the cold air with indifference.
This was the day that Neddy Merrill swam across the county.
That was the day! He started off then for his most difficult
portage.

Had you gone for a Sunday afternoon ride that day you
might have seen him, close to naked, standing on the shoulders of route 424, waiting for a chance to cross. You might
have wondered if he was the victim of foul play, had his car
broken down, or was he merely a fool. Standing barefoot in
the deposits of the highway—beer cans, rags, and blowout
patches—exposed to all kinds of ridicule, he seemed pitiful.
He had known when he started that this was a part of his
journey—it had been on his maps—but confronted with the
lines of traffic, worming through the summery light, he found
himself unprepared. He was laughed at, jeered at, a beer can
was thrown at him, and he had no dignity or humor to bring
to the situation. He could have gone back, back to the Westerhazys', where Lucinda would still be sitting in the sun. He
had signed nothing, vowed nothing, pledged nothing not
even to himself. Why, believing as he did, that all human
obduracy was susceptible to common sense, was he unable to
turn back? Why was he determined to complete his journey
even if it meant putting his life in danger? At what point had
this prank, this joke, this piece of horseplay become serious?
He could not go back, he could not even recall with any clearness the green water at the Westerhazys', the sense of inhaling
the day's components, the friendly and relaxed voices saying

that they had *drunk* too much. In the space of an hour, more or less, he had covered a distance that made his return impossible.

An old man, tooling down the highway at fifteen miles an hour, let him get to the middle of the road, where there was a grass divider. Here he was exposed to the ridicule of the northbound traffic, but after ten or fifteen minutes he was able to cross. From here he had only a short walk to the Recreation Center at the edge of the Village of Lancaster, where there were some handball courts and a public pool.

The effect of the water on voices, the illusion of brilliance and suspense, was the same here as it had been at the Bunkers' but the sounds here were louder, harsher, and more shrill, and as soon as he entered the crowded enclosure he was confronted with regimentation. "ALL SWIMMERS MUST TAKE A SHOWER BEFORE USING THE POOL. ALL SWIMMERS MUST USE THE FOOTBATH. ALL SWIMMERS MUST WEAR THEIR IDENTIFICATION DISKS." He took a shower, washed his feet in a cloudy and bitter solution and made his way to the edge of the water. It stank of chlorine and looked to him like a sink. A pair of lifeguards in a pair of towers blew police whistles at what seemed to be regular intervals and abused the swimmers through a public address system. Neddy remembered the sapphire water at the Bunkers' with longing and thought that he might contaminate himself—damage his own prosperousness and charm—by swimming in this murk, but he reminded himself that he was an explorer, a pilgrim, and that this was merely a stagnant bend in the Lucinda River. He dove, scowling with distaste, into the chlorine and had to swim with his head above water to avoid collisions, but even so he was bumped into, splashed and jostled. When he got to the shallow end both lifeguards were shouting at him: "Hey, you, you without the identification disk, get outa the water." He did, but they had no way of pursuing him and he went through the reek of suntan oil and chlorine out through the hurricane fence and passed the handball courts. By crossing the road he entered the wooded part of the Halloran estate. The woods were not cleared and the footing was treacherous and difficult until he reached the lawn and the clipped beech hedge that encircled their pool.

The Hallorans were friends, an elderly couple of enormous wealth who seemed to bask in the suspicion that they might be Communists. They were zealous reformers but they were not Communists, and yet when they were accused, as they sometimes were, of subversion, it seemed to gratify and excite them. Their beech hedge was yellow and he guessed this had been blighted like the Levys' maple. He called hullo, hullo, to warn the Hallorans of his approach, to palliate his invasion of their privacy. The Hallorans, for reasons that had never been explained to him, did not wear bathing suits. No explanations were in order, really. Their nakedness was a detail in their uncompromising zeal for reform and he stepped politely out of his trunks before he went through the opening in the hedge.

Mrs. Halloran, a stout woman with white hair and a serene face, was reading the *Times*. Mr. Halloran was taking beech leaves out of the water with a scoop. They seemed not surprised or displeased to see him. Their pool was perhaps the oldest in the county, a fieldstone rectangle, fed by a brook. It had no filter or pump and its waters were the opaque gold of the stream.

"I'm swimming across the county," Ned said.

"Why, I didn't know one could," exclaimed Mrs. Halloran.
"Well, I've made it from the Westerhazys'," Ned said.
"That must be about four miles."

He left his trunks at the deep end, walked to the shallow
end, and swam this stretch. As he was pulling himself out of
the water he heard Mrs. Halloran say: "We've been *terribly*
sorry to hear about all your misfortunes, Neddy."

"My misfortunes?" Ned asked. "I don't know what you
mean."

"Why, we heard that you'd sold the house and that your
poor children . . ."

"I don't recall having sold the house," Ned said, "and the
girls are at home."

"Yes," Mrs. Halloran sighed. "Yes . . ." Her voice filled the
air with an unseasonable melancholy and Ned spoke briskly.
"Thank you for the swim."

"Well, have a nice trip," said Mrs. Halloran.

Beyond the hedge he pulled on his trunks and fastened
them. They were loose and he wondered if, during the space
of an afternoon, he could have lost some weight. He was cold
and he was tired and the naked Hallorans and their dark
water had depressed him. The swim was too much for his
strength but how could he have guessed this, sliding down
the banister that morning and sitting in the Westerhazys'
sun? His arms were lame. His legs felt rubbery and ached at
the joints. The worst of it was the cold in his bones and the
feeling that he might never be warm again. Leaves were
falling down around him and he smelled woodsmoke on
the wind. Who would be burning wood at this time of year?

He needed a drink. Whiskey would warm him, pick him up,
carry him through the last of his journey, refresh his feeling

that it was original and valorous to swim across the county. Channel swimmers took brandy. He needed a stimulant. He crossed the lawn in front of the Hallorans' house and went down a little path to where they had built a house for their only daughter Helen and her husband Eric Sachs. The Sachses' pool was small and he found Helen and her husband there.

"Oh, *Neddy*," Helen said. "Did you lunch at Mother's?"

"Not *really*," Ned said. "I *did* stop to see your parents." This seemed to be explanation enough. "I'm terribly sorry to break in on you like this but I've taken a chill and I wonder if you'd give me a drink."

"Why, I'd *love* to," Helen said, "but there hasn't been anything in this house to drink since Eric's operation. That was three years ago."

Was he losing his memory, had his gift for concealing painful facts let him forget that he had sold his house, that his children were in trouble, and that his friend had been ill? His eyes slipped from Eric's face to his abdomen, where he saw three pale, sutured scars, two of them at least a foot long. Gone was his navel, and what, Neddy thought, would the roving hand, bed-checking one's gifts at 3 A.M. make of a belly with no navel, no link to birth, this breach in the succession?

"I'm sure you can get a drink at the Biswangers'," Helen said. "They're having an enormous do. You can hear it from here. Listen!"

She raised her head and from across the road, the lawns, the gardens, the woods, the fields, he heard again the brilliant noise of voices over water. "Well, I'll get wet," he said, still feeling that he had no freedom of choice about his means of travel. He dove into the Sachses' cold water and, gasping, close to drowning, made his way from one end of the pool to the other. "Lucinda and I want *terribly* to see you," he said over his shoulder, his face set toward the Biswangers'. "We're sorry it's been so long and we'll call you *very* soon."

He crossed some fields to the Biswangers' and the sounds of revelry there. They would be honored to give him a drink, they would be happy to give him a drink, they would in fact be lucky to give him a drink. The Biswangers invited him and Lucinda for dinner four times a year, six weeks in advance. They were always rebuffed and yet they continued to send out their invitations, unwilling to comprehend the rigid and undemocratic realities of their society. They were the sort of people who discussed the price of things at cocktails, exchanged market tips during dinner, and after dinner told dirty stories to mixed company. They did not belong to Neddy's set—they were not even on Lucinda's Christmas card list. He went toward their pool with feelings of indifference, charity, and some unease, since it seemed to be getting dark and these were the longest days of the year. The party when he joined it was noisy and large. Grace Biswanger was the kind of hostess who asked the optometrist, the veterinarian, the real-estate dealer and the dentist. No one was swimming and the twilight, reflected on the water of the pool, had a wintry gleam. There was a bar and he started for this. When Grace Biswanger saw him she came toward him, not affectionately as he had every right to expect, but bellicosely.

"Why, this party has everything," she said loudly, "including a gate crasher."

She could not deal him a social blow—there was no question about this and he did not flinch. "As a gate crasher," he asked politely, "do I rate a drink?"

"Suit yourself," she said. "You don't seem to pay much attention to invitations."

She turned her back on him and joined some guests, and he went to the bar and ordered a whiskey. The bartender served him but he served him rudely. His was a world in which the caterer's men kept the social score, and to be rebuffed by a part-time barkeep meant that he had suffered some loss of social esteem. Or perhaps the man was new and uninformed. Then he heard Grace at his back say: "They went for broke overnight—nothing but income—and he showed up drunk one Sunday and asked us to loan him five thousand dollars. . . ." She was always talking about money. It was worse than eating your peas off a knife. He dove into the pool, swam its length and went away.

The next pool on his list, the last but two, belonged to his old mistress, Shirley Adams. If he had suffered any injuries at the Biswangers' they would be cured here. Love—sexual roughhouse in fact—was the supreme elixir, the painkiller, the brightly colored pill that would put the spring back into his step, the joy of life in his heart. They had had an affair last week, last month, last year. He couldn't remember. It was he who had broken it off, his was the upper hand, and he stepped through the gate of the wall that surrounded her pool with nothing so considered as self-confidence. It seemed in a way to be his pool as the lover, particularly the illicit lover, enjoys the possessions of his mistress with an authority unknown to holy matrimony. She was there, her hair the color of brass, but her figure, at the edge of the lighted, cerulean water, excited in him no profound memories. It had been, he thought, a lighthearted affair, although she had wept when he broke it off. She seemed confused to see him and he wondered if she was still wounded. Would she, God forbid, weep again?

"What do you want?" she asked.

"I'm swimming across the county."

"Good Christ. Will you ever grow up?"

"What's the matter?"

"If you've come here for money," she said, "I won't give you another cent."

"You could give me a drink."

"I could but I won't. I'm not alone."

"Well, I'm on my way."

He dove in and swam the pool, but when he tried to haul himself up onto the curb he found that the strength in his arms and his shoulders had gone, and he paddled to the ladder and climbed out. Looking over his shoulder he saw, in the lighted bathhouse, a young man. Going out onto the dark lawn he smelled chrysanthemums or marigolds—some stubborn autumnal fragrance—on the night air, strong as gas. Looking overhead he saw that the stars had come out, but why should he seem to see Andromeda, Cepheus, and Cassiopeia? What had become of the constellations of midsummer? He began to cry.

It was probably the first time in his adult life that he had ever cried, certainly the first time in his life that he had ever felt so miserable, cold, tired, and bewildered. He could not understand the rudeness of the caterer's barkeep or the rudeness of a mistress who had come to him on her knees and showered his trousers with tears. He had swum too long, he had been immersed too long, and his nose and his throat were sore from the water. What he needed then was a drink, some company, and some clean dry clothes, and while he could have cut directly across the road to his home he went on to the Gilmartins' pool. Here, for the first time in his life, he did not dive but went down the steps into the icy water and swam a hobbled side stroke that he might have learned as a youth. He staggered with fatigue on his way to the Clydes' and paddled the length of their pool, stopping again and again with his hand on the curb to rest. He climbed up the ladder and wondered if he had the strength to get home. He had done what he wanted, he had swum the county, but he was so stupefied with exhaustion that his triumph seemed vague. Stooped, holding onto the gateposts for support, he turned up the driveway of his own house.

The place was dark. Was it so late that they had all gone to bed? Had Lucinda stayed at the Westerhazys' for supper? Had the girls joined her there or gone someplace else? Hadn't they agreed, as they usually did on Sunday, to regret all their invitations and stay at home? He tried the garage doors to see what cars were in but the doors were locked and rust came off the handles onto his hands. Going toward the house, he saw that the force of the thunderstorm had knocked one of the rain gutters loose. It hung down over the front door like an umbrella rib, but it could be fixed in the morning. The house was locked, and he thought that the stupid cook or the stupid maid must have locked the place up until he remembered that it had been some time since they had employed a maid or a cook. He shouted, pounded on the door, tried to force it with his shoulder, and then, looking in at the windows, saw that the place was empty.

Metamorphoses

❦

I

LARRY ACTAEON WAS BUILT ALONG CLASSICAL LINES: curly hair, a triangulated nose, and a large and supple body, and he had what might be described as a Periclean interest in innovation. He designed his own sailboat (it had a list to port), ran for mayor (he was defeated), bred a Finnish wolf bitch to a German shepherd dog (the American Kennel Club refused to list the breed), and organized a drag hunt in Bullet Park, where he lived with his charming wife and three children. He was a partner in the investment-banking firm of Lothard and Williams, where he was esteemed for his shrewd and boisterous disposition.

Lothard and Williams was a highly conservative shop with an unmatched reputation for probity, but it was unconventional in one respect. One of the partners was a woman. This was a widow named Mrs. Vuiton. Her husband had been a senior partner, and when he died she had asked to be taken into the firm. In her favor were her intelligence, her beauty, and the fact that, had she withdrawn her husband's interest

77

from the partnership, it would have been missed. Lothard, the most conservative of them all, supported her candidacy, and she was taken in. Her intellect was formidable, and was fortified by her formidable and immaculate beauty. She was a stunning woman, in her middle thirties, and brought more than her share of business to the firm. Larry didn't dislike her—he didn't quite dare to—but that her good looks and her musical voice were more effective in banking than his own shrewd and boisterous manner made him at least uneasy.

The partners in Lothard and Williams—they were seven—had their private offices arranged around the central offices of Mr. Lothard. They had the usual old-fashioned appurtenances—walnut desks, portraits of dead partners, dark walls and carpets. The six male partners all wore watch chains, stickpins, and high-crowned hats. Larry sat one afternoon in this atmosphere of calculated gloom, weighing the problems of a long-term bond issue that was in the house and having a slow sale, and suddenly it crossed his mind that they might unload the entire issue on a pension-fund customer. Moved by his enthusiasm, his boisterousness, he strode through Mr. Lothard's outer office and impetuously opened the inner door. There was Mrs. Vuiton, wearing nothing but a string of beads. Mr. Lothard was at her side wearing a wristwatch. "Oh, I'm terribly sorry!" Larry said, and he closed the door and returned to his own desk.

The image of Mrs. Vuiton seemed incised in his memory, burnt there. He had seen a thousand naked women, but he had never seen one so stunning. Her skin had a luminous and pearly whiteness that he could not forget. The pathos and beauty of the naked woman established itself in his memory like a strain of music. He had beheld something that he should not have seen, and Mrs. Vuiton had glared at him with a look that was wicked and unholy. He could not shake or rationalize away the feeling that his blunder was disastrous; that he had in some way stumbled into a trans-gression that would demand compensation and revenge. Pure enthusiasm had moved him to open the door without knock-ing; pure enthusiasm, by his lights, was a blameless impulse. Why should he feel himself surrounded by trouble, misfor-tune, and disaster? The nature of man was concupiscent; the same thing might be going on in a thousand offices. What he had seen was commonplace, he told himself. But there had been nothing commonplace about the whiteness of her skin or her powerful and collected stare. He repeated to himself that he had done nothing wrong, but underlying all his fancies of good and evil, merits and rewards, was the stub-born and painful nature of things, and he knew that he had seen something that it was not his destiny to see.

He dictated some letters and answered the telephone when it rang, but he did nothing worthwhile for the rest of that afternoon. He spent some time trying to get rid of the litter that his Finnish wolf bitch had whelped. The Bronx Zoo was not interested. The American Kennel Club said that he had not introduced a breed, he had produced a monstrosity. Some-one had informed him that jewelers, department stores, and museums were policed by savage dogs, and he telephoned the security departments of Macy's, Cartier's, and the Mu-seum of Modern Art, but they all had dogs. He spent the last of the afternoon at his window, joining that vast population of the blunderers, the bored—the empty-handed barber, the clerk in the antique store nobody ever comes into, the idle insurance salesman, the failing haberdasher—all of those thousands who stand at the windows of the city and watch the afternoon go down. Some nameless doom seemed to threaten his welfare, and he was unable to refresh his boisterousness, his common sense.

He had a directors' dinner meeting on the East Side at seven. He had brought his evening clothes to town in a suit box, and had been invited to bathe and change at his host's. He left his office at five and, to kill time and if possible cheer himself, walked the two or three miles to Fifty-seventh Street. Even so, he was early, and he stopped in a bar for a drink. It was one of those places where the single women of the neighborhood congregate and are made welcome; where, having tippled sherry for most of the day, they gather to observe the cocktail hour. One of the women had a dog. As soon as Larry entered the place, the dog, a dachshund, sprang at him. The leash was attached to a table leg, and he struck at Larry so vigorously that he dragged the table a foot or two and upset a couple of drinks. He missed Larry, but there was a great deal of confusion, and Larry went to the end of the bar farthest from the ladies. The dog was excited, and his harsh, sharp barking filled the place. "What are you thinking of, Smoky?" his mistress asked. "What in the world are you thinking of? What's become of my little doggy? This can't be my little Smoky. This must be another doggy. . . ." The dog went on barking at Larry.

"Dogs don't like you?" the bartender asked.

"I breed dogs," Larry said. "I get along very well with dogs."

"It's a funny thing," the bartender said, "but I never heard that dog bark before. She's in here every afternoon, seven days a week, and that dog's always with her, but this is the first time there's ever been a peep out of him. Maybe if you took your drink into the dining room."

"You mean I'm disturbing Smoky?"

"Well, she's a regular customer. I never saw you before."

"All right," Larry said, putting as much feeling as he could into his consent. He carried his drink through a doorway into the empty dining room and sat at a table. The dog stopped barking as soon as he was gone. He finished his drink and looked around for another way to leave the place, but there was none. Smoky sprang at him again when he went out through the bar, and everyone was glad to see such a troublemaker go.

The apartment house where he was expected was one he had been in many times, but he had forgotten the address. He had counted on recognizing the doorway and the lobby, but when he stepped into the lobby he was faced with the sameness of those places. There was a black-and-white floor, a false fireplace, two English chairs, and a framed landscape. It was all familiar, but he realized that it could have been one of a dozen lobbies, and he asked the elevator man if this was the Fullmers' house. The man said "Yes," and Larry stepped into the car. Then, instead of ascending to the tenth floor where the Fullmers lived, the car went down. The first idea that crossed Larry's mind was that the Fullmers might be having their vestibule painted and that, for this or for some other inconvenience or change, he would be expected to use the back elevator. The man slid the door open onto a kind of infernal region, crowded with heaped ashcans, broken perambulators, and steampipes covered with ruptured asbestos sleeving. "Go through the door there and get the other elevator," the man said.

"But why do I have to take the back elevator?" Larry asked.

"It's a rule," the man said.

"I don't understand," Larry said.

"Listen," the man said. "Don't argue with me. Just take the back elevator. All you deliverymen always want to go in the front door like you owned the place. Well, this is one building where you can't. The management says all deliveries at the back door, and the management is boss."

"I'm not a deliveryman," Larry said. "I'm a guest."

"What's the box?"

"The box," Larry said, "contains my evening clothes. Now take me up to the tenth floor where the Fullmers live."

"I'm sorry, Mister, but you *look* like a deliveryman."

"I am an investment banker," Larry said, "and I am on my way to a directors' meeting, where we are going to discuss the underwriting of a forty-four-million-dollar bond issue. I am worth nine hundred thousand dollars. I have a twenty-two-room house in Bullet Park, a kennel of dogs, two riding horses, three children in college, a twenty-two-foot sailboat, and five automobiles."

"Jesus," the man said.

After Larry had bathed, he looked at himself in the mirror to see if he could detect any change in his appearance, but the face in the glass was too familiar; he had shaved and washed it too many times for it to reveal any secrets. He got through dinner and the meeting, and afterward had a whiskey with the other directors. He was still, in a way that he could not have defined, troubled at having been mistaken for a deliveryman, and hoping to shift his unease a little he said to the man beside him, "You know, when I was coming up

in the elevator tonight I was mistaken for a deliveryman."
His confidant either didn't hear, didn't comprehend, or
didn't care. He laughed loudly at something that was being
said across the room, and Larry, who was used to command-
ing attention, felt that he had suffered another loss.

He took a taxi to Grand Central and went home on one
of those locals that seem like a roundup of the spiritually way-
ward, the drunken, and the lost. The conductor was a corpu-
lent man with a pink face and a fresh rose in his buttonhole.
He had a few words to say to most of the travelers.

"You working the same place?" he asked Larry.

"Yes."

"You rush beer up in Yorktown, isn't that it?"

"No," Larry said, and he touched his face with his hands to
see if he could feel there the welts, lines, and other changes
that must have been worked in the last few hours.

"You work in a restaurant, don't you?" the conductor
asked.

"No," Larry said quietly.

"That's funny," the conductor said. "When I saw the soup-
and-fish I thought you was a waiter."

It was after one o'clock when he got off the train. The
station and the cabstand were shut, and only a few cars were
left in the parking lot. When he switched on the lights of the
small European car he used for the station, he saw that they
burned faintly, and as soon as he pressed the starter they
faded to nothing with each revolution of the motor. In the
space of a few minutes, the battery gave up the ghost. It was
only a little less than a mile to his house, and he really didn't
mind the walk. He strode briskly along the empty streets and
unfastened the gates to his driveway. He was fastening them

when he heard the noise of running and panting and saw that the dogs were out.

The noise woke his wife, who, thinking that he had already come home, called to him for help. "Larry! Larry, the dogs are out! The dogs are out! Larry, please come quickly, the dogs are out and I think they're after someone!" He heard her calling him as he fell, and saw the yellow lights go on in the windows, but that was the last he saw.

II

Orville Betman spent the three summer months alone in New York, as he had done ever since his marriage. He had a large apartment, a good housekeeper, and a host of friends; but he had no wife. Now, some men have a sexual disposition as vigorous, indiscriminate, and demanding as a digestive tract, and to invest these drives with the crosslights of romantic agony would be as tragic as it would be to invent rituals and music for the bronchial tree. These men do not, when they are eating a piece of pie, consider themselves involved in a sacred contract; no more do they in the bounding act of love. This was not Betman. He loved his wife, and he loved no other woman in the world. He loved her voice, her tastes, her face, her grace, her presence, and her memory. He was a good-looking man, and when he was alone other women pursued him. They asked him up to their apartments, they tried to force their way into his apartment, they seized him in corridors and garden paths, and one of them, on the beach at East Hampton, pulled off his bathing trunks, but, thus, incommoded, the only love he had was for Victoria.

Betman was a singer. His voice was distinguished not by its range and beauty but by its persuasiveness. He gave one recital of eighteenth-century music early in his career and was roasted by the critics. He drifted into television and for a while dubbed voices for animated cartoons. Then, by chance, someone asked him to do a cigarette commercial. It was four lines. The result was explosive. Cigarette sales shot up eight hundred percent, and from this single commercial he made, with residuals, more than fifty thousand dollars. The element of persuasiveness in his voice could not be isolated or imitated, but it was infallible. Whatever he praised in song—shoe polish, toothpaste, floor wax—hundreds and thousands of men and women would find his praise irresistible. Even little children heeded his voice. He was very wealthy, of course, and the work was light.

He first saw his wife on a Fifth Avenue bus on a rainy night. She was then a young and slender woman with yellow hair, and the instant he saw her he felt a singular attraction or passion that he had never felt before and would never, as it happened, feel again. The strenuousness of his feeling made him follow her when she left the bus, somewhere on upper Fifth Avenue. He suffered, as any lover will who, moved by a pure and impetuous heart, well knows that his attentions, whatever they are, will be mistaken for a molestation, and usually a revolting one. She walked toward the door of an apartment house and hesitated under the awning long enough to shake the raindrops out of her umbrella.

"Miss?" he asked.

"Yes?"

"Could I speak with you for a minute?"

"What about?"

"My name is Orville Betman," he said. "I sing television commercials. You may have heard me. I . . ." Her attention wandered from him to the lighted lobby, and then he sang, in a true, sweet, and manly voice, a commercial he had taped that afternoon:

> "Gream takes the ish
> Out of washing a dish."

His voice touched her as it seemed to have touched the rest of the world, but it touched her glancingly. "I don't look at television," she said. "What is it you want?"

"I want to marry you," he said sincerely.

She laughed and went on into the lobby and the elevator. The doorman, for five dollars, gave him her name and circumstances. She was Victoria Heatherstone and lived with her invalid father in 14-B. In the space of a morning, the research department in the station where he worked reported that she had graduated from Vassar that spring, and was doing volunteer work in an East Side hospital. One of the apprentice script girls had been in her class and knew her roommate intimately. In a few days, Betman was able to go to a cocktail party where he met her, and he took her out to dinner. His instinct when he first glimpsed her on the bus had been unerring. She was the woman life meant him to have; she was his destiny. She resisted his claims on her for a week or two, and then she succumbed. But there was a problem. Her old father—a Trollope scholar—was indeed an invalid, and she felt that if she left him he would die. She could not, even if it meant constricting her own life, hold the burden of his death upon her conscience. He was not expected to live for long, and she would marry Betman when her father died; she became, to express the genuineness of her promise, his mistress. Betman's happiness was exalted. But the old man did not die.

Betman wanted to marry; wanted to have the union blessed, celebrated, and announced. He was not content to have Victoria come to his apartment two or three times a week as she did. Then the old man had a stroke and was urged by his doctor to leave New York. He moved to a house he owned in Albany, and this then left Victoria free—or free at least for nine months of the year. She married Betman, and they were vastly happy together, although they had no children. However, on the first of June she left for an island in Lake St. Francis, where the dying old man summered, and she did not return to her husband until September. The old man still thought his daughter unmarried, and Betman was forbidden to visit her. He wrote her three times a week to a post-office box, and she replied much less frequently, since, as she explained, there was nothing to report but her father's blood pressure, temperature, digestion, and night sweats. He always appeared to be dying. Since he had never seen either the island or the old man, the place naturally took on for Betman legendary proportions, and his three months alone each year was agony.

He woke one summer Sunday morning to feel such love for his wife that he called out her name: "Victoria, Victoria!" He went to church, dismissed the housekeeper after lunch, and late in the afternoon went for a walk. It was inhumanly hot, and the high temperature seemed to draw the city closer to the heart of time; the smell of hot pavings seemed to belong to history. From an open car window he heard himself singing a song about peanut butter. Traffic was heavy on the

East River Drive, and this respiratory and melancholy sound came up to where he walked. Traffic would be heavy on all the approaches to the city—and the thought of these lines of cars at Sunday's end made it seem as if the day conformed to some rigid script, part of which was the traffic, part the golden light that poured through the city's parallel streets, part a distant rumble of thunder, as if some leaf had been peeled away from the bulk of sound, and part the unendurable spiritual winter of his months alone. He was overwhelmed by the need for his only love. He got his car and started north a little after dark.

He spent the night in Albany and got to the town of Lake St. Francis in the middle of the morning. It was a small and pleasant resort town, neither booming nor dead. He asked at the boat livery how he could get out to Temple Island. "She comes over once a week," the boatman said. "She comes over to get groceries and medicine, but I don't expect she'll be over today." He pointed across the water to where the island lay, a mile or so distant. Betman rented an outboard and started across the lake. He circled the island and found a landing in a cove, where he made the boat fast. The house above him was a preposterous and old-fashioned cottage, highly inflammable, black with creosote and ornamented with outrageous medieval fancies. There was a round tower of shingles and a wooden parapet that wouldn't have withstood the fire of a .22. Tall firs surrounded the wooden castle and covered it in darkness. It was so dark on that bright morning that lights were burning in most of the rooms.

He crossed the porch and saw, through a glass panel in the door, a long hall ending in a staircase with newel posts. Venus stood on one, a lustreless bronze. In one hand she held a branch of two electric candles, lighted against the gloom of the firs. There was no trace of modesty in her stance, and that her legs were apart made her seem utterly defenseless and a little pathetic, as is sometimes the case with Venus. On the other newel post was Hermes; Hermes in flight. He, too, carried a pair of lighted electric candles. The stairs, carpeted in dark green, led up to a stained-glass window. The colors of the glass, even in the gloom, were of astonishing brilliance and discord. After he had rung, an elderly maid came down the stairs, keeping one hand on the banister. She limped. She came up to the door and, looking out at him through the glass panel, simply shook her head.

He opened the door; it opened easily. "I'm Mr. Betman," he said softly. "I want to see my wife."

"You can't see her now. Nobody can. She's with *him*."

"I must see her."

"You can't. Please go. Please go away." Her pleading seemed frightened.

Beyond the firs he could see the lake, flat as glass, but the wind in the trees made a sound so like the sea that had he been blindfold he would have guessed that the house stood on a headland. Then he thought or felt that this was that instant where death enters the terrain of love. These were not the bare facts of life but its ancient and invisible storms, and they moved him like the weight of water. Then he sang:

> "Wher-e'er you walk,
>   cool gales shall fan the glade;
> Trees, where you sit,
>   shall crowd in-to a shade . . ."

The elderly maid, too courteous perhaps to interrupt or moved perhaps by Handel's air and the words, said nothing.

Upstairs he heard a door close and footsteps on the carpet. She hastened past the brilliant, ugly window down to where he waited. There was nothing in all the world so sweet to him as her kiss.

"Come back with me now," he said.

"I can't, darling, my darling. He's dying."

"How many times have you thought this before?"

"Oh, I know, but now he *is* dying."

"Come with me."

"I can't. He's dying."

"Come."

He took her hand and led her out the door, down over the treacherous, pungent carpet of pine needles, to the landing. They crossed the lake without speaking but in such a somberness of feeling that the air, the hour, and the light seemed solid. He paid for the boat, opened the car door for her, and they started south. He did not look at her until they were on the main highway, and then he turned to bask in her freshness, her radiance. It was because he loved her too well that her white arms, the color of her hair, her smile distracted him. He veered from one lane into another and the car was crushed by a truck.

She died, of course. He was in the hospital eight months, but when he was able to walk again he found that the persuasiveness of his voice had not been injured. You can still hear him singing about table polish, bleaches, and vacuum cleaners. He always sings of inessentials, never about the universality of suffering and love, but thousands of men and women go off to the stores as if he had, as if this was his song.

III

To watch Mrs. Peranger enter the club was a little like choosing up sides for a sand-lot ballgame; it was exciting. On her way toward the dining room she would give Mrs. Bebe, who had worked with her on the hospital committee, a fleeting and absent-minded smile. She would cut Mrs. Binger, who was waving and calling her name loudly, dead. She would kiss Mrs. Evans lightly on both cheeks, but she would seem to have forgotten poor Mrs. Budd, at whose house she sometimes dined. She would also seem to have forgotten the Wrights, the Hugginses, the Frames, the Logans, and the Halsteads. A white-haired woman, beautifully dressed, she wielded the power of rudeness so adroitly that she was never caught in an exposed position, and when people asked one another how she got away with it they only increased her advantage. She had been a beauty, and had been painted by Paxton in the twenties. She stood in front of a mirror. The wall was luminous, an imitation of Vermeer, and, as in a Vermeer, the light was put on without its source. There were the usual appurtenances—the ginger jar, the gilt chair, and in the farther room, seen in the glass, a harp on a rug. Her hair had been the color of fire. But this static portrait was only half a world. She had introduced the maxixe to Newport, played golf with Bobby Jones, closed speakeasies at dawn, played strip poker at a Baltimore houseparty, and even now—an old woman—should she hear on the aromatic summer air the music of a Charleston, she would get up from the sofa and begin to dance with a vigorous pivot step, throwing first one leg out in front of her and then the other, cracking her thumbs and singing, "Charleston! Charleston!"

Mr. Peranger and her only son, Patrick, were dead. Of her only daughter, the nymphlike Nerissa, she would say, "Nerissa is giving me a few days of her time. I don't feel that I can ask her for more. She is *so* sought after that I sometimes think she has never married because she has never found the time. She showed her dogs last week in San Francisco, and hopes to take them to Rome for the dog show there. Everyone *loves* Nerissa. Everyone *adores* her. She is *too* attractive for *words*."

Enter Nerissa then, into her mother's drawing room. She is a thin and wasted spinster of thirty. Her hair is gray. Her slip shows. Her shoes are caked with mud. She is plainly one of those children who, without bitterness or rancor, seem burdened with the graceless facts of life. It is their destiny to point out that the elegance and chic of the world their mothers have mastered is not, as it might appear to be, the end of bewilderment and pain. They are a truly pure and innocent breed, and it would never cross their minds or their hearts to upset or contravene the plans, the dreams, the worldly triumphs that their elders hold out for them. It seems indeed to be the hand of God that leads them to take a pratfall during the tableaux at the débutante cotillion. Stepping from a gondola to the water stairs of some palace in Venice where they are expected for dinner, they will lose their balance and fall into the Grand Canal. They spill food and wine, they knock over vases, they step into dog manure, they shake hands with butlers, they have coughing fits during the chamber music, their taste for disreputable friends is unerring, and yet they are like Franciscans in their goodness and simplicity. Thus, enter Nerissa. In the process of being introduced, she savages an end table with her hipbone, tracks mud onto the rug, and drops a lighted cigarette into a chair.

By the time the fire is extinguished, she seems to have satisfactorily ruffled the still waters of her mother's creation. But this is not perversity; it is not even awkwardness. It is her nearly sacred call to restate the pathos and clumsiness of mankind.

The nymphlike Nerissa bred Townsend terriers. Her mother's descriptions of the claims upon her time were, of course, transparent and pathetic. Nerissa was a shy and a lonely woman, mostly occupied with her dogs. Her heart was not unsusceptible, but she always fell in love with gardeners, deliverymen, waiters, and janitors. Late one evening, when her best bitch (Ch. Gaines-Clansman) was about to whelp, she asked the help of a new veterinary, who had just opened a dog-and-cat hospital on Route 14. He came to the kennels at once, and had been there only a few minutes when the bitch threw the first of her litter. He opened the sack and put the dog to suck. His touch with animals, Nerissa thought, was quick and natural, and, standing above him as he knelt at the whelping box, Nerissa felt a strong compulsion to touch his dark hair. She asked if he was married, and when he said that he was not she let herself luxuriate in the fact that she was in love again. Now, Nerissa never anticipated her mother's censure. When she announced her engagement to a garage mechanic or a tree surgeon, she was always surprised at her mother's rage. It never occurred to her that her mother might not like her new choice. She beamed at the veterinary, brought him water, towels, whiskey, and sandwiches. The whelping took most of the night, and it was dawn when they were done. The puppies were sucking; the bitch was proud and requited. All of the litter were well favored and well marked. When Nerissa and the veterinary left the kennels, a cold white light was beating up beyond the dark trees of the estate. "Would you like some coffee?" Nerissa asked, and then, hearing in the distance the sound of running water, she asked, "Or would you like to swim? I sometimes swim in the morning."

"You know, I would," he said. "That's what I'd like. I'd like a swim. I have to go back to the hospital, and a swim would wake me up."

The pool, built by her grandfather, was of marble and had a deep and graceful curb, curved like the frame of a mirror. The water was limpid, and here and there a sunken leaf threw a shadow, edged with the strong colors of the spectrum. It was the place on her mother's estate that had always seemed to Nerissa—more than any room or garden— her home. When she was away, it was the pool she missed, and when she came back it was to the pool—this watery home-sweet-home—that she returned. She found a pair of trunks in the bathhouse, and they took an innocent swim. They dressed and walked back across the lawns to his car. "You know, you're awfully nice," he said. "Did anyone ever tell you that?" Then he kissed her lightly and tenderly and drove away.

Nerissa didn't see her mother until four the next afternoon, when she went down to tea wearing two left shoes, one brown and one black. "Oh, Mother, Mother," she said, "I've found the man I want to marry."

"Really," said Mrs. Peranger. "Who is this paragon?"

"His name is Dr. Johnson," said Nerissa. "He runs the new dog-and-cat hospital on Route 14."

"But you cannot marry a veterinary, sweet love," said Mrs. Peranger.

"He calls himself an animal hygienist," said Nerissa.

"How revolting!" said Mrs. Peranger.

"But I love him, Mother. I love him, and I'm going to marry him."

"Go to hell!" said Mrs. Peranger.

That night, Mrs. Peranger called the mayor and asked to speak with his wife. "This is Louisa Peranger," she said. "I am going to put someone up for the Tilton Club this fall, and I was thinking of you." There was a sigh of excitement from the wife of the mayor. Her head would be swimming. But why? But why? The clubrooms were threadbare, the maids were surly, and the food was bad. Why was there a ferocious waiting list of thousands? "I drive a hard bargain," said Mrs. Peranger, "as everyone knows. There is a dog-and-cat hospital on Route 14 that I would like to have shut down. I'm sure your husband can discover that some sort of zoning violation is involved. It must be some sort of nuisance. If you will speak to your husband about the dog-and-cat hospital, I will get the membership list to you so that you can decide on your other sponsors. I will arrange a luncheon party for the middle of September. Goodbye."

Nerissa pined away, died, and was buried in the little Episcopal church whose windows had been given in memory of her grandfather. Mrs. Peranger looked imperious and patrician in her mourning, and as she left the church she was heard to sob loudly, "She was *so* attractive—she was so *frightfully* attractive."

Mrs. Peranger rallied from her loss, and kept up with her work, which, at that time of year, consisted of screening candidates for a débutante cotillion. Three weeks after Nerissa's funeral, a Mrs. Pentason and her daughter were shown into the drawing room.

Mrs. Peranger knew how hard Mrs. Pentason had worked for this interview. She had done hospital work; she had organized theatre parties, strawberry festivals, and antique fairs. But Mrs. Peranger looked at her callers harshly. They would have learned their manners from a book. They would have studied the chapter on how to drink tea. They were the sort who dreamed in terms of invitations that would never be received. *Mr. and Mrs. William Paley request the honor . . .* Their mail, instead, would consist of notices of private sales, trial offers from the Book-of-the-Month Club, and embarrassing letters from Aunt Minnie, who lived in Waco, Texas, and used a spittoon. Nora passed the tea and Mrs. Peranger kept a sharp eye on the girl. The noise of water from the swimming pool sounded very loud, and Mrs. Peranger asked Nora to close the window.

"We have so many applicants for the cotillion these days that we expect a little more than we used to," Mrs. Peranger said. "We not only want attractive and well-bred young women, we want interesting young women." Even with the windows shut, she could hear the sound of water. It seemed to put her at a disadvantage. "Do you sing?" she asked.

"No," the girl said.

"Do you play any musical instruments?"

"I play the piano a little."

"How little?"

"I play some of the Chopin. I mean, I used to. And 'Für Elise.' But mostly I play popular music."

"Where do you summer?"

"Dennis Port," the girl said.

"Ah yes," said Mrs. Peranger. "Dennis Port, poor Dennis Port. There really isn't any place left to go, is there? The Adriatic Coast is crowded. Capri, Ischia, and Amalfi are all ruined. The Princess of Holland has spoiled the Argentario. The Riviera is jammed. Brittany is so cold and rainy. I love Skye, but the food is dreadful. Bar Harbor, the Cape, the Islands—they've all gotten to seem so shabby." She heard again the noise of running water from the pool, as if a breeze carried the sound straight up to the shut windows. "Tell me, are you interested in the theatre?" she asked.

"Oh, yes. Very much."

"What plays did you see last season?"

"None."

"You ride, play tennis, and so forth?"

"Yes."

"What in New York is your favorite museum?"

"I don't know."

"What books have you read recently?"

"I read *The Seersucker Plague*. It was on the best-seller list. They bought it for the movies. And *Seven Roads to Heaven*. That was on the best-seller list, too."

"Please take these things away, Nora," Mrs. Peranger said, making a broad gesture of distaste, as if she expected the maid to remove the Pentasons with the dirty cups and the slop jar. The tea was over, and she walked her guests down the length of the room. If she meant to be cruel, it would have been cruelest to let them wait; to prey upon the common weakness of men and women who look for glad tidings in the mail. She drew Mrs. Pentason aside and said, "I'm *terribly* afraid . . ."

"Well, thank you just the same," said Mrs. Pentason, and

she began to cry. The daughter put an arm around the stricken mother and led her out the door.

Mrs. Peranger noticed again the sound of water from the pool. Why was it so loud, and why did it seem to say: *Mother, Mother, I've found the man I want to marry.* . . . Why did it sound so true, and make her task of cutting the Pentasons seem so harsh and senseless? She went down the stairs to the lawn and crossed the lawn to the pool. Standing on the curb, she called, "Nerissa! Nerissa! Nerissa!" but all the water said was, *Mother, Mother, I've found the man I want to marry.*

Her only daughter had been turned into a swimming pool.

IV

Mr. Bradish wanted a change. He did not mean at all by this that he wanted to change himself—only his scenery, his pace, and his environment, and that for only a space of eighteen or twenty days. He could leave his office for that long. Bradish was a heavy smoker, and the Surgeon General's report had made him self-conscious about his addiction. It seemed to him that strangers on the street regarded the cigarette in his fingers with disapproval and sometimes with commiseration. This was manifestly absurd, and he needed to get away. He would take a trip. He was divorced at the time, and would go alone.

One day after lunch he stopped in a travel agency on Park Avenue to see what rates were in force. A receptionist directed him to a desk at the back of the office, where a young woman offered him a chair and lit his cigarette from a matchbook flying the ensign of the Corinthian Yacht Club. She had, he noticed, a dazzling smile and a habit of biting it off when it had served its purpose, as a tailor bites off a thread. He had England in mind. He would spend ten days in London and ten in the country with friends. When he mentioned England, the clerk said that she had recently come back from England herself. From Coventry. She flashed her smile, bit it off. He did not want to go to Coventry, but she was a young woman with the determination and single-mindedness of her time of life, and he saw that he would have to hear her out on the beauties of Coventry, where she seemed to have had an aesthetic and spiritual rebirth. She took from her desk drawer an illustrated magazine to show him pictures of the cathedral. What impressed him, as it happened, was a blunt advertisement in the magazine, stating that cigarettes caused lung cancer. He dismissed England from his mind—the clerk was still on Coventry—and thought that he would go to France. He would go to Paris. The French government had not censured smoking, and he could inhale his Gauloise without feeling subversive. However, the memory of a Gauloise stopped him. Gauloises, Bleues and Jaunes. He recalled how their smoke seemed to drop from an altitude into his lungs and double him up with paroxysms of coughing. In his imagination clouds of rank French tobacco smoke seemed to settle like a bitter fog over the City of Light, making it appear to him an unsavory and despondent place. So he would go to the Tyrol, he thought. He was about to ask for information on the Tyrol when he remembered that tobacco was a state monopoly in Austria and that all you could get to smoke there were flavorless ovals that came in fancy boxes and smelled of perfume. Italy, then. He would cross the Brenner and go down to Venice. But he remembered Italian cigarettes—Esportaziones and Giubeks—remembered how the

crude tobacco stuck to his tongue and how the smoke, like
a winter wind, made him shiver and think of death. He
would go on to Greece, then; he would take a cruise through
the islands, he thought—until he recalled the taste of that
Egyptian tobacco that is all you can get to smoke in Greece.
Russia. Turkey. India. Japan. Glancing above the clerk's
head to a map of the world, he saw it all as a chain of tobacco
stores. There was no escape. "I think I won't go anywhere,"
he said. The clerk flashed her smile, bit it off like a thread,
and watched him go out the door.

The quality of discipline shines through a man's life
and all his works, giving them a probity and a fineness that
preclude disorder, or so Bradish thought. The time had come
for him to discipline himself. He put out his last cigarette and
walked up Park Avenue with the straitened, pleasant,
and slightly dancy step of an old athlete who has his shoes
and his suits made in England. As a result of his decision,
toward the end of the afternoon he began to suffer from something that resembled a mild case of the bends. His circulatory
system was disturbed. His capillaries seemed abraded, his lips
were swollen, and now and then his right foot would sting.
There was a marked unfreshness in his mouth that seemed
too various and powerful to be contained by that small organ;
seemed by its power and variety to enlarge his mouth, giving
it, in fact, the dimensions and malodorousness of some ancient burlesque theatre like the Howard Athenaeum. Fumes
seemed to rise from his mouth to his brain, leaving him with
an extraordinary sense of light-headedness. Since he felt himself committed to this discipline, he decided to think of
these symptoms in the terms of travel. He would observe

them as they made themselves felt, as one would observe from the windows of a train the changes in geology and vegetation in a strange country.

As the day changed to night, the country through which he traveled seemed mountainous and barren. He seemed to be on a narrow-gauge railroad traveling through a rocky pass. Nothing but thistles and wire grass grew among the rocks. He reasoned that once they were over the pass they would come onto a fertile plain with trees and water, but when the train rounded a turn on the summit of the mountain, he saw that what lay ahead was an alkali desert scored with dry stream beds. He knew that if he smoked, tobacco would irrigate this uninhabitable place, the fields would bloom with flowers, and water would run in the streams, but since he had chosen to take this particular journey, since it was quite literally an escape from an intolerable condition, he settled down to study the unrelieved aridity. When he made himself a cocktail in his apartment that night, he smiled—he actually smiled—to observe that there was nothing to be seen in the ashtrays but a little dust and a leaf he had picked off his shoe.

He was changing, he was changing, and like most men he had wanted to change, it seemed. In the space of a few hours, he had become more sagacious, more comprehensive, more mature. He seemed to feel the woolly mantle of his time of life come to rest on his shoulders. He felt himself to be gaining some understanding of the poetry of the force of change in life, felt himself involved in one of those intimate, grueling, and unseen contests that make up the story of a man's soul. If he stopped smoking, he might stop drinking. He might even curtail his erotic tastes. Immoderation had been the cause of his divorce. Immoderation had alienated his beloved children. If they could only see him now, see the clean ashtrays in his room, mightn't they invite him to come home? He could charter a schooner and sail up the coast of Maine with them. When he went, later that night, to see his mistress, the smell of tobacco on her breath made her seem to him so depraved and unclean that he didn't bother to take off his clothes and went home early to his bed and his clean ashtrays.

Bradish had never had any occasion to experience self-righteousness other than the self-righteousness of the sinner. His censure had been aimed at people who drank clam juice and cultivated restrained tastes. Walking to work the next morning, he found himself jockeyed rudely onto the side of the angels; found himself perforce an advocate of abstemiousness, and discovered that some part of this condition was an involuntary urge to judge the conduct of others—a sensation so strange to him, so newly found, so unlike his customary point of view that he thought it exciting. He watched with emphatic disapproval a stranger light a cigarette on a street corner. The stranger plainly had no will power. He was injuring his health, trimming his life span, and betraying his dependents, who might suffer hunger and cold as a result of this self-indulgence. What's more, the man's clothing was shabby, his shoes were unshined, and if he could not afford to dress himself decently he could surely not afford the vice of tobacco. Should Bradish take the cigarette out of his hand? Lecture him? Awaken him? It seemed a little early in the game, but the impulse was there and he had never experienced it before. Now he walked up Fifth Avenue with his newly possessed virtuousness, looking neither at the sky nor at the pretty women but instead raking the population like a lieutenant of the vice squad employed to seek out malefactors. Oh, there were so many! A disheveled old lady, colorless but for a greasy smear of crimson lipstick, stood on the corner of Forty-fourth Street, lighting one cigarette from another. Men in doorways, girls on the steps of the library, boys in the park all seemed determined to destroy themselves.

His light-headedness continued through the morning, so that he found it difficult to make business decisions, and there was some definite injury to his eyesight. He felt as if he had taken his eyes through a dust storm. He went to a business lunch where drinks were served, and when someone passed him a cigarette he said, "Not right now, thank you." He blushed with self-righteousness, but he was not going to demean his struggle by confiding in anyone. Having abstained triumphantly for nearly twenty-four hours, he thought he deserved a reward, and he let the waiter keep filling his cocktail glass. In the end he drank too much, and when he got back to his office he was staggering. This, on top of his disturbed circulatory system, his swollen lips, his bleary eyes, the stinging sensation in his right foot, and the feeling that his brain was filled with the fumes and the malodorousness of an old burlesque theatre made it impossible for him to work, and he floundered through the rest of the day. He seldom went to cocktail parties, but he went to one that afternoon, hoping that it would distract him. He definitely felt unlike himself. The damage by this time had reached his equilibrium, and he found crossing streets difficult and hazardous, as if he were maneuvering over a high and narrow bridge.

The party was large, and he kept going to the bar. He

thought that gin would quench his craving. It was hardly a craving, he noticed—nothing like hunger or thirst or the need for love. It felt like some sullen and stubborn ebbing in his bloodstream. The lightness in his head had worsened. He laughed, talked, and behaved himself up to a point, but this was merely mechanical. Late in the party, a young woman wearing a light sack or tube-shaped dress, her long hair the color of Virginia tobacco, came in at the door. In his ardor to reach her he knocked over a table and several glasses. It was, or had been up to that point, a decorous party, but the noise of broken glass, followed by the screaming of the stranger when he wrapped his legs around her and buried his nose in her tobacco-colored hair, were barbarous. Two guests pried him loose, He stood there, crouched with ardor, snorting through his distended nostrils. Then he flung away the arms of the men who held him and strode out of the room.

He went down in the elevator with a stranger whose brown suit looked and smelled like a Havana Upman, but Bradish kept his eyes on the floor of the carriage and contented himself with breathing in the stranger's fragrance. The elevator man smelled of a light, cheap blend that had been popular in the fifties. The doorman, he noticed, looked and smelled like a briar pipe with a Burley mixture. And on Fifty-seventh Street he saw a woman whose hair was the the color of his favorite blend and who seemed to trail after her its striking corrupt perfume. Only by grinding his teeth and bracing his muscles did he keep from seizing her, but he realized that his behavior at the party, repeated on the street, would take him to jail, and there were, as far as he knew, no cigarettes in jail. He had changed—he had changed, and so had his world, and watching the population of the city pass him in the dusk, he saw them as Winstons, Chesterfields, Marlboros, Salems, hookahs, meerschaums, cigarillos, Corona-Coronas, Camels, and Players. It was a young woman—really a child—whom he mistook for a Lucky Strike that was his undoing. She screamed when he attacked her, and two strangers knocked him down, striking and kicking him with just moral indignation. A crowd gathered. There was pandemonium, and presently the sirens of the police car that took him away.

The Bella Lingua

WILSON STREETER, LIKE MANY AMERICANS WHO LIVE IN
Rome, was divorced. He worked as a statistician for the
F.R.U.P.C. agency, lived alone, and led a diverting social life
with other expatriates and those Romans who were drawn
into expatriate circles, but he spoke English all day long at
his office and the Italians he met socially spoke English so
much better than he spoke Italian that he could not bring
himself to converse with them in their language. It was his
feeling that in order to understand Italy he would have to
speak Italian. He did speak it well enough when it was a
question of some simple matter of shopping or making arrangements of one kind or another, but he wanted to be able
to express his sentiments, to tell jokes, and to follow overheard conversations on trolley cars and buses. He was keenly
conscious of the fact that he was making his life in a country
that was not his own, but this sense of being an outsider
would change, he thought, when he knew the language.

For the tourist, the whole experience of traveling through

a strange country is on the verge of the past tense. Even as the days are spent, these *were* the days in Rome, and every- thing—the sightseeing, souvenirs, photographs, and presents —is commemorative. Even as the traveler lies in bed waiting for sleep, these *were* the nights in Rome. But for the expa- triate there is no past tense. It would defeat his purpose to think of this time in another country in relation to some town or countryside that was and might again be his perma- nent home, and he lives in a continuous and unrelenting present. Instead of accumulating memories, the expatriate is offered the challenge of learning a language and understand- ing a people. So they catch a glimpse of one another in the Piazza Venezia—the expatriates passing through the square on their way to their Italian lessons, the tourists occupying, by prearrangement, all the tables at a sidewalk café and drinking Campari, which they have been told is a typical Roman *operitivo*.

Streeter's teacher was an American woman named Kate Dresser, who lived in an old palace near the Piazza Firenze, with an adolescent son. Streeter went there for his lessons on Tuesday and Friday evenings and on Sunday afternoons. He enjoyed the walk in the evening from his office, past the Pan- theon, to his Italian lesson. Among the rewards of his expatri- ation were a heightened awareness of what he saw and an exhilarating sense of freedom. Mixed with the love we hold for our native country is the fact that it is the place where we were raised, and, should anything have gone a little wrong in this process, we will be reminded of this fault, by the scene of the crime, until the day we die. Some such unhappiness may have accounted for Streeter's sense of freedom, and his height- ened awareness may have been nothing but what is to be expected of a man with a good appetite walking through the back streets of a city in the autumn. The air was cold and smelled of coffee—sometimes of incense, if the doors to a church stood open—and chrysanthemums were for sale everywhere. The sights were exciting and confusing—the ruins of Republican and Imperial Rome, and the ruins of what the city had been the day before yesterday—but the whole thing would be revealed to him when he could speak Italian.

It was not easy, Streeter knew, for a man his age to learn anything, and he had not been fortunate in his search for a good Italian teacher. He had first gone to the Dante Alighieri Institute, where the classes were so large that he made no progress. Then he had taken private lessons from an old lady. He was supposed to read and translate Collodi's *Pinocchio,* but when he had done a few sentences the teacher would take the book out of his hands and do the reading and translating herself. She loved the story so much that she laughed and cried, and sometimes whole lessons passed in which Streeter did not open his mouth. It disturbed his sense of fitness that he, a man of fifty, should be sitting in a cold flat at the edge of Rome, being read a children's tale by a woman of seventy, and after a dozen lessons he told his teacher that he had to go to Perugia on business. After this he enrolled in the Tauchnitz School and had private lessons. His teacher was an astonishingly pretty young woman who wore the tight-waisted clothes that were in fashion that year, and a wedding ring—a prop, he guessed, because she seemed so openly flirtatious and gay. She wore a sharp perfume, rattled her bracelets, pulled down her jacket, swung her hips when she walked to the blackboard, and gave Streeter, one evening, such a dark look that he took her in his arms. What she did then was to shriek, kick over a little desk, and run through three intervening classrooms to the lobby, screaming that she had been attacked by a beast. After all his months of study, "beast" was the only word in her tirade that Streeter understood. The whole school was alerted, of course, and all he could do was to wipe the sweat off his forehead and start through the classrooms toward the lobby. People stood on chairs to get a better look at him, and he never went back to Tauchnitz.

His next teacher was a very plain woman with gray hair and a lavender shawl that she must have knitted herself, it was so full of knots and tangles. She was an excellent teacher for a month, and then one evening she told him that her life was difficult. She waited to be encouraged to tell him her troubles, and when he did not give her any encouragement, she told them to him anyhow. She had been engaged to be married for twenty years, but the mother of her betrothed disapproved of the match and, whenever the subject was raised, would climb up onto the window sill and threaten to jump into the street. Now her betrothed was sick, he would have to be cut open (she gestured) from the neck to the navel, and if he died she would go to her grave a spinster. Her wicked sisters had got pregnant in order to force their marriages—one of them had walked down the aisle eight months gone (more gestures)—but she would rather (with a hitch at her lavender shawl) solicit men in the street than do that. Streeter listened helplessly to her sorrow, as we will listen to most human troubles, having some of our own, but she was still talking when her next student, a Japanese, came in for his lesson, and Streeter had learned no Italian that night. She had not told Streeter all of the story, and she continued it when he came again. The fault might have been his—he should have discouraged her rudely—but now that she had made him her confidant, he saw that he could not change this relationship. The force he had to cope with was the loneliness that is to be found in any large city, and he invented another trip to Perugia. He had two more teachers, two more trips to Perugia, and then, in the late autumn of his second year in Rome, someone from the Embassy recommended Kate Dresser.

An American woman who teaches Italian in Rome is unusual, but then all arrangements in Rome are so complicated that lucidity and skepticism give way when we try to follow the description of a scene in court, a lease, a lunch, or anything else. Each fact or detail breeds more questions than it answers, and in the end we lose sight of the truth, as we were meant to do. Here comes Cardinal Micara with the True Finger of Doubting Thomas—that much is clear—but is the man beside us in church asleep or dead, and what are all the elephants doing in the Piazza Venezia?

The lessons took place at one end of a huge *sala*, by the fireplace. Streeter spent an hour and sometimes two hours preparing for them. He finished *Pinocchio* and began to read *I Promessi Sposi*. After this would come the *Divine Comedy*. He was as proud as a child of his completed homework, loved to be given tests and dictation, and usually came into Kate's apartment with a big, foolish smile on his face, he was so pleased with himself. She was a very good teacher. She understood his fatuousness, the worn condition of his middle-aged memory, and his desire to learn. She spoke an Italian that he could almost always understand, and by keeping a wristwatch on the table to mark the period, by sending him bills through the mail, and by never speaking of herself, she conducted the lessons in an atmosphere that was practical and impersonal. He thought she was a good-looking woman—intense, restless, overworked, perhaps, but charming.

Among the things that Kate Dresser did not tell him, as they sat in this part of the room that she had staked out for herself with a Chinese screen and some rickety gold chairs, was the fact that she was born and raised in the little town of Krasbie, Iowa. Her father and mother were both dead. In a place where almost everybody worked in the chemical-fertilizer factory, her father had happened to be a trolley conductor. When she was growing up, Kate could never bring herself to admit that her father took fares in a trolley car. She could never even admit that he was her father, although she had inherited his most striking physical feature—a nose that turned up so spectacularly at the tip that she was called Roller Coaster and Pug. She had gone from Krasbie to Chicago, from Chicago to New York, where she married a man in the Foreign Service. They lived in Washington and then Tangier. Shortly after the war, they moved to Rome, where her husband died of food poisoning, leaving her with a son and very little money. So she made her home in Rome. The only preparation Krasbie had given her for Italy was the curtain in the little movie theatre where she had spent her Saturday afternoons when she was a girl. Skinny then, dressed no better than most rebellious children and smelling no sweeter, her hair in braids, her pockets full of peanuts and candy and her mouth full of chewing gum, she had put down her quarter every Saturday afternoon, rain or shine, and spread herself out in a seat in the front row. There were shouts of "Roller Coaster!" and "Pug!" from all over the theatre, and, what with the high-heeled shoes (her sister's) that she sometimes wore and the five-and-ten-cent-store diamonds on her fingers, it was no wonder that people made fun of her. Boys dropped chewing gum into her hair and shot spitballs at the back of her skinny neck, and, persecuted in body and spirit, she would raise her eyes to the curtain and see a remarkably precise vision of her future. It was painted on canvas, very badly cracked from having been rolled and unrolled so many times—a vision of an Italian garden, with cypress trees, a terrace, a pool and fountain, and a marble balustrade with roses spilling from marble urns. She seemed literally to have risen up from her seat and to have entered the cracked scene, for it was almost exactly like the view from her window into the courtyard of the Palazzo Tarominia, where she lived.

Now, you might ask why a woman who had so little money was living in the Palazzo Tarominia, and there was a Roman answer. The Baronessa Tramonde—the old Duke of Rome's sister—lived in the west wing of the palace, in an apartment that had been built for Pope Andros X and that was reached by a great staircase with painted walls and ceilings. It had pleased the Baronessa, before the war, to stand at the head of this staircase and greet her friends and relations, but things had changed. The Baronessa had grown old, and so had her friends; they could no longer climb the stairs. Oh, they tried. They had straggled up to her card parties like a patrol under machine-gun fire, the gentlemen pushing the ladies and sometimes vice versa, and old marchesas and princesses—the cream of Europe—huffing and puffing and sitting down on the steps in utter exhaustion. There was a lift in the other wing of the place—the wing Kate lived in—but a lift could not be installed in the west wing, because it would ruin the paintings. The only other way to enter the Baronessa's quarters was to take the lift to Kate's apartment and walk through it and out a service door that led into the other wing. By giving the Duke of Rome, who also had an apartment in the Palazzo, a kind of eminent domain, Kate had a palace apartment at a low rent. The Duke usually passed through twice a day to visit his sister, and on the first Thursday of every month, at five minutes after eight, a splendid and elderly company would troop through Kate's rooms to the Baronessa's card party. Kate did not mind. In fact, when she heard the doorbell ring on Thursdays her heart would begin a grating beat of the deepest excitement. The old Duke always led the procession. His right hand had been chopped off at the wrist by one of Mussolini's public executioners, and now that the old man's enemies were dead, he carried the stump proudly. With him would come Don Fernando Marchetti, the Duke of Treno, the Duke and Duchess Ricotto-Sporci, Count Ambro di Albentiis, Count and Countess Fabrizio Daromeo, Princess Urbana Tessoro, Princess Isabella Tessoro, and Federico, Cardinal Baldova. They had all distinguished themselves in one way or another. Don Fernando had driven a car from Paris to Peking, via the Gobi Desert. Duke Ricotto-Sporci had broken most of his bones in a steeplechase accident, and the Countess Daromeo had operated an Allied radio station in the middle of Rome during the German Occupation. The old Duke of Rome would present Kate with a little bouquet of flowers, and then he and his friends would file through the kitchen and go out the service door.

Kate spoke an admirable Italian, and had done some translating and given lessons, and for the past three years she had supported herself and her son by dubbing parts of English dialogue into old Italian movies, which were then shown over British TV. With her cultivated accent, she played mostly dowagers and the like, but there seemed to be plenty of work, and she spent much of her time in a sound studio near the Tiber. With her salary and the money her husband had left her, she had barely enough to get by on. Her elder sister, in Krasbie, wrote her a long lament two or three times a year: "Oh, you lucky, lucky dog, Kate! Oh, how I envy you being away from all the tiresome, nagging, stupid, petty details of life at home." Kate Dresser's life was not lacking in stupid and nagging details, but instead of mentioning such things in her letters, she inflamed her sister's longing to travel by sending home photographs of herself in gondolas, or cards from Florence, where she always spent Easter with friends.

Streeter knew that under Kate Dresser's teaching he was making progress with his Italian, and usually when he stepped out of the Palazzo Tarominia into the street after his lesson, he was exhilarated at the thought that in another month—at the end of the season, anyhow—he would understand everything that was going on and being said. But his progress had its ups and downs.

The beauty of Italy is not easy to come by any longer, if it ever was, but, driving to a villa below Anticoli for a weekend with friends, Streeter saw a country of such detail and loveliness that it could not be described. They had reached the villa early on a rainy night. Nightingales sang in the trees, the double doors of the villa stood open, and in all the rooms there were bowls of roses and olivewood fires. It had seemed, with the servants bowing and bringing in candles and wine, like some gigantic and princely homecoming in a movie, and, going out onto the terrace after dinner to hear the nightingales and see the lights of the hill towns, Streeter felt that he had never been put by dark hills and distant lights into a mood of such tenderness. In the morning, when he stepped out onto his bedroom balcony, he saw a barefoot maid in the garden, picking a rose to put in her hair. Then she began to sing. It was like a flamenco—first guttural and then falsetto—and poor Streeter found his Italian still so limited that he couldn't understand the words of the song, and this brought him around to the fact that he couldn't quite understand the landscape, either. His feeling about it was very much what he might have felt about some excellent resort or summer place—a scene where, perhaps as children, we have thrown ourselves into a temporary relationship with beauty and simplicity that will be rudely broken off on Labor Day. It was the evocation of a borrowed, temporary, bittersweet happiness that he rebelled against—but the maid went on singing, and Streeter did not understand a word.

When Streeter took his lessons at Kate's, her son, Charlie, usually passed through the *sala* at least once during the hour. He was a baseball fan, and had a bad complexion and an owlish laugh. He would say hello to Streeter and pass on some sports news from the Rome *Daily American*. Streeter had a son of his own of about the same age, and was enjoined by the divorce settlement from seeing the boy, and he never looked at Charlie without a pang of longing for his own son. Charlie was fifteen, and one of those American boys you see waiting for the school bus up by the Embassy, dressed in black leather jackets and Levis, and with sideburns or ducktail haircuts, and fielder's mitts—anything that will stamp

them as American. These are the real expatriates. On
Saturdays after the movies they go into one of those bars
called Harry's or Larry's or Jerry's, where the walls are
covered with autographed photographs of unknown electric-
guitar players and unknown soubrettes, to eat bacon and eggs
and talk baseball and play American records on the jukebox.
They are Embassy children, and the children of writers and
oil-company and airline employees and divorcées and Ful-
bright Fellows. Eating bacon and eggs, and listening to the
jukebox, they have a sense of being far, far from home that
is a much sweeter and headier distillation than their parents
ever know. Charlie had spent five years of his life under a
ceiling decorated with gold that had been brought from
the New World by the first Duke of Rome, and he had seen
old marchesas with diamonds as big as acorns slip the cheese
parings into their handbags when the lunch was finished. He
had ridden in gondolas and played softball on the Palatine.
He had seen the Palio at Siena, and had heard the bells of
Rome and Florence and Venice and Ravenna and Verona.
But it wasn't about these things that he wrote in a letter to his
mother's Uncle George in Krasbie toward the middle of
March. Instead, he asked the old man to take him home and
let him be an American boy. The timing was perfect. Uncle
George had just retired from the fertilizer factory and had
always wanted to bring Kate and her son home. Within two
weeks he was on board a ship bound for Naples.

Streeter, of course, knew nothing of this. But he had suspected that there was some tension between Charlie and his
mother. The boy's hoedown American clothes, the poses he
took as a rail splitter, pitcher, and cowboy, and his mother's
very Italianate manners implied room for sizable disagree-

ment, at least, and, going there one Sunday afternoon, Streeter stepped into a quarrel. Assunta, the maid, let him in, but he stopped at the door of the *sala* when he heard Kate and her son shouting at one another in anger. Streeter could not retreat. Assunta had gone on ahead to say he was there, and all he could do was wait in the vestibule. Kate came out to him then—she was crying—and said, in Italian, that she could not give him a lesson that afternoon. She was sorry. Something had come up, and there had not been time to telephone him. He felt like a fool, confronted with her tears, holding his grammar, his copybook, and *I Promessi Sposi* under one arm. He said it didn't matter about the lesson, it was nothing, and could he come on Tuesday? She said yes, yes, would he come on Tuesday—and would he come on Thursday, not for a lesson but to do her a favor? "My father's brother—my Uncle George—is coming, to try and take Charlie home. I don't know what to do. I don't know what I *can* do. But I would appreciate it if there was a man here; I would feel so much better if I weren't alone. You don't have to say anything or do anything but sit in a chair and have a drink, but I would feel so much better if I weren't alone."

Streeter agreed to come, and went away then, wondering what kind of a life it was she led if she had to count in an emergency on a stranger like him. With his lesson canceled and nothing else that he had to do, he took a walk up the river as far as the Ministry of the Marine, and then came back through a neighborhood that was neither new nor old nor anything else you could specify. Because it was Sunday afternoon, the houses were mostly shut. The streets were deserted. When he passed anyone, it was usually a family group returning from an excursion to the zoo. There were also a few of those lonely men and women carrying pastry boxes that you see everywhere in the world at dusk on Sunday—unmarried aunts and uncles going out to tea with their relations and bringing a little pastry to sweeten the call. But mostly he was alone, mostly there was no sound but his own footsteps and, in the distance, the iron ringing of iron trolley-car wheels on iron tracks—a lonely sound on Sunday afternoons for many Americans; a lonely one for him, anyhow, and reminding him of some friendless, loveless, galling Sunday in his youth. As he came closer to the city, there were more lights and people—flowers and the noise of talk—and under the gate of Santa Maria del Popolo a whore spoke to him. She was a beautiful young woman, but he told her, in his broken Italian, that he had a friend, and walked on.

Crossing the Piazza, he saw a man struck by a car. The noise was loud—that surprising loudness of our bones when they are dealt a mortal blow. The driver of the car slipped out of his seat and ran up the Pincian Hill. The victim lay in a heap on the paving, a shabbily dressed man but with a lot of oil in his black, wavy hair, which must have been his pride. A crowd gathered—not solemn at all, although a few women crossed themselves—and everyone began to talk excitedly. The crowd, garrulous, absorbed in its own opinions and indifferent, it seemed, to the dying man, was so thick that when the police came they had to push and struggle to reach the victim. With the words of the whore still in his ears, Streeter wondered why it was that they regarded a human life as something of such dubious value.

He turned away from the Piazza then, toward the river, and, passing the Tomb of Augustus, he noticed a young man calling to a cat and offering it something to eat. The cat was one of those thousands of millions that live in the ruins of Rome and eat leftover spaghetti, and the man was offering the cat a piece of bread. Then, as the cat approached him, the man took a firecracker out of his pocket, put it into the piece of bread, and lit the fuse. He put the bread on the sidewalk, and just as the cat took it the powder exploded. The animal let out a hellish shriek and leaped into the air, its body all twisted, and then it streaked over the wall and was lost in the darkness of Augustus's Tomb. The man laughed at his trick, and so did several people who had been watching.

Streeter's first instinct was to box the man's ears and teach him not to feed lighted firecrackers to stray cats. But, with such an appreciative audience, this would have amounted to an international incident, and he realized there wasn't anything he could do. The people who had laughed at the prank were good and kind—most of them affectionate parents. You might have seen them earlier in the day on the Palatine, picking violets.

Streeter walked on into a dark street and heard at his back the hoofs and trappings of horses—it sounded like cavalry— and stepped aside to let a hearse and a mourner's carriage pass. The hearse was drawn by two pairs of bays with black plumes. The driver wore funerary livery, with an admiral's hat, and had the brutish red face of a drunken horse thief. The hearse banged, slammed, and rattled over the stones in such a loose-jointed way that the poor soul it carried must have been in a terrible state of disarrangement, and the mourner's carriage that followed was empty. The friends of the dead man had probably been too late or had got the wrong date or had forgotten the whole thing, as was so often the case in Rome. Off the hearse and carriage rattled toward the Servian Gate.

Streeter knew one thing then: He did not want to die in Rome. He was in excellent health and had no reason to think about death; nevertheless, he was afraid. Back at his flat, he poured some whiskey and water into a glass and stepped out onto his balcony. He watched the night fall and the street lights go on with complete bewilderment at his own feelings. He did not want to die in Rome. The power of this idea could only stem from ignorance and stupidity, he told himself—for what could such a fear represent but the inability to respond to the force of life? He reproached himself with arguments and consoled himself with whiskey, but in the middle of the night he was waked by the noise of a carriage and horses' hoofs, and again he sweated with fear. The hearse, the horse thief, and the empty mourner's carriage, he thought, were rattling back, under his balcony. He got up out of bed and went to the window to see, but it was only two empty carriages going back to the stables.

When Uncle George landed in Naples, on Tuesday, he was excited and in a good humor. His purpose in coming abroad was twofold—to bring Charlie and Kate home, and to take a vacation, the first in forty-three years. A friend of his in Krasbie who had been to Italy had written an itinerary for him: "Stay at the Royal in Naples. Go to the National Museum. Have a drink in the Galleria Umberto. Eat supper at the California. Good American food. Take the Roncari *auto-pullman* in the morning for Rome. This goes through two interesting villages and stops at Nero's villa. In Rome stay at the Excelsior. Make reservations in advance. . . ."

On Wednesday morning, Uncle George got up early and went down to the hotel dining room. "Orange juice and ham and eggs," he said to the waiter. The waiter brought him orange juice, coffee, and a roll. "Where's my ham and eggs?" Uncle George asked, and then realized, when the waiter bowed and smiled, that the man did not understand English. He got out his phrase book, but there was nothing about ham and eggs. "You gotta no hamma?" he asked loudly. "You gotta no eggsa?" The waiter went on smiling and bowing, and Uncle George gave up. He ate the breakfast he hadn't ordered, gave the waiter a twenty-lira tip, cashed four hundred dollars' worth of traveler's checks at the desk, and checked out. All this money in lire made a bump in his suit jacket, and he held his left hand over his wallet as if he had a pain there. Naples, he knew, was full of thieves. He took a cab to the bus station, which was in a square near the Galleria Umberto. It was early in the morning, the light was slanting, and he enjoyed the smell of coffee and bread and the stir of people hurrying along the streets to work. A fine smell of the sea rose up the streets from the bay. He was early and was shown his seat in the bus by a red-faced gentleman who spoke English with a British accent. This was the guide—one of those who, whatever conveyance you take and wherever you go, make travel among the monuments bizarre. Their command of languages is extraordinary, their knowledge of antiquity is impressive, and their love of beauty is passionate, but when they separate themselves from the party for a moment it is to take a pull from a hip flask or to pinch a young pilgrim. They praise the ancient world in four languages, but their clothes are threadbare, their linen is dirty, and their hands tremble with thirst and lechery. While the guide chatted about the weather with Uncle George, the whiskey could already be smelled on his breath. Then the guide left Uncle George to greet the rest of the party, now coming across the square.

There were about thirty—they moved in a flock, or mass, understandably timid about the strangeness of their surroundings—and they were mostly old women. As they came into the bus, they cackled (as we all will when we grow old), and made the fussy arrangements of elderly travelers. Then, with the guide singing the praises of ancient Naples, they started on their way.

They first went along the coast. The color of the water reminded Uncle George of postcards he had received from Honolulu, where one of his friends had gone for a vacation. It was green and blue. He had never seen anything like it himself. They passed some resorts only half open and sleepy, where young men sat on rocks in their bathing trunks, waiting patiently for the sun to darken their skins. What did they think about, Uncle George wondered. During all those hours that they sat on rocks, what on earth did they think about? They passed a ramshackle colony of little bathhouses no bigger than privies, and Uncle George remembered—how many years ago—the thrill of undressing in such briny sea chambers as these when he had been taken to the seashore as a boy. As they turned inland, he craned his neck to get a last look at the sea, wondering why it should seem, shining and blue, like something that he remembered in his bones. Then they went into a tunnel and came out in farm land. Uncle George was interested in farming methods and admired the way that vines were trained onto trees. He admired the ter-

racing of the land, and was troubled by the traces of soil
erosion that he saw. And he recognized that he was separated
only by a pane of glass from a life that was as strange to him
as life on the moon.

The bus, with its glass roof and glass windows, was like a
fishbowl, and the sunlight and cloud shadows of the day fell
among the travelers. Their way was blocked by a flock of
sheep. Sheep surrounded the bus, isolated this little island
of elderly Americans, and filled the air with dumb, harsh
bleating. Beyond the sheep they saw a girl carrying a water
jug on her head. A man lay sound asleep in the grass by the
side of the road. A woman sat on a doorstep, suckling a child.
Within the dome of glass the old ladies discussed the high
price of airplane luggage. "Grace got ringworm in Palermo,"
one of them said. "I don't think she'll ever be cured."

The guide pointed out fragments of old Roman road,
Roman towers and bridges. There was a castle on a hill—a
sight that delighted Uncle George, and no wonder, for there
had been castles painted on his supper plate when he was a
boy, and the earliest books that had been read to him and
that he had been able to read had been illustrated with
castles. They had meant everything that was exciting and
strange and wonderful in life, and now, by raising his eyes,
he could see one against a sky as blue as the sky in his picture
books.

After traveling for an hour or two, they stopped in a village where there were a coffee bar and toilets. Coffee cost one
hundred lire a cup, a fact that filled the ladies' conversation
for some time after they had started again. Coffee had been
sixty lire at the hotel. Forty at the corner. They took pills and
read from their guidebooks, and Uncle George looked out

of the windows at this strange country, where the spring flowers and the autumn flowers seemed to grow side by side in the grass. It would be miserable weather in Krasbie, but here everything was in bloom—fruit trees, mimosa—and the pastures were white with flowers and the vegetable gardens already yielding crops.

They came into a town or city then—an old place with crooked and narrow streets. He didn't catch the name. The guide explained that there was a *festa*. The bus driver had to blow his horn continuously to make any progress, and two or three times came to a full stop, the crowd was so dense. The people in the streets looked up at this apparition —this fishbowl of elderly Americans—with such incredulity that Uncle George's feelings were hurt. He saw a little girl take a crust of bread out of her mouth to stare at him. Women held their children up in the air to see the strangers. Windows were thrown open, bars were emptied, and people pointed at the curious tourists and laughed. Uncle George would have liked to address them, as he so often addressed the Rotary. "Don't stare," he wanted to say to them. "We are not so queer and rich and strange. Don't stare at us."

The bus turned down a side street, and there was another stop for coffee and toilets. Most of the travelers scattered to buy postcards. Uncle George, seeing an open church across the street, decided to go inside. The air smelled of spice when he pushed the door open. The stone walls inside were bare— it was like an armory—and only a few candles burned in the chapels at the sides. Then Uncle George heard a loud voice and saw a man kneeling in front of one of the chapels, saying his prayers. He carried on in a way that Uncle George had never seen before. His voice was strong, supplicatory, sometimes angry. His face was wet with tears. He was beseeching the Cross for something—an explanation or an indulgence or a life. He waved his hands, he wept, and his voice and his sobs echoed in the barny place. Uncle George went out and got back into his seat on the bus.

They left the city for the country again, and a little before noon they stopped at the gates to Nero's villa, bought their tickets, and went in. It was a large ruin, fanciful, and picked clean of everything but its brick supports. The place had been vast and tall, and now the walls and archways of roofless rooms, the butts of towers stood in a stretch of green pasture, with nothing leading anywhere any more except to nothing, and all the many staircases mounting and turning stopped in midair. Uncle George left the party and wandered happily through these traces of a palace. The atmosphere seemed to him pleasant and tranquil—a little like the feeling in a forest —and he heard a bird singing and the noise of water. The forms of the ruins, all bristling with plants like the hair in an old man's ears, seemed pleasantly familiar, as if his unremembered dreams had been played out against a scene like this. He found himself then in a place that was darker than the rest. The air was damp, and the senseless brick rooms, opening onto one another, were full of brush. It might have been a dungeon or a guardhouse or a temple where obscene rites were performed, for he was suddenly stirred licentiously by the damp. He turned back, looking for the sun, the water, and the bird, and found a guide standing in his path.

"You wish to see the special place?"

"What do you mean?"

"Very special," the guide said. "For men only. Only for strong men. Such pictures. Very old."

"How much?"

"Two hundred lire."

"All right." Uncle George took two hundred lire out of his change pocket.

"Come," the guide said. "This way." He walked on briskly —so briskly that Uncle George nearly had to run to keep up with him. He saw the guide go through a narrow opening in the wall, a place where the brick had crumbled, but when Uncle George followed him the guide seemed to have disappeared. It was a trap. He felt an arm around his throat, and his head was thrown back so violently that he couldn't call for help. He felt a hand lift the wallet out of his pocket—a touch as light as the nibble of a fish on a line—and then he was thrown brutally to the ground. He lay there dazed for a minute or two. When he sat up, he saw that he had been left his empty wallet and his passport.

Then he roared with anger at the thieves, and hated Italy, with its thieving population of organ grinders and bricklayers. But even during this outburst his anger was not as strong as a feeling of weakness and shame. He was terribly ashamed of himself, and when he picked up his empty wallet and put it in his pocket, he felt as if his heart had been plucked out and broken. Who could he blame? Not the damp ruins. He had asked for something that was by his lights all wrong, and he could only blame himself. The theft might happen every day—some lecherous old fool like him might be picked clean each time the bus stopped. He got to his feet, weary and sick of the old bones that had got him into trouble. He dusted the dirt off his clothes. Then he realized that he might be late. He might have missed the bus and be stranded in the ruins without a cent. He began to walk and run through the rooms, until he came out into a clearing and saw in the distance the flock of old ladies, still clinging to one another.

The guide came out from behind a wall, and they all got in the bus and started off again.

Rome was ugly; at least, the outskirts were: trolley cars and cut-rate furniture stores and torn-up streets and the sort of apartment houses that nobody ever really wants to live in. The old ladies began to gather their guidebooks and put on their coats and hats and gloves. Journey's end is the same everywhere. Then, dressed for their destination, they all sat down again, with their hands folded in their laps, and the bus was still. "Oh, I wish I'd never come," one old lady said to another. "I just wish I'd never left home." She was not the only one.

"*Ecco, ecco Roma,*" the guide said, and so it was.

Streeter went to Kate's at seven on Thursday. Assunta let him in, and, for the first time, he walked down the *sala* without his copy of *I Promessi Sposi*, and sat down by the fireplace. Charlie came in then. He had on the usual outfit— the tight Levis, with cuffs turned up, and a pink shirt. When he moved, he dragged or banged the leather heels of his loafers on the marble floor. He talked about baseball and exercised his owlish laugh, but he didn't mention Uncle George. Neither did Kate, when she came in, nor did she offer Streeter a drink. She seemed to be in the throes of an emotional storm, with all her powers of decision suspended. They talked about the weather. At one point, Charlie came and stood by his mother, and she took both of his hands in one of hers. Then the doorbell rang, and Kate went down the room to meet her uncle. They embraced very tenderly—the members of a family—and when this was over he said, "I was robbed, Katie. I was robbed yesterday of four hundred dollars. Coming up from Naples on the bus."

"Oh, I'm so sorry!" she said. "Wasn't there anything you could do, George? Wasn't there anyone you could speak to?"

"Speak to, Katie? There hasn't been anyone I could speak to since I got off the boat. No speaka da English. If you cut off their hands, they wouldn't be able to say anything. I can afford to lose four hundred dollars—I'm not a poor man— but if I could only have given it to some worth-while cause."

"I'm terribly sorry."

"You've got quite a place here, Katie."

"And, Charlie, this is Uncle George."

If she had counted on their not getting along, this chance was lost in a second. Charlie forgot his owlish laugh and stood so straight, so earnest, so in need of what America could do for him that the rapport between the man and the boy was instantaneous, and Kate had to separate them in order to introduce Streeter. Uncle George shook hands with her student and came to a likely but erroneous conclusion.

"Speaka da English?" he asked.

"I'm an American," Streeter said.

"How long is your sentence?"

"This is my second year," Streeter said. "I work at F.R.U.-P.C."

"It's an immoral country," Uncle George said, sitting down in one of the golden chairs. "First they rob me of four hundred dollars, and then, walking around the streets here, all I see is statues of men without any clothes on. Nothing."

Kate rang for Assunta, and when the maid came in she ordered whiskey and ice, in very rapid Italian. "It's just another way of looking at things, Uncle George," she said.

"No, it isn't," Uncle George said. "It isn't natural. Not even in locker rooms. There's very few men who'd choose to parade around a locker room stark naked if a towel was handy. It's not natural. Everywhere you look. Up on the roofs. At the main traffic intersections. When I was coming over here, I passed through a little garden—playground, I guess you'd say— and right in the middle of it, right in the middle of all these little children is one of these men without anything on."

"Will you have some whiskey?"

"Yes, please. . . . The boat sails on Saturday, Katie, and I want you and the boy to come home with me."

"I don't want Charlie to leave," Kate said.

"He wants to leave—don't you, Charlie? He wrote me a nice letter. Nicely worded, and he's got a nice handwriting. That was a nice letter, Charlie. I showed it to the high-school superintendent, and he said you can enter the Krasbie high school whenever you want. And I want you to come, too, Kate. It's your home, and you've only got one. The trouble with you, Katie, is that when you were a kid they used to make fun of you in Krasbie, and you just started running, that's all, and you never stopped."

"If that's true—and it may be," she said quickly, "why should I want to go back to a place where I will seem ridiculous."

"Oh, Katie, you won't seem ridiculous. I'll take care of that."

"I want to go home, Mama," Charlie said. He was sitting on a stool by the fireplace—not so straight-backed any more. "I'm homesick all the time."

"How could you possibly be homesick for America?" Her voice was very sharp. "You've never seen it. This is your home."

"How do you mean?"

"Your home is with your mother."

"There's more to it than that, Mama. I feel strange here all the time. Everybody on the street speaking a different language."

"You've never even tried to learn Italian."

"Even if I had, it wouldn't make any difference. It would still sound strange. I mean it would still remind me that it wasn't my language. I just don't understand the people, Mama. I like them all right, but I just don't understand them. I never know what they're going to do next."

"Why don't you try and understand them?"

"Oh, I do, but I'm no genius, and you don't understand them either. I've heard you say so, and sometimes you're homesick, too, I know. I can tell by the way you look."

"Homesickness is nothing," she said angrily. "It is absolutely nothing. Fifty per cent of the people in the world are homesick all the time. But I don't suppose you're old enough to understand. When you're in one place and long to be in another, it isn't as simple as taking a boat. You don't really long for another country. You long for something in yourself that you don't have, or haven't been able to find."

"Oh, I don't mean that, Mama. I just mean if I was with people who spoke my language, people who understood me, I'd be more comfortable."

"If comfort is all you expect to get out of life, God help you."

Then the doorbell rang and Assunta answered it. Kate glanced at her watch and saw that it was five after eight. It was also the first Thursday in the month. Before she could get out an explanation, they had started down the *sala*, with the old Duke of Rome in the lead, holding some flowers in his left hand. A little behind him was the Duchess, his wife—a tall, willowy, gray-haired woman wearing a lot of jewelry that had been given to the family by Francis I. An assortment of nobles brought up the rear, looking like a country circus, gorgeous and travel-worn. The Duke gave Kate her flowers. They all bowed vaguely to her company and went out through the kitchen, with its smell of gas leaks, to the service door.

"Oh, Giuseppe the barber he gotta the cash," Uncle George sang loudly, "He gotta the bigga the blacka mustache." He waited for someone to laugh, and when no one did he asked, "What was that?"

Kate told him, but her eyes were brighter, and he noticed this.

"You like that kind of thing, don't you?" he said.

"Possibly," she said.

"It's crazy, Katie," he said. "It's crazy, it's crazy. You come home with me and Charlie. You and Charlie can live in the other half of my house, and I'll have a nice American kitchen put in for you."

Streeter saw that she was touched by this remark, and he thought she was going to cry. She said quickly, "How in hell do you think America would have been discovered if everybody stayed home in places like Krasbie?"

"You're not discovering anything, Katie."

"I am. I am."

"We'll all be happier, Mama," Charlie said. "We'll all be happier if we have a nice clean house and lots of nice friends and a nice garden and kitchen and stall shower."

She stood with her back to them, by the mantelpiece, and

said loudly, "No nice friends, no kitchen, no garden, no shower bath or anything else will keep me from wanting to see the world and the different people who live in it." Then she turned to her son and spoke softly. "You'll miss Italy, Charlie."

The boy laughed his owlish laugh. "I'll miss the black hairs in my food," he said. She didn't make a sound. She didn't even sigh. Then the boy went to her and began to cry. "I'm sorry, Mummy," he said. "I'm sorry. That was a dumb thing to say. It's just an old joke." He kissed her hands and the tears on her cheeks, and Streeter got up and left.

"Tal era ciò che di meno deforme e di men compassion-evole si faceva vedere intorno, i sani, gli agiati," Streeter read when he went again for his lesson on Sunday. *"Chè, dopo tante immagini di miseria, e pensando a quella ancor più grave, per mezzo alla quale dovrem condurre il lettore, no ci fermeremo ora a dir qual fosse lo spettacolo degli appestati che si strascicavano o giacevano per le strade, de' poveri, de' fanciulli, delle donne."*

The boy had gone, he could tell—not because she said so but because the place seemed that much bigger. In the middle of his lesson, the old Duke of Rome came through in his bathrobe and slippers, carrying a bowl of soup to his sister, who was sick. Kate looked tired, but then she always did, and when the lesson ended and Streeter stood up, wondering if she would mention Charlie or Uncle George, she complimented him on the progress he had made and urged him to finish *I Promessi Sposi* and to buy a copy of the *Divine Comedy* for next week.

Clementina

❦

SHE WAS BORN AND BROUGHT UP IN NASCOSTA, IN THE time of the wonders—the miracle of the jewels and the winter of the wolves. She was ten years old when thieves broke into the shrine of the Holy Virgin after the last Mass on San Giovanni and stole the jewels that had been given to the Madonna by a princess who was cured there of a malady of the liver. On the next day, when Uncle Serafino was walking up from the fields, he saw, in the mouth of the cave where the Etruscans had buried their dead, a youth of great radiance, who beckoned to him, but he was afraid and ran away. Then Serafino was stricken with a fever, and he called for the priest and told him what he had seen, and the priest went to the cave and found the jewels of the Madonna there in the dead leaves where the angel had been standing. That same year, on the road below the farm, her Cousin Maria saw the Devil, with horns, a pointed tail, and a tight red suit, just as in the pictures. She was fourteen at the time of the big snow, and she went that night after dark to the fountain and, turning back toward the tower where they then lived, she saw the wolves. It was a pack of six or seven, trotting up the stairs of the Via Cavour in the snow. She dropped her pitcher and ran into the tower, and her tongue was swollen with terror, but she looked out the cracks in the door and saw them, more churlish than dogs, more ragged, their ribs showing in their mangy coats and the blood of the sheep they had murdered falling from their mouths. She was terrified and she was rapt, as if the sight of the wolves moving over the snow was the spirits of the dead or some other part of the mystery that she knew to lie close to the heart of life, and when they had passed she would not have believed she had seen them if they had not left their tracks in the snow. She was seventeen when she went to work as a donna di servizio for the baron of little importance who had a villa on the hill, and it was the same summer that Antonio, in the dark field, called her his dewy rose and made her head swim. She confessed to the priest and did her penance and was absolved, but when this had happened six times the priest said they should become engaged, and so Antonio became her fidanzato. The mother of Antonio was not sympathetic, and after three years Clementina was still his rose and he was still her fidanzato and whenever the marriage was mentioned the mother of Antonio would hold her head and scream. In the autumn, the baron asked her to come to Rome as a donna and how could she say no when she had dreamed all the nights of her life of seeing the Pope with her own eyes and walking on streets that were lighted after dark with electricity?

In Rome she slept on straw and washed in a bucket, but the streets were a spectacle, although she had to work such hours that she was not often able to walk in the city. The baron promised to pay her twelve thousand lire a month, but he paid her nothing at the end of the first month and nothing at the end of the second, and the cook said that he often brought girls in from the country and paid them nothing. Opening the door for him one evening, she asked with great courtesy for her wages, and he said he had given her a room, a change of air, and a visit to Rome and that she was badly educated to ask for more. She had no coat to wear in the street, and there were holes in her shoes, and all she was given to eat was the leftovers from the baron's table. She saw that she would have to find another post, because she didn't have the money to go back to Nascosta. That next week, the cousin of the cook found her a place where she was both seamstress and donna, and here she worked even harder, but when the month was over there were no wages. Then she refused to finish a dress the signora had asked her to make for a reception. She said she would not finish the dress until she had her wages. The signora angered herself and tore her hair, but she paid the wages. Then that night the cousin of the cook said that some Americans needed a donna. She put all the dirty dishes in the oven to give a false appearance of cleanliness, said her prayers in San Marcello, and flew across Rome to where the Americans lived, feeling that every girl on the street that night was looking for the same post. The Americans were a family with two boys—well-educated people, although she could see that they were sad and foolish. They offered her twenty thousand lire in wages and showed her a very commodious room where she would live and said they hoped she would not be uncomfortable, and in the morning she moved her things to the Americans'.

She had heard much about Americans, about how they

were generous and ignorant, and some of this was true, for they were very generous and treated her like a guest in the house, always asking her if she had time to do this and that and urging her to take a passage in the streets on Thursdays and Sundays. The signore was meager and tall and worked in the Embassy. His hair was cropped close like a German or a prisoner or someone recovering from an operation of the brain. His hair was black and strong, and if he had let it go and waved it with frissone the girls in the street would have admired him, but he went each week to the barber and had himself disfigured. He was very modest in other things and wore at the beach a concealing bathing costume, but he walked through the streets of Rome with the shape of his head naked for everyone to see. The signora was fine, with a skin like marble and many clothes, and it was a commodious and a diverting life, and Clementina prayed at San Marcello's that it would never end. They left all the lights burning as if electricity cost nothing, and they burned wood in the fireplace only to take off the evening chill, and they drank iced gin and vermouth before dinner. They smelled different. It was a pale smell, she thought—a weak smell—and it might have had something to do with the blood of northerners, or it might be because they took so many hot baths. They took so many hot baths that she could not understand why they were not neurasthenics. They ate Italian food and drank wine, and she hoped that if they ate enough pasta and oil they would have a strong and wholesome smell. Sometimes when she waited on table, she smelled them, but it was always a very weak smell and sometimes nothing. They spoiled their children, and sometimes the children spoke sharply or in an ill temper to their genitori, for which they should have been

whipped, but they never whipped their children, these strangers, or even raised their voices in anger, or did anything
else that would explain to the children the importance of
their genitori, and once when the smallest boy was very badly
disposed and should have been whipped, his mother took him
instead to a toy store and bought him a sailboat. And sometimes when they were dressing to go out in the evening the
signore would fasten his wife's clothes or her pearls, like a
cafone, instead of ringing for Clementina. And once when
there was no water in the flat and she had gone down the stairs
to the fountain to get some, he came after her to help, and
when she said that it was not possible for him to carry water,
he said that it was not possible for him to sit by his fire while a
young woman carried a heavy demijohn up and down the
stairs. Then he took the demijohn out of her hands and
went down to the fountain, where he could be seen getting
water by the porter and all the other servants in the palace,
and she watched this from the kitchen window and was so
angry and ashamed that she had to take some wine for her
stomach, for everyone would say that she was lazy and that she
worked for a vulgar and badly educated family. And they did
not believe in the dead. Once, walking down the sala in the
dusk, she saw the spirit of a dead man before her so clearly
that at first she thought it was the signore, until she saw him
standing in the door. Then she screamed and dropped the
tray with the glasses and bottles on it, and when the signore
asked her why she had screamed and she said it was because
she had seen a ghost he was not sympathetic. And once, in the
back hall, she saw another ghost, the ghost of a bishop with a
mitre, and when she screamed and told the signore what she
had seen he was not sympathetic.

But the children were sympathetic, and in the evening, when they were in bed, she told them the stories of Nascosta. The story they liked best was of the young farmer in Nascosta who was married to a beautiful woman named Assunta. When they had been married a year, they had a fine son with dark curls and a golden skin, but from the first he was sickly, and he cried, and they thought there was a spell on him, and they took him to the doctor in Conciliano, riding all the way there on an asino, and the doctor said the baby was dying of starvation. But how could this be, they asked, for the breasts of Assunta were so full of milk they stained her blouse. But the doctor said to watch at night, and they went home by asino and ate their supper, and Assunta fell asleep, but the husband stayed awake to watch, and then at midnight he saw in the moonlight a great viper come over the threshold of the farmhouse and come into the bed and suck the milk from the breasts of the woman, but the husband could not move, for if he moved, the viper would have put his fangs into her breast and killed her, and when the serpent had sucked her breasts dry he went back across the floor and over the threshold in the moonlight, and then the farmer gave the alarm, and all the farmers from around came, and they found against the wall of the farm a nest of eight great serpents, fat with milk, who were so poisonous that even their breath was mortal, and they beat them to death with clubs, and this was a true story, because she had passed the farm where it happened a hundred times. And the story they preferred after this was of the lady in Conciliano who became the lover of a handsome stranger from America. But one night she noticed on his back a small mark like a leaf and remembered that the son who had been taken away from her many years

ago was so marked, and knew then that this lover was her
son. She ran then to the church to ask forgiveness in the confessional, but the priest—he was a fat and a haughty man—
said there was no forgiveness for her sin and, subito, there
was in the confessional a loud clatter of bones. Then the
people came and opened the confessional and saw that where
there had been a proud and a haughty priest there was nothing but bones. And she also told the children about the
miracle of the jewels of the Madonna, and the tempo infame
when she had seen the wolves coming up the Via Cavour, and
the time her Cousin Maria had seen the Devil in his red suit.

She went with this American family to the mountains
in July, and in August to Venice and, coming back to Rome
in the fall, she understood them to say that they were leaving Italy, and they had the trunks brought up from the
cellar, and she helped the signora with the packing. Now she
had five pairs of shoes and eight dresses and money in the
bank, but the thought of looking for another post with a
Roman signora who might spit in her eye whenever she felt
like it was discouraging, and one day when she was repairing
a dress for the signora she became so discouraged that she
cried. Then she explained to the signora how hard the life
of a donna was working for Romans, and the signora said
they would take her to the new world if she liked. They
would take her for six months on an impermanent visa; it
would be diverting for her and a help to them. Then all the
arrangements were made, and she went to Nascosta, and the
Mamma cried and asked her not to go, and everyone in the
village said she should not go, but this was jealousy, because
they had never had a chance to go anywhere—not even
Conciliano. And for once the world where she had lived and

been so happy seemed to her truly to be an old world where the customs and the walls were older than the people, and she felt that she would be happier in a world where the walls were all new, even if the people were savage.

When the time came to go, they drove to Naples, stopping whenever the signore felt like it to have a little coffee and cognac, traveling very commodiously like millionaires and staying in a di-lusso hotel in Naples, where she had a room to herself. But on the morning when they sailed she felt a great sadness, for who can live out a good life but in his own country? Then she told herself that it was only a voyage—she would come home in six months—and what had the good God made the world so strange and various for if it was not to be seen? She had her passport stamped and went aboard the ship feeling very emotional. It was an American ship, as cold as winter, and at lunch there was ice water on the table, and what was not cold was flavorless and badly cooked, and she came back to her deep feeling that, while these people were kind and generous, they were ignorant and the men fastened their wives' pearls and, with all their money, they did not know any better than to eat platefuls of raw steak washed down with coffee that tasted like medicine. They were not beautiful or elegant and they had pale eyes, but what disgusted her most on the ship were the old women, who in her country would be wearing black in memory of their numerous dead and, as suited their time of life, would move slowly and inspire dignity. But here the old ladies spoke in shrill voices and wore bright clothes and as much jewelry, all of it false, as you would find on the Madonna of Nascosta, and painted their faces and tinted their hair.

But who was deceived, for you could see how haggard under the paint were their cheeks, and that their necks were rucked and seamed like the necks of turtles, and although they smelled like the campagna in spring they were as withered and dry as the flowers on a tomb. They were like straw, and this must be a savage country where the old had no wisdom or taste and did not deserve or receive the respect of their children and their grandchildren and had forgotten their dead.

But it would be beautiful, she thought, because she had seen in magazines and newspapers photographs of the towers of the city of New York, towers of gold and silver, against the blue sky, in a city that had never once been touched by the damage of war. But it was raining when they came up the Narrows, and when she looked for the towers they were not to be seen, and when she asked for the towers she was told they were lost in the rain. She was disappointed, for what she could see of this new world seemed ugly, and all the people who dreamed of it were deceived. It was like Naples in the time of the war, and she wished she had not come. The customs man who went through her bags was badly educated. They took a taxi and a train to Washington, the capital of the new world, and then another taxi, and she could see out of the window that all the buildings were copies of the buildings of Imperial Rome, and they looked ghostly to her in the night lights, as if the Forum had risen again from the dust. They drove into the country where the houses were all of wood and all new and where the washbasins and bathtubs were very commodious, and in the morning her signora showed her the machines and how to work them.

At first she was suspicious of the washing machine, for it

used a fortune in soap and hot water and did not clean the clothes, and it reminded her of how happy she had been at the fountain in Nascosta, talking with her friends and making everything as clean as new. But little by little the machine seemed to her more carina, for it was after all only a machine, and it filled itself and emptied itself and turned around and around, and it seemed marvelous to her that a machine could remember so much and was always there, ready and waiting to do its work. And then there was the machine for washing the dishes, and you could wash the dishes in a costume for the evening without getting a drop of water on your gloves. When the signora was away and the boys were at school, first she would put some dirty clothes in the washing machine and start that, and then she would put some dirty dishes in the other machine and start that, and then she would put a nice saltimbocca alla romana in the electric frying pan and start that, and then she would sit in the salone in front of the TV and listen to all the machines around her doing the work, and it delighted her and made her feel powerful. Then there was the frigidario in the kitchen, making ice and keeping the butter as hard as stone, and there was the deep freeze full of lamb and beef as fresh as the day when they had been killed, and there was an electric egg beater, and a machine for squeezing the oranges, and a machine for breathing in the dust, and she would have them all going at once, and a machine for making the toast—all bright silver—where you put in the plain bread and turned your back and allora, there were two pieces of toast just the color you had asked for, and all done by the machine.

During the day, her signore was away at the office, but her signora, who in Rome had lived like a princess, seemed in the new world to be a secretary, and she thought perhaps that they were poor and the signora must work. She was always talking on the telephone and making computations and writing letters like a secretary. She was always hurried during the day and tired at night, like a secretary. Because they were both tired at night, the house was not as peaceful as it had been in Rome. Finally she asked the signora to explain what she was a secretary for, and the signora said that she was not a secretary but that she was kept busy raising money for the poor and the sick and the mad. This seemed to Clementina very strange. The climate also seemed to her strange and humid, bad for the lungs and the liver, but the trees at that season were very colorful—she had never seen this before; they were gold and red and yellow, and their leaves fell through the air as in some great hall in Rome or Venice where the paint is flaking from the pictures on the ceiling.

There was a paisano, an old man they called Joe, from bas-Italia, who delivered the milk. He had sixty years or more and was bent with carrying milk bottles, but she went with him to the movies, where he could explain the story to her in Italian and where he pinched her and asked her to marry him. This was a joke, as far as Clementina was concerned. There were strange festas in the new world—one with a turkey and no saints—and then there was the festa of the Natale, and she herself had never seen anything so discourteous to the Holy Virgin and the sainted baby. First they bought a green tree and then they put it up in the salone and hung it with shining necklaces, as if it were a holy saint with the power of curing evil and hearing prayers. Mamma mia. A tree! She was confessed by a priest who gave her the tail of the Devil for not coming to church every Sunday of her life and who was very rigid. When she went to Mass, they took the collection three times. She thought that when she returned to Rome she would write an article for the paper about the church in this new world where there was not even the wristbone of a saint to kiss and where they made offerings to a green tree and forgot the travail of the Holy Virgin and took the collection three times. And then there was the snow, but it was more carina than the snow in Nascosta—there were no wolves, and the signori skied in the mountains, and the children played in the snow and the house was always warm.

She still went with Joe every Sunday to the movies, where he told her the story, asked her to marry him, and pinched her. Once, before the movies, he stopped at a fine house all made of wood and neatly painted, and he unlocked the door and took her upstairs to a nice apartment with paper on the walls, the floor shining with varnish, and five rooms in all, with a modern bathroom, and he said that if she would marry him it would all be hers. He would buy her a machine for washing the dishes and a machine for beating the eggs and a frying pan like the signora had that knew when to turn off the saltimbocca alla romana. When she asked him where he would find all the money to do this, he said that he had saved seventeen thousand dollars, and he took a book out of his pocket, a bankbook, and there was stamped in it seventeen thousand two hundred and thirty dollars and seventeen cents. It would all be hers if she would come and be his wife. She said no, but after the movies, when she was in bed, it made her sad to think of all the machinery and she wished that she had never come to the new world. Nothing would ever be the same again. When she went back to Nascosta and told them that a man—not a beautiful man, but one who was honest and gentle—had offered her seventeen thousand dollars and a place with five rooms, they would never believe her. They would think she was crazy, and how could she lie again on straw in a cold room and be contented? Her impermanent visa expired in April and she would have to go home then, but the signore said that he could apply for an extension if she liked, and she begged him to do this. In the kitchen one night, she heard them speaking in low voices and she guessed they were speaking about her affairs, but he did not speak to her until much later when the others had gone up and she came into the room to say good night.

"I'm very sorry, Clementina," he said, "but they won't give me an extension."

"It doesn't matter," she said. "If I am not wanted in this country, I will go home."

"It isn't that, Clementina, it's the law. I'm very sorry. Your visa expires on the twelfth. I'll get your passage on a boat before then."

"Thank you, Signore," she said. "Good night."

She would go back, she thought. She would take the boat, she would debark at Naples, she would catch a train at the Mergellina and in Rome a *pullman,* and go out the Tiburtina with the curtains of the bus swaying and the purple clouds of exhaust rolling out behind them when they climbed the hill at Tivoli. Her eyes filled with tears when she thought of kissing Mamma and giving her the silver-framed photograph of Dana Andrews that she had bought at Woolworth's for her present. Then she would sit on the piazza with such a ring of people around her as would form for an accident, speaking in her own tongue and drinking the wine they had made and talking about the new world where there were frying pans with brains and where even the powder for cleaning the gabinetti smelled of roses. She saw the scene distinctly, the fountain spray blowing on the wind, but then she saw gathering in the imagined faces of her townsmen a look of disbelief. Who would believe her tales? Who would listen? They would have admired her if she had seen the Devil, like Cousin Maria, but she had seen a sort of paradise and no one cared. In leaving one world and coming to another she had lost both.

Then she opened and reread a package of letters written from Nascosta by her Uncle Sebastiano. That night, his letters all seemed dolorous. The autumn had come on quickly, he wrote, and it was cold, even in September, and many of the olives and the grapes were lost, and la bomba atomica had ruined the seasons of Italy. Now the shadow of the town fell over the valley earlier, and she remembered herself the beginnings of winter—the sudden hoarfrost lying on the grapes and wild flowers, and the contadini coming in at dark on their asini, loaded down with roots and other scraps of wood, for wood was hard to find in that country and one would ride ten kilometri for a bundle of green olive cuttings, and she could remember the cold in her bones and see the asini against the yellow light of evening and hear the lonely noise of stones falling down the steep path, falling away from their hoofs. And in December Sebastiano wrote that it was again the time of the wolves. The tempo infame had come again to Nascosta, and wolves had killed six of the padrone's sheep, and there was no abbacchio, and no eggs, either, for pasta, and the piazza was buried in snow up to the edge of the fountain, and they knew hunger and cold, and she could remember both.

The room where she read these letters was warm. The lights were pink. She had a silver ashtray like a signora, and, if she had wanted, in her private bathroom she could have drawn a hot bath up to her neck. Did the Holy Virgin mean for her to live in a wilderness and die of starvation? Was it wrong to take the comforts that were held out to her? The faces of her people appeared to her again, and how dark were their skin, their hair, and their eyes, she thought, as if through living with fair people she had taken on the dispositions and the prejudices of the fair. The faces seemed to regard her with reproach, with earthen patience, with a sweet, dignified, and despairing regard, but why should she be compelled to return and drink sour wine in the darkness of the hills? In this new world they had found the secret of youth, and would the saints in Heaven have refused a life of youthfulness if it had been God's will? She remembered how in Nascosta even the most beautiful fell quickly under the darkness of time, like flowers without care; how even the most beautiful became bent and toothless, their dark clothes smelling, as the Mamma's did, of smoke and manure. But in this country she could have forever white teeth and color in her hair. Until the day she died she would have shoes with heels and rings on her fingers, and the attention of men, for in this new world one lived ten lifetimes and never felt the pinch of age; no, never. She would marry Joe. She would stay here and live ten lives, with a skin like marble and always the teeth with which to bite the meat.

On the next night, her signore told her when the boats were leaving, and when he had finished she said, "I am not going back."

"I don't understand."

"I will marry Joe."

"But Joe's a great deal older than you, Clementina."

"Joe is sixty-three."

"And you?"

"I am twenty-four."

"Do you love Joe?"

"Oh no, Signore. How could I love him, with his big paunch like a sackful of apples and so many wrinkles at the back of his neck you could tell your fortune there? It is not possible."

"Clementina, I admire Joe," the signore said. "He's an honest man. If you marry him, you must care for him."

"Oh, I'll care for him, Signore. I'll make his bed and cook his supper, but I will never let him touch me."

He deliberated, looked down at the floor, and finally said, "I will not let you marry Joe, Clementina."

"But why?"

"I won't let you marry him unless you'll be his wife. You must love him."

"But, Signore, in Nascosta there would be no sense in marrying a man whose land did not adjoin yours, and does that mean then that your heart will fly out to him?"

"This is not Nascosta."

"But all marriages are like this, Signore. If people married for love, the world would not be a place in which to live, it would be a hospital for the mad. Did not the Signora marry you because of the money and the conveniences you bring her?" He did not answer, but she saw his face flush dark with blood. "Oh Signore, my Signore," she said, "you talk like a boy with stars in your eyes, a thin boy at the fountain, his head full of the poesia. I am only trying to unfold to you that I am only marrying Joe so that I can stay in this country, and you are talking like a boy."

"I am not talking like a boy," he said. Then he rose from the chair. "I am not talking like a boy. Who do you think you are? When you came to us in Rome you didn't have shoes or a coat."

"Signore, you do not understand me. Perhaps I will love him, but I am only trying to unfold to you that I am not marrying for love."

"And that's what I'm trying to explain to you. I won't stand for it."

"I will leave your house, Signore."

"I'm responsible for you."

"No, Signore. Joe is responsible for me now."

"Then get out of my house."

She went upstairs to her room and cried and cried, in anger and pity for this grown fool, but she packed her things. In the morning she cooked the breakfast, but she stayed in the kitchen until the signore had gone to work, and then the signora came down and cried, and the children cried, and at noon Joe came to get her in his car and took her to the Pelluchis', who were paisani and with whom she would stay until she and Joe were married. Maria Pelluchi explained to her that in the new world one was married like a princess, and this was so. For three weeks she was in and out of the stores with Maria—first to buy the wedding dress for herself, all white and the latest mode, with a tail of satin to drag along the ground, but economical, too, because the tail could be adjusted, making the dress like a costume for the grand evening. Then there were the costumes for Maria and her sister, who would be the attendants, and these were yellow and lavender and could be used later as costumes for the evening. Then there were the shoes and the flowers and the clothes for traveling and the suitcase, and nothing was rented. And when the day of the wedding arrived she was so tired that she had milk in the knees and walked through it all like a dream, of which she could remember very little. There were many paisani at the reception and much wine, food, and music, and then she took with Joe a train to New York, where the buildings were so tall they made her feel homesick and of little importance. In New York, they spent the night in a hotel, and the next day they took a di-lusso train, only for signori who were going to Atlantic City, with a special chair for each passenger and a waiter to bring things to eat and drink. She hung behind her chair the mink stole that Joe had given her for a present, and everyone saw it and admired it and judged her to be a rich signora. Joe called the waiter over and told him to bring some whiskey and seltz, but the waiter pretended not to understand what Joe was saying and to be so busy waiting on other people that they would have to be the last, and she felt again that shame and anger at discovering that because they could not speak elegantly the language of this new country they would be treated with great discourtesy, as if they were pigs. And that is the way they were treated on the passage, for the waiter did not come near them again, as if their money was not as good as the money of the others. They went first through a great, dark galleria and then out into a country that was ugly and potent with fire exploding from many chimneys, and there were trees and rivers and places for boating. She looked out of the window at the country that streamed by as swiftly and gently as water, to see if it was as fair as Italy, but what she saw was that it was not her country, her earth. Near the cities they passed those places where the poor lived and where washing was hung on lines, and she thought that this was the same—that washing on lines must be the same all over the world. And the houses of the poor were the same, too, the way they leaned against one another and had gardens that were not commodious but that were cultivated, you could see, with gentleness and love. It was in the middle of the day or later when they left, and, as they sped through the country and the afternoon, she saw that the schools were closing and that on the streets there were many children carrying books and riding bicycles and playing games, and many of them waved to the train as it rolled along and she waved back to them. She waved to some children who were walking through the high grass in a field, and she waved to two boys on a bridge, and she waved to an old man, and they all waved back to her, and she waved to three girls, and she waved to a lady who was pushing a baby carriage, and she waved to a little boy who was wearing a yellow coat and carrying a valise, and he waved back. They all waved back. Then she could see that they were coming close to the ocean, for there was a bareness in the air and not so many trees and many pictures of hotels painted on wood saying how many hundreds of rooms they had and how many different kinds of places for drinking cocktails, and she was happy to see the name of their hotel on one of these signs and to be sure that it was di lusso. Then the train stopped and it was the end of the passage and she felt shy and timid, but Joe said andiamo, and the waiter who had been so discourteous to them took their bags away and reached for her mink stole, but she said, "No, thank you," and got it away from him, the pig. And then there was the largest black car she had ever seen in her life, with a sign on it saying the name of their hotel, and they got into this with some other people, but they did not speak to one another on the passage, because she did not want the others to know that she could not speak the language of this country.

The hotel was very di lusso, and they ascended in an elevator, and walked down a hall that was covered with thick carpet, into a fine room, also with thick carpet everywhere, and a toilet—only with no bidet—and when the waiter had gone Joe got a bottle of whiskey out of his valise and had a drink and asked her to come and sit in his lap, and she said a little later, later, for it was unlucky in the daylight, and it would be better to wait for the moon to rise, and she would like to go down and see the dining rooms and lounges. She wondered if the salt air would be bad for the mink, and Joe had another drink, and out of the window she could see the ocean and the lines of white waves coming in, and because the windows were closed and she could not hear the sound the waves made when they broke it seemed like something she was dreaming. They went down again, not speaking, because she had distinctly come to feel that it was better not to speak the bella lingua in such a luxurious place, and they looked in the bars and dining rooms, which were grand, and then went out onto a broad walk beside the sea and there was salt in the air, like Venice, and it smelled like Venice, and there was also a smell of frying food in the air, which reminded her of the feast of San Giuseppe in Rome. On one side of them was the green, cold sea, which she had crossed to come to this new world, and on the other side of them there were many diverting things. They walked along until they came to the gypsies, where there was in the window a drawing of the human hand and where one's fortune could be told, and when she asked if they could speak Italian they said, "Si, si, si, non c'è dubbio!" and Joe gave her a dollar, and she went behind a curtain with the gypsy, who looked at her hand and began to tell her fortune, but it was not Italian she was speaking, it was a bastard language of a little Spanish and a little something that Clementina had never heard before, and she could only understand a word here and there, like "the sea" and "the voyage," but she could not tell if this was a voyage she would make or a voyage she had made, and she became impatient with the gypsy, who had made a lie in saying that she spoke in Italian, and she asked for her money back, but the gypsy said that if the money was given back there would be a curse on it. And, knowing what strong curses the gypsies make, she did not create a further disturbance, and went out where Joe was waiting for her on the wooden walk, and walked along again between the green sea and the diversions of frying food, where people called to them to come in and spend their money, smiling and beckoning wickedly like the angels of Hell. And then there was the tramonto, and the lights went on gloriously like pearls, and, looking back, she could see the pink windows of the hotel where they were known, where they had a room of their own they could return to when they pleased, and the noise of the sea sounded like distant blasting in the mountains.

She was a good wife to him, and in the morning he was so grateful that he bought her a silver dish for the butter and a cover for the ironing board and a pair of red pants, laced with gold. The mother would give her the tail of the Devil, she knew, for wearing pants, and in Rome she herself would spit in the eye of a woman who was so badly educated as to wear pants, but this was a new world and it was no sin, and in the afternoon she wore the mink stole and the red pants and went with Joe up and down the wooden walk above the sea. On Saturday they went home, and on Monday they bought the furniture, and on Tuesday it was delivered, and on Friday she put on the red pants and went to the supermarket with Maria Pelluchi, who explained the labels on the boxes to her, and she looked so much like an American that people were surprised when she could not speak the language.

But if she could not speak the language she could do everything else, and she even learned to drink whiskey without coughing and spitting. In the morning, she would turn on all the machines and watch the TV, learning the words of the songs, and in the afternoons Maria Pelluchi came to her house and they watched the TV together, and in the evening she watched it with Joe. She tried to write the mother about the things she had bought—much finer things than the Pope possessed—but she realized that the letter would only bewilder the mother, and in the end she sent her nothing but postcards. No one could describe how diverting and commodious her life had become. In the summer, in the evenings, Joe took her to the races in Baltimore, and she had never seen anything so carina—the little horses and the lights and the flowers and the red coat of the marshal with his bugle. That summer, they went to the races every

Friday and sometimes oftener, and it was one night there, when she was wearing her red pants and drinking whiskey, that she saw her signore for the first time since they had quarreled.

She asked him how he was, and how was his family, and he said, "We are not together. We are divorced." Looking into his face then, she saw not the end of his marriage but the end of his happiness. The advantage was hers, because hadn't she explained to him that he was like a boy with stars in his eyes, but some part of his loss seemed to be hers as well. Then he went away, and, although the race was beginning, she saw instead the white snow and the wolves of Nascosta, the pack coming up the Via Cavour and crossing the piazza as if they were bent on some errand of that darkness that she knew to lie at the heart of life, and, remembering the cold on her skin and the whiteness of the snow and the stealth of the wolves, she wondered why the good God had opened up so many choices and made life so strange and diverse.

A Woman Without a Country

❦

I SAW HER THAT SPRING BETWEEN THE THIRD AND FOURTH races at Campino with the Conte de Capra—the one with the mustache—drinking *Campari* at that nice easygoing track, with the mountains in the distance and beyond the mountains a mass of cumulus clouds that at home would have meant a tree-splitting thunderstorm by supper but that amounts to nothing over there. I next saw her at the Tennerhof in Kitzbühel, where a Frenchman was singing American cowboy songs to an audience that included the Queen of the Netherlands, but I never saw her in the mountains, and I don't think she skied, but just went there, like so many others, for the crowds and the excitement. Then I saw her at the Lido, and again in Venice late one morning when I was taking a gondola to the station and she was sitting on the terrace of the Gritti, drinking coffee. I saw her at the Passion Play in Erl—not at the Passion Play, actually, but at the inn in the village, where you have lunch during the intermission, and I saw her at the horse show in the Piazza di

Siena, and that autumn in Treviso, boarding the plane for London. Blooey.

But it all might have happened. She was one of those tireless wanderers who go to bed night after night to dream of bacon-lettuce-and-tomato sandwiches. Although she came from a small lumber-mill town in the north where they manufactured wooden spoons, the kind of lonely place where international society is spawned, this had nothing to do with her wanderings. Her father was the mill agent, and the mill was owned by the Tonkin family—they owned a great deal, they owned whole counties, and their divorce proceedings were followed by the tabloids—and young Marchand Tonkin, learning the business, spent a month there and fell in love with Anne. She was a plain girl with a sweet and modest disposition—qualities that she never lost—and they were married at the end of a year. Though immensely rich, the Tonkins were poor-mouthed, and the young couple lived modestly in a small town near New York where Marchand worked in the family office. They had one child and lived a contented and uneventful life until one humid morning in the seventh year of their marriage.

Marchand had a meeting in New York, and he had to catch an early train. He planned to have breakfast in the city. It was about seven when he kissed Anne goodbye. She had not dressed and was lying in bed when she heard him grinding the starter on the car that he used to take to the station. Then she heard the front door open and he called up the stairs. The car wouldn't start, and could she drive him to the station in the Buick? There was no time to dress, so she drew a jacket over her shoulders and drove him to the station. What was visible of her was properly clad, but below the jacket her nightgown was transparent. Marchand kissed her goodbye and urged her to get some clothes on, and she drove away from the station, but at the junction of Alewives' Lane and Hill Street she ran out of gas.

She was stopped in front of the Beardens', and they would give her some gasoline, she knew, or at least lend her a coat. She blew her horn and blew it and blew it, until she remembered that the Beardens were in Nassau. All she could do then was to wait in the car, virtually naked, until some friendly housewife came by and offered her help. First, Mary Pym drove by, and although Anne waved to her, she did not seem to notice. Then Julia Weed raced by, rushing Francis to the train, but she was going too fast to notice anything. Then Jack Burden, the village rake, who, without being signaled to or appealed to in any way, seemed drawn magnetically to the car. He stopped and asked if he could help. She got into his car—what else could she do—thinking of Lady Godiva and St. Agnes. The worst of it was that she didn't seem able to wake up—to accomplish the transition between the shades of sleep and the lights of day. And it was a lightless day, close and oppressive, like the climate of a harrowing dream. Their driveway was sheltered from the road by some shrubbery, and when she got out of the car and thanked Jack Burden, he followed her up the steps and took advantage of her in the hallway, where they were discovered by Marchand when he came back to get his briefcase.

Marchand left the house then, and Anne never saw him again. He died of a heart attack in a New York hotel ten days later. Her parents-in-law sued for the custody of the only child, and during the trial Anne made the mistake, in her innocence, of blaming her malfeasance on the humidity.

The tabloids picked this up—"IT WASN'T ME, IT WAS THE
HUMIDITY"—and it swept the country. There was a popular
song, "Humid Isabella." It seemed that everywhere she went
she heard them singing:

> Oh, Humid Isabella
> Never kissed a fellah
> Unless there was moisture in the air,
> But when the skies were cloudy,
> She got very rowdy . . .

In the middle of the trial she surrendered her claims, put
on smoked glasses, and sailed incognito for Genoa, the out-
cast of a society that seemed to her to modify its invincible
censoriousness only with a ribald sense of humor.

Of course, she had a boodle—her sufferings were only
spiritual—but she had been burned, and her memories were
bitter. From what she knew of life she was entitled to forgiveness, but she had received none, and her own country, remembered across the Atlantic, seemed to have passed on her
a moral judgment that was unrealistic and savage. She had
been made a scapegoat; she had been pilloried; and because
she was genuinely purehearted she was deeply incensed. She
based her expatriation not on cultural but on moral grounds.
By impersonating a European she meant to express her disapproval of what had gone on at home. She drifted all over
Europe, but she finally bought a villa in Tavola-Calda, and
spent at least half the year there. She not only learned Italian,
she learned all the grunting noises and hand signals that
accompany the language. In the dentist's chair she would
say *"aiiee"* instead of "ouch," and she could wave a hornet
away from her wineglass with great finesse. She was proprie-
tary about her expatriation—it was her demesne, achieved

through uncommon sorrow—and it irritated her to hear other foreigners speaking the language. Her villa was charming—nightingales sang in the oak trees, fountains played in the garden, and she stood on the highest terrace, her hair dyed the shade of bronze that was fashionable in Rome that year, calling down to her guests, *"Ben tornati. Quanto piacere!"* but the image was never quite right. It seemed like a reproduction, with the slight imperfections that you find in an enlargement—the loss of quality. The sense was that she was not so much here in Italy as that she was no longer there in America.

She spent much of her time in the company of people who, like herself, claimed to be the victims of an astringent and repressive moral climate. Their hearts were on the shipping lanes, running away from home. She paid for her mobility with some loneliness. The party of friends she was planning to meet in Wiesbaden moved on without leaving an address. She looked for them in Heidelberg and Munich, but she never found them. Wedding invitations and weather reports ("Snow Blankets the Northeast U.S.") made her terribly homesick. She continued to polish her impersonation of a European, and while her accomplishments were admirable, she remained morbidly sensitive to criticism and detested being taken for a tourist. One day at the end of the season in Venice, she took a train south, reaching Rome late on a hot September afternoon. Most of the people of Rome were asleep, and the only sign of life was the tourist buses, grinding tirelessly through the streets like some basic piece of engineering—like the drains or the light conduits. She gave her luggage check to a porter and described her bags to him in fluent Italian, but he seemed to see through her and he mumbled something about the Americans. Oh, there were so *many*. This irritated her and she snapped at him, "I am not an American."

"Excuse me, Signora," he said. "What, then, is your country?"

"I am," she said, "a *Greek*."

The enormity, the tragedy of her lie staggered her. What have I done, she asked herself wildly. Her passport was as green as grass, and she traveled under the protectorate of the Great Seal of the United States. Why had she lied about such an important part of her identity?

She took a cab to a hotel on the Via Veneto, sent her bags upstairs, and went into the bar for a drink. There was a single American at the bar—a white-haired man wearing a hearing aid. He was alone, he seemed lonely, and finally he turned to the table where she sat and asked most courteously if she was American.

"Yes."

"How come you speak the language?"

"I live here."

"Stebbins," he said, "Charlie Stebbens. Philadelphia."

"How do you do," she said. "Where in Philadelphia?"

"Well, I was born in Philadelphia," he said, "but I haven't been back in forty years. Shoshone, California's my real home. They call it the gateway to Death Valley. My wife came from London. London, Arkansas. Ha ha. My daughter went to school in six states of the Union. California. Washington. Nevada. North and South Dakota, and Louisiana. Mrs. Stebbins passed away last year, and so I thought I'd see a little of the world."

The Stars and Stripes seemed to break out in the air

above his head, and she realized that in America the leaves were turning.

"Where have you been?" she asked.

"You know, it's a funny thing, but I'm not sure myself. This agency in California planned the trip for me, and they told me I'd be traveling with a group of Americans, but as soon as I get on the high seas I find that I'm traveling alone. I'll never do it again. Sometimes there's whole days in which I don't hear any decent American spoken. Why, sometimes I just sit up in my room and talk to myself for the pleasure of hearing American. Why, I took a bus from Frankfurt to Munich, and you know there wasn't anybody on that bus who spoke a word of English? Then I took a bus from Munich to Innsbruck, and there wasn't anybody on that bus who spoke English, either. Then I took a bus from Innsbruck to Venice, and there wasn't anybody on that bus who spoke English, either, until some Americans got on at Cortina. But I don't have any complaints about the hotels. They usually speak English in the hotels, and I've stayed in some very nice ones."

Sitting on a bar stool in a Roman basement, the stranger seemed to Anne to redeem her country. He seemed to gleam with shyness and honesty. The radio was tuned to the Armed Forces station in Verona, where they were playing a recording of "Star Dust."

" 'Star Dust,' " the stranger said. "But I guess you know. It was written by a friend of mine. Hoagy Carmichael. He makes six, seven thousand dollars a year on royalties from that song alone. He's a good friend of mine. I've never met him, but I've corresponded with him. I guess it must seem

funny to you that I have a friend I've never met, but Hoagy's
a real friend of mine."

This statement seemed much more melodic and expressive
to Anne than the music. Its juxtaposition, its apparent point-
lessness, and the rhythm with which it was spoken seemed to
her like the music of her own country, and she remembered
walking, as a girl, past the piles of sawdust at the spoon
factory to the house of her best friend. If she made the walk
in the afternoon, she would sometimes have to wait at the
grade crossing for a freight to pass. First there would be a
sound in the distance like a cave of winds, and then the iron
thunder, the clangor of the wheels. The freights went through
there at full speed; they stormed through. But reading the
lettering on the cars used to move her; used to remind her
not of any glamorous promise at the end of the line but of
the breadth and vastness of her own country, as if the states
of the Union—wheat states, oil states, coal states, maritime
states—were being drawn down the track near where she
stood and where she read Southern Pacific, Baltimore & Ohio,
Nickel Plate, New York Central, Great Western, Rock Island,
Santa Fe, Lackawanna, Pennsylvania, clackety-clack and out
of sight.

"Don't cry, lady," Mr. Stebbins said. "Don't cry."

It was time to go home, and she got a plane for Orly that
night and another plane for Idlewild the next evening. She
was shaking with excitement long before they saw land. She
was going home; she was going home. Her heart was in her
throat. How dark and fresh the water of the Atlantic looked,
after those years away. In the morning light, the low-lying
islands with Indian names passed under their starboard wing,

and even the houses of Long Island, arranged like the grids on a waffle iron, excited her. They circled the field once and came down. She planned to find a lunch counter in the airport and order a bacon-lettuce-and-tomato sandwich. She gripped her umbrella (Parisian) and her handbag (Sienese) and waited her turn to leave the plane, but as she was coming down the steps, even before her shoes (Roman) had touched her native earth, she heard a mechanic who was working on a DC-7 at the next gate singing:

> Oh, Humid Isabella
> Never kissed a fellah . . .

She never left the airport. She took the next plane back to Orly and joined those hundreds, those thousands of Americans who stream through Europe, gay or sad, as if they were a truly homeless people. They round a street corner in Innsbruck, thirty strong, and vanish. They swarm over a bridge in Venice and are gone. They can be heard asking for ketchup in a Gasthaus above the clouds on the great massif, and be seen poking among the sea caves, with masks and snorkels, in the deep waters off Porto San Stefano. She spent the autumn in Paris. Kitzbühel saw her. She was in Rome for the horse show and in Siena for the Palio. She was always on the move, dreaming of bacon-lettuce-and-tomato sandwiches.

Reunion

❦

THE LAST TIME I SAW MY FATHER WAS IN GRAND CENTRAL
Station. I was going from my grandmother's in the Adiron-
dacks to a cottage on the Cape that my mother had rented,
and I wrote my father that I would be in New York between
trains for an hour and a half, and asked if we could have lunch
together. His secretary wrote to say that he would meet me at
the information booth at noon, and at twelve o'clock sharp I
saw him coming through the crowd. He was a stranger to
me—my mother divorced him three years ago and I hadn't
been with him since—but as soon as I saw him I felt that he
was my father, my flesh and blood, my future and my doom.
I knew that when I was grown I would be something like
him; I would have to plan my campaigns within his limitations. He was a big, good-looking man, and I was terribly
happy to see him again. He struck me on the back and shook
my hand. "Hi, Charlie," he said. "Hi, boy. I'd like to take
you up to my club, but it's in the Sixties, and if you have to
catch an early train I guess we'd better get something to eat

around here." He put his arm around me, and I smelled my father the way my mother sniffs a rose. It was a rich compound of whiskey, after-shave lotion, shoe polish, woolens, and the rankness of a mature male. I hoped that someone would see us together. I wished that we could be photographed. I wanted some record of our having been together.

We went out of the station and up a side street to a restaurant. It was still early, and the place was empty. The bartender was quarreling with a delivery boy, and there was one very old waiter in a red coat down by the kitchen door. We sat down, and my father hailed the waiter in a loud voice. "*Kellner!*" he shouted. "*Garçon! Cameriere! You!*" His boisterousness in the empty restaurant seemed out of place. "Could we have a little service here!" he shouted. "Chop-chop." Then he clapped his hands. This caught the waiter's attention, and he shuffled over to our table.

"Were you clapping your hands at me?" he asked.

"Calm down, calm down, *sommelier*," my father said. "If it isn't too much to ask of you—if it wouldn't be too much above and beyond the call of duty, we would like a couple of Beefeater Gibsons."

"I don't like to be clapped at," the waiter said.

"I should have brought my whistle," my father said. "I have a whistle that is audible only to the ears of old waiters. Now, take out your little pad and your little pencil and see if you can get this straight: two Beefeater Gibsons. Repeat after me: two Beefeater Gibsons."

"I think you'd better go somewhere else," the waiter said quietly.

"That," said my father, "is one of the most brilliant sug-

gestions I have ever heard. Come on, Charlie, let's get the hell
out of here."

I followed my father out of that restaurant into another.
He was not so boisterous this time. Our drinks came, and he
cross-questioned me about the baseball season. He then
struck the edge of his empty glass with his knife and began
shouting again. *"Garçon! Kellner! Cameriere! You!* Could
we trouble you to bring us two more of the same."

"How old is the boy?" the waiter asked.

"That," my father said, "is none of your God-damned
business."

"I'm sorry, sir," the waiter said, "but I won't serve the boy
another drink."

"Well, I have some news for you," my father said. "I have
some very interesting news for you. This doesn't happen to
be the only restaurant in New York. They've opened another
on the corner. Come on, Charlie."

He paid the bill, and I followed him out of that restaurant
into another. Here the waiters wore pink jackets like hunting
coats, and there was a lot of horse tack on the walls. We sat
down, and my father began to shout again. "Master of the
hounds! Tallyhoo and all that sort of thing. We'd like a
little something in the way of a stirrup cup. Namely, two
Bibson Geefeaters."

"Two Bibson Geefeaters?" the waiter asked, smiling.

"You know damned well what I want," my father said
angrily. "I want two Beefeater Gibsons, and make it snappy.
Things have changed in jolly old England. So my friend the
duke tells me. Let's see what England can produce in the way
of a cocktail."

"This isn't England," the waiter said.

"Don't argue with me," my father said. "Just do as you're told."

"I just thought you might like to know where you are," the waiter said.

"If there is one thing I cannot tolerate," my father said, "it is an impudent domestic. Come on, Charlie."

The fourth place we went to was Italian. *"Buon giorno,"* my father said. *"Per favore, possiamo avere due cocktail americani, forti, forti. Molto gin, poco vermut."*

"I don't understand Italian," the waiter said.

"Oh, come off it," my father said. "You understand Italian, and you know damned well you do. *Vogliamo due cocktail americani. Subito."*

The waiter left us and spoke with the captain, who came over to our table and said, "I'm sorry, sir, but this table is reserved."

"All right," my father said. "Get us another table."

"All the tables are reserved," the captain said.

"I get it," my father said. "You don't desire our patronage. Is that it? Well, the hell with you. *Vada all'inferno.* Let's go, Charlie."

"I have to get my train," I said.

"I'm sorry, sonny," my father said. "I'm terribly sorry." He put his arm around me and pressed me against him. "I'll walk you back to the station. If there had only been time to go up to my club."

"That's all right, Daddy," I said.

"I'll get you a paper," he said. "I'll get you a paper to read on the train."

Then he went up to a newsstand and said, "Kind sir, will

you be good enough to favor me with one of your God-damned, no-good, ten-cent afternoon papers?" The clerk turned away from him and stared at a magazine cover. "Is it asking too much, kind sir," my father said, "is it asking too much for you to sell me one of your disgusting specimens of yellow journalism?"

"I have to go, Daddy," I said. "It's late."

"Now, just wait a second, sonny," he said. "Just wait a second. I want to get a rise out of this chap."

"Goodbye, Daddy," I said, and I went down the stairs and got my train, and that was the last time I saw my father.

The Chaste Clarissa

ঙঃৡৡ৯

THE EVENING BOAT FOR VINEYARD HAVEN WAS LOADING freight. In a little while, the warning whistle would separate the sheep from the goats—that's the way Baxter thought of it —the islanders from the tourists wandering through the streets of Woods Hole. His car, like all the others ticketed for the ferry, was parked near the wharf. He sat on the front bumper, smoking. The noise and movement of the small port seemed to signify that the spring had ended and that the shores of West Chop, across the Sound, were the shores of summer, but the implications of the hour and the voyage made no impression on Baxter at all. The delay bored and irritated him. When someone called his name, he got to his feet with relief.

It was old Mrs. Ryan. She called to him from a dusty station wagon, and he went over to speak to her. "I knew it," she said. "I knew that I'd see someone here from Holly Cove. I had that feeling in my bones. We've been traveling since nine this morning. We had trouble with the brakes outside

Worchester. Now I'm wondering if Mrs. Talbot will have cleaned the house. She wanted seventy-five dollars for opening it last summer and I told her I wouldn't pay her that again, and I wouldn't be surprised if she's thrown all my letters away. Oh, I hate to have a journey end in a dirty house, but if worst comes to worst, we can clean it ourselves. Can't we, Clarissa?" she asked, turning to a young woman who sat beside her on the front seat. "Oh, excuse me, Baxter!" she exclaimed. "You haven't met Clarissa, have you? This is Bob's wife, Clarissa Ryan."

Baxter's first thought was that a girl like that shouldn't have to ride in a dusty station wagon; she should have done much better. She was young. He guessed that she was about twenty-five. Red-headed, deep-breasted, slender, and indolent, she seemed to belong to a different species from old Mrs. Ryan and her large-boned, forthright daughters. " 'The Cape Cod girls, they have no combs. They comb their hair with codfish bones,' " he said to himself. But Clarissa's hair was well groomed. Her bare arms were perfectly white. Woods Hole and the activity on the wharf seemed to bore her and she was not interested in Mrs. Ryan's insular gossip. She lighted a cigarette.

At a pause in the old lady's monologue, Baxter spoke to her daughter-in-law. "When is Bob coming down, Mrs. Ryan?" he asked.

"He isn't coming at all," the beautiful Clarissa said. "He's in France. He's—"

"He's gone there for the government," old Mrs. Ryan interrupted, as if her daughter-in-law could not be entrusted with this simple explanation. "He's working on this terribly interesting project. He won't be back until autumn. I'm going abroad myself. I'm leaving Clarissa alone. Of course," she added forcefully, "I expect that she will *love* the island. Everyone does. I expect that she will be kept very busy. I expect that she—"

The warning signal from the ferry cut her off. Baxter said goodbye. One by one, the cars drove aboard, and the boat started to cross the shoal water from the mainland to the resort. Baxter drank a beer in the cabin and watched Clarissa and old Mrs. Ryan, who were sitting on deck. Since he had never seen Clarissa before, he supposed that Bob Ryan must have married her during the past winter. He did not understand how this beauty had ended up with the Ryans. They were a family of passionate amateur geologists and bird-watchers. "We're all terribly keen about birds and rocks," they said when they were introduced to strangers. Their cottage was a couple of miles from any other and had, as Mrs. Ryan often said, "been thrown together out of a barn in 1922." They sailed, hiked, swam in the surf, and organized expeditions to Cuttyhunk and Tarpaulin Cove. They were people who emphasized *corpore sano* unduly, Baxter thought, and they shouldn't leave Clarissa alone in the cottage. The wind had blown a strand of her flame-colored hair across her cheek. Her long legs were crossed. As the ferry entered the harbor, she stood up and made her way down the deck against the light salt wind, and Baxter, who had returned to the island indifferently, felt that the summer had begun.

Baxter knew that in trying to get some information about Clarissa Ryan he had to be careful. He was accepted in Holly Cove because he had summered there all his life. He could be pleasant and he was a good-looking man, but his two divorces, his promiscuity, his stinginess, and his Latin complexion had left with his neighbors a vague feeling that he was unsavory. He learned that Clarissa had married Bob Ryan in November and that she was from Chicago. He heard people say that she was beautiful and stupid. That was all he did find out about her.

He looked for Clarissa on the tennis courts and the beaches. He didn't see her. He went several times to the beach nearest the Ryans' cottage. She wasn't there. When he had been on the island only a short time, he received from Mrs. Ryan, in the mail, an invitation to tea. It was an invitation that he would not ordinarily have accepted, but he drove eagerly that afternoon over to the Ryans' cottage. He was late. The cars of most of his friends and neighbors were parked in Mrs. Ryan's field. Their voices drifted out of the open windows into the garden, where Mrs. Ryan's climbing roses were in bloom. "Welcome aboard!" Mrs. Ryan shouted when he crossed the porch. "This is my farewell party. I'm going to Norway." She led him into a crowded room.

Clarissa sat behind the teacups. Against the wall at her back was a glass cabinet that held the Ryans' geological specimens. Her arms were bare. Baxter watched them while she poured his tea. "Hot? . . . Cold? . . . Lemon? . . . Cream?" seemed to be all she had to say, but her red hair and her white arms dominated that end of the room. Baxter ate a sandwich. He hung around the table.

"Have you ever been to the island before, Clarissa?" he asked.

"Yes."

"Do you swim at the beach at Holly Cove?"

"It's too far away."

"When your mother-in-law leaves," Baxter said, "you must let me drive you there in the mornings. I go down at eleven."

"Well, thank you." Clarissa lowered her green eyes. She seemed uncomfortable, and the thought that she might be susceptible crossed Baxter's mind exuberantly. "Well, thank you," she repeated, "but I have a car of my own and—well, I don't know, I don't—"

"What are *you* two talking about?" Mrs. Ryan asked, coming between them and smiling wildly in an effort to conceal some of the force of her interference. "I know it isn't geology," she went on, "and I know that it isn't birds, and I know that it can't be books or music, because those are all things that Clarissa doesn't like, aren't they, Clarissa? Come with me, Baxter," and she led him to the other side of the room and talked to him about sheep raising. When the conversation had ended, the party itself was nearly over. Clarissa's chair was empty. She was not in the room. Stopping at the door to thank Mrs. Ryan and say goodbye, Baxter said that he hoped she wasn't leaving for Europe immediately.

"Oh, but I am," Mrs. Ryan said. "I'm going to the mainland on the six-o'clock boat and sailing from Boston at noon tomorrow."

At half past ten the next morning, Baxter drove up to the Ryans' cottage. Mrs. Talbot, the local woman who helped the Ryans with their housework, answered the door. She said that young Mrs. Ryan was home, and let him in. Clarissa came downstairs. She looked more beautiful than ever, although she seemed put out at finding him there. She accepted his invitation to go swimming, but she accepted it unenthusiastically. "Oh, all right," she said.

When she came downstairs again, she had on a bathrobe over her bathing suit, and a broad-brimmed hat. On the drive to Holly Cove, he asked about her plans for the summer. She was noncommittal. She seemed preoccupied and unwilling to talk. They parked the car and walked side by side over the dunes to the beach, where she lay in the sand with her eyes closed. A few of Baxter's friends and neighbors stopped to pass the time, but they didn't stop for long, Baxter noticed. Clarissa's unresponsiveness made it difficult to talk. He didn't care.

He went swimming. Clarissa remained on the sand, bundled in her wrap. When he came out of the water, he lay down near her. He watched his neighbors and their children. The weather had been fair. The women were tanned. They were all married women and, unlike Clarissa, women with children, but the rigors of marriage and childbirth had left them all pretty, agile, and contented. While he was admiring them, Clarissa stood up and took off her bathrobe.

Here was something else, and it took his breath away. Some of the inescapable power of her beauty lay in the whiteness of her skin, some of it in the fact that, unlike the other women, who were at ease in bathing suits, Clarissa seemed humiliated and ashamed to find herself wearing so little. She walked down toward the water as if she were naked. When she first felt the water, she stopped short, for, again unlike the others, who were sporting around the pier like seals, Clarissa didn't like the cold. Then, caught for a second between nakedness and the cold, Clarissa waded in and swam a few feet. She came out of the water, hastily wrapped herself in the robe, and lay down in the sand. Then she spoke, for the first time that morning—for the first time in Baxter's experience—with warmth and feeling.

"You know those stones on the point have grown a lot since I was here last," she said.

"What?" Baxter said.

"Those stones on the point," Clarissa said. "They've grown a lot."

"Stones don't grow," Baxter said.

"Oh yes they do," Clarissa said. "Didn't you know that? Stones grow. There's a stone in Mother's rose garden that's grown a foot in the last few years."

"I didn't know that stones grew," Baxter said.

"Well, they do." Clarissa said. She yawned; she shut her eyes. She seemed to fall asleep. When she opened her eyes again, she asked Baxter the time.

"Twelve o'clock," he said.

"I have to go home," she said. "I'm expecting guests."

Baxter could not contest this. He drove her home. She was unresponsive on the ride, and when he asked her if he could drive her to the beach again, she said no. It was a hot, fair day and most of the doors on the island stood open, but when Clarissa said goodbye to Baxter, she closed the door in his face.

Baxter got Clarissa's mail and newspapers from the post office the next day, but when he called with them at the cottage, Mrs. Talbot said that Mrs. Ryan was busy. He went that week to two large parties that she might have attended, but she was not at either. On Saturday night, he went to a barn dance, and late in the evening—they were dancing "Lady of the Lake"—he noticed Clarissa, sitting against the wall.

She was a striking wallflower. She was much more beautiful than any other woman there, but her beauty seemed to have intimidated the men. Baxter dropped out of the dance when he could and went to her. She was sitting on a packing case. It was the first thing she complained about. "There isn't even anything to sit on," she said.

"Don't you want to dance?" Baxter asked.

"Oh, I love to dance," she said. "I could dance all night, but I don't think *that's* dancing." She winced at the music of the fiddle and the piano. "I came with the Hortons. They just told me there was going to be a dance. They didn't tell me it was going to be this kind of a dance. I don't like all that skipping and hopping."

"Have your guests left?" Baxter asked.

"What guests?" Clarissa said.

"You told me you were expecting guests on Tuesday. When we were at the beach."

"I didn't say they were coming on Tuesday, did I?" Clarissa asked. "They're coming tomorrow."

"Can't I take you home?" Baxter asked.

"Well," Clarissa said, "I came with the Hortons."

"Let me take you home," Baxter said.

"All right."

He brought the car around to the barn and turned on the radio. She got in and slammed the door with spirit. He raced the car over the back roads, and when he brought it up to the Ryans' cottage, he turned off the lights. He watched her hands. She folded them on her purse. "Well, thank you very much," she said. "I was having an awful time and you saved my life. I just don't understand this place, I guess. I've always had plenty of partners, but I sat on that hard box for nearly an hour and nobody even spoke to me. You saved my life."

"You're lovely, Clarissa," Baxter said.

"Well," Clarissa said, and she sighed. "That's just my outward self. Nobody knows the real me."

That was it, Baxter thought, and if he could only adjust his flattery to what she believed herself to be, her scruples would dissolve. Did she think of herself as an actress, he wondered, a Channel swimmer, an heiress? The intimations of susceptibility that came from her in the summer night were so powerful, so heady, that they convinced Baxter that here was a woman whose chastity hung by a thread.

"I think I know the real you," Baxter said.

"Oh no you don't," Clarissa said. "Nobody does."

The radio played some lovelorn music from a Boston hotel. By the calendar, it was still early in the summer, but it seemed, from the stillness and the hugeness of the dark trees, to be much later. Baxter put his arms around Clarissa and planted a kiss on her lips.

She pushed him away violently and reached for the door. "Oh, now you've spoiled everything," she said as she got out of the car. "Now you've spoiled everything. I know what you've been thinking. I know you've been thinking it all along." She slammed the door and spoke to him across the window. "Well, you needn't come around here any more, Baxter," she said. "My girl friends are coming down from New York tomorrow on the morning plane and I'll be too busy to see you for the rest of the summer. Good night."

Baxter was aware that he had only himself to blame; he had moved too quickly. He knew better. He went to bed feeling angry and sad, and slept poorly. He was depressed when he woke, and his depression was deepened by the noise of a sea rain, blowing in from the northeast. He lay in bed listening to the rain and the surf. The storm would metamorphose the island. The beaches would be empty. Drawers would stick. Suddenly he got out of bed, went to the telephone, called the airport. The New York plane had been unable to land, they told him, and no more planes were expected that day. The storm seemed to be playing directly into his hands. At noon, he drove in to the village and bought a Sunday paper and a box of candy. The candy was for Clarissa, but he was in no hurry to give it to her.

She would have stocked the icebox, put out the towels, and planned the picnic, but now the arrival of her friends had been postponed, and the lively day that she had anticipated had turned out to be rainy and idle. There were ways, of course, for her to overcome her disappointment, but on the evidence of the barn dance he felt that she was lost without her husband or her mother-in-law, and that there were few, if any, people on the island who would pay her a chance call or ask her over for a drink. It was likely that she would spend the day listening to the radio and the rain and that by the end of it she would be ready to welcome anyone, including Baxter. But as long as the forces of loneliness and idleness were working on his side, it was shrewder, Baxter knew, to wait. It would be best to come just before dark, and he waited until then. He drove to the Ryans' with his box of candy. The windows were lighted. Clarissa opened the door.

"I wanted to welcome your friends to the island," Baxter said. "I—"

"They didn't come," Clarissa said. The plane couldn't land. They went back to New York. They telephoned me. I had planned such a nice visit. Now everything's changed."

"I'm sorry, Clarissa," Baxter said. "I've brought you a present."

"Oh!" She took the box of candy. "What a beautiful box! What a lovely present! What—" Her face and her voice were, for a minute, ingenuous and yielding, and then he saw the force of resistance transform them. "You shouldn't have done it," she said.

"May I come in?" Baxter asked.

"Well, I don't know," she said. "You can't come in if you're just going to sit around."

"We could play cards," Baxter said.

"I don't know how," she said.

"I'll teach you," Baxter said.

"No," she said. "No, Baxter, you'll have to go. You just don't understand the kind of a woman I am. I spent all day writing a letter to Bob. I wrote and told him that you kissed me last night. I can't let you come in." She closed the door.

From the look on Clarissa's face when he gave her the box of candy, Baxter judged that she liked to get presents. An inexpensive gold bracelet or even a bunch of flowers might do it, he knew, but Baxter was an extremely stingy man, and while he saw the usefulness of a present, he could not bring himself to buy one. He decided to wait.

The storm blew all Monday and Tuesday. It cleared on Tuesday night, and by Wednesday afternoon the tennis courts were dry and Baxter played. He played until late. Then, when he had bathed and changed his clothes, he stopped at a cocktail party to pick up a drink. Here one of his neighbors, a married woman with four children, sat down beside him and began a general discussion of the nature of married love.

It was a conversation, with its glances and innuendoes, that Baxter had been through many times, and he knew roughly what it promised. His neighbor was one of the pretty mothers that Baxter had admired on the beach. Her hair was brown. Her arms were thin and tanned. Her teeth were sound. But while he appeared to be deeply concerned with her opinions on love, the white image of Clarissa loomed up in his mind, and he broke off the conversation and left the party. He drove to the Ryans'.

From a distance, the cottage looked shut. The house and the garden were perfectly still. He knocked and then rang. Clarissa spoke to him from an upstairs window.

"Oh, hello, Baxter," she said.

"I've come to say goodbye, Clarissa," Baxter said. He couldn't think of anything better.

"Oh, dear," Clarissa said. "Well, wait just a minute. I'll be down."

"I'm going away, Clarissa," Baxter said when she opened the door. "I've come to say goodbye."

"Where are you going?"

"I don't know." He said this sadly.

"Well, come in, then," she said hesitantly. "Come in for a minute. This is the last time that I'll see you, I guess, isn't it? Please excuse the way the place looks. Mr. Talbot got sick on Monday and Mrs. Talbot had to take him to the hospital on the mainland, and I haven't had anybody to help me. I've been all alone."

He followed her into the living room and sat down. She

was more beautiful than ever. She talked about the problems that had been presented by Mrs. Talbot's departure. The fire in the stove that heated the water had died. There was a mouse in the kitchen. The bathtub wouldn't drain. She hadn't been able to get the car started.

In the quiet house, Baxter heard the sound of a leaky water tap and a clock pendulum. The sheet of glass that protected the Ryans' geological specimens reflected the fading sky outside the window. The cottage was near the water, and he could hear the surf. He noted these details dispassionately and for what they were worth. When Clarissa finished her remarks about Mrs. Talbot, he waited a full minute before he spoke.

"The sun is in your hair," he said.

"What?"

"The sun is in your hair. It's a beautiful color."

"Well, it isn't as pretty as it used to be," she said. "Hair like mine gets dark. But I'm not going to dye it. I don't think that women should dye their hair."

"You're so intelligent," he murmured.

"You don't mean that?"

"Mean what?"

"Mean that I'm intelligent."

"Oh, but I do," he said. "You're intelligent. You're beautiful. I'll never forget that night I met you at the boat. I hadn't wanted to come to the island. I'd made plans to go out West."

"I can't be intelligent," Clarissa said miserably. "I must be stupid. Mother Ryan says that I'm stupid, and Bob says that I'm stupid, and even Mrs. Talbot says that I'm stupid, and—" She began to cry. She went to a mirror and dried her eyes. Baxter followed. He put his arms around her. "Don't put your arms around me," she said, more in despair than in anger. "Nobody ever takes me seriously until they get their arms around me." She sat down again and Baxter sat near her. "But you're not stupid, Clarissa," he said. "You have a wonderful intelligence, a wonderful mind. I've often thought so. I've often felt that you must have a lot of very interesting opinions."

"Well, that's funny," she said, "because I do have a lot of opinions. Of course, I never dare say them to anyone, and Bob and Mother Ryan don't ever let me speak. They always interrupt me, as if they were ashamed of me. But I do have these opinions. I mean I think we're like cogs in a wheel. I've concluded that we're like cogs in a wheel. Do you think we're like cogs in a wheel?"

"Oh, yes," he said. "Oh, yes, I do!"

"I think we're like cogs in a wheel," she said. "For instance, do you think that women should work? I've given that a lot of thought. My opinion is that I don't think married women should work. I mean unless they have a lot of money, of course, but even then I think it's a full-time job to take care of a man. Or do you think that women should work?"

"What do you think?" he asked. "I'm terribly interested in knowing what you think."

"Well, my opinion is," she said timidly, "that you just have to hoe your row. I don't think that working or joining the church is going to change everything, or special diets, either. I don't put much stock in fancy diets. We have a friend who eats a quarter of a pound of meat at every meal. He has a scales right on the table and he weighs the meat. It makes the table look awful and I don't see what good it's going to do him. I buy what's reasonable. If ham is reasonable, I buy ham. If lamb is reasonable, I buy lamb. Don't you think that's intelligent?"

"I think that's very intelligent."

"And progressive education," she said. "I don't have a good opinion of progressive education. When we go to the How-ards' for dinner, the children ride their tricycles around the table all the time, and it's my opinion that they get this way from progressive schools, and that children ought to be told what's nice and what isn't."

The sun that had lighted her hair was gone, but there was still enough light in the room for Baxter to see that as she aired her opinions, her face suffused with color and her pupils dilated. Baxter listened patiently, for he knew by then that she merely wanted to be taken for something that she was not—that the poor girl was lost. "You're very intelligent," he said, now and then. "You're so intelligent."

It was as simple as that.

The Music Teacher

❧

IT ALL SEEMED TO HAVE BEEN ARRANGED—SETON SENSED
this when he opened the door of his house that evening and
walked down the hall into the living room. It all seemed to
have been set with as much care as, in an earlier period of his
life, he had known girls to devote to the flowers, the candles,
and the records for the phonograph. This scene was not arranged for his pleasure, nor was it arranged for anything so
simple as reproach. "Hello," he said loudly and cheerfully.
Sobbing and moaning rent the air. In the middle of the small
living room stood an ironing board. One of his shirts was
draped over it, and his wife, Jessica, wiped away a tear as
she ironed. Near the piano stood Jocelin, the baby. Jocelin
was howling. Sitting in a chair near her little sister was Millicent, his oldest daughter, sobbing and holding in her hands
the pieces of a broken doll. Phyllis, the middle child, was on
her hands and knees, prying the stuffing out of an armchair
with a beer-can opener. Clouds of smoke from what smelled
like a burning leg of lamb drifted out of the open kitchen
door into the living room.

He could not believe that they had passed the day in such disorder. It must all have been planned, arranged—including the conflagration in the oven—for the moment of his homecoming. He even thought he saw a look of inner tranquillity on his wife's harassed face as she glanced around the room and admired the effectiveness of the scene. He felt routed but not despairing, and, standing on the threshold, he made a quick estimate of his remaining forces and settled on a kiss as his first move; but as he approached the ironing board his wife waved him away, saying, "Don't come near me. You'll catch my cold. I have a *terrible* cold." He then got Phyllis away from the armchair, promised to mend Millicent's doll, and carried the baby into the bathroom and changed her diapers. From the kitchen came loud oaths as Jessica fought her way through the clouds of smoke and took the meat out of the stove.

It was burned. So was almost everything else—the rolls, the potatoes, and the frozen apple tart. There were cinders in Seton's mouth and a great heaviness in his heart as he looked past the plates of spoiled food to Jessica's face, once gifted with wit and passion but now dark and lost to him. After supper he helped with the dishes and read to the children, and the purity of their interest in what he read and did, the power of trust in their love, seemed to make the taste of burned meat sad as well as bitter. The smell of smoke stayed in the air long after everyone but Seton had gone up to bed. He sat alone in the living room, recounting his problems to himself. He had been married ten years, and Jessica still seemed to him to possess an unusual loveliness of person and nature, but in the last year or two something grave and mysterious had come between them. The burned roast was not unusual; it was routine. She burned the chops, she burned the hamburgers, she even burned the turkey at Thanksgiving, and she seemed to burn the food deliberately, as if it was a means of expressing her resentment toward him. It was not rebellion against drudgery. Cleaning women and mechanical appliances—the lightening of her burden—made no difference. It was not, he thought, even resentment. It was like some subterranean sea change, some sexual campaign or revolution stirring—unknown perhaps to her—beneath the shining and common appearance of things.

He did not want to leave Jessica, but how much longer could he cope with the tearful children, the dark looks, and the smoky and chaotic house? It was not discord that he resisted but a threat to the most healthy and precious part of his self-esteem. To be long-suffering under the circumstances seemed to him indecent. What could he do? Change, motion, openings seemed to be what he and Jessica needed, and it was perhaps an indication of his limitations that, in trying to devise some way of extending his marriage, the only thing he could think of was to take Jessica to dinner in a restaurant where they had often gone ten years ago, when they were lovers. But even this, he knew, would not be simple. A point-blank invitation would only get him a point-blank, bitter refusal. He would have to be wary. He would have to surprise and disarm her.

This was in the early autumn. The days were clear. The yellow leaves were falling everywhere. From all the windows of the house and through the glass panes in the front door, one saw them coming down. Seton waited for two or three days. He waited for an unusually fine day, and then he called Jessica from his office, in the middle of the morning. There was a cleaning woman at the house, he knew. Millicent and Phyllis would be in school, and Jocelin would be asleep. Jessica would not have too much to do. She might even be idle and reflective. He called her and told her—he did not invite her—to come to town and to have dinner with him. She hesitated; she said it would be difficult to find someone to stay with the children; and finally she succumbed. He even seemed to hear in her voice when she agreed to come a trace of the gentle tenderness he adored.

It was a year since they had done anything like dining together in a restaurant, and when he left his office that night and turned away from the direction of the station he was conscious of the mountainous and deadening accrual of habit that burdened their relationship. Too many circles had been drawn around his life, he thought; but how easy it was to overstep them. The restaurant where he went to wait for her was modest and good—polished, starched, smelling of fresh bread and sauces, and in a charming state of readiness when he reached it that evening. The hat-check girl remembered him, and he remembered the exuberance with which he had come down the flight of steps into the bar when he was younger. How wonderful everything smelled. The bartender had just come on duty, freshly shaved and in a white coat. Everything seemed cordial and ceremonious. Every surface was shining, and the light that fell onto his shoulders was the light that had fallen there ten years ago. When the headwaiter stopped to say good evening, Seton asked to have a bottle of wine—*their* wine—iced. The door into the night was the door he used to watch in order to see Jessica come in with snow in her hair, to see her come in with a new dress and new shoes, to see her come in with good news, worries, apologies for being late. He could remember the way she glanced at the bar to see if he was there, the way she stopped to speak with the hat-check girl, and then lightly crossed the floor to put her hand in his and to join lightly and gracefully in his pleasure for the rest of the night.

Then he heard a child crying. He turned toward the door in time to see Jessica enter. She carried the crying baby against her shoulder. Phyllis and Millicent followed in their worn snowsuits. It was still early in the evening, and the restaurant was not crowded. This entrance, this tableau, was not as spectacular as it would have been an hour later, but it was—for Seton, at least—powerful enough. As Jessica stood in the doorway with a sobbing child in her arms and one on each side of her, the sense was not that she had come to meet her husband and, through some breakdown in arrangements, had been forced to bring the children; the sense was that she had come to make a public accusation of the man who had wronged her. She did not point her finger at him, but the significance of the group was dramatic and accusatory.

Seton went to them at once. It was not the kind of restaurant one brought children to, but the hat-check girl was kindly and helped Millicent and Phyllis out of their snowsuits. Seton took Jocelin in his arms, and she stopped crying.

"The baby-sitter couldn't come," Jessica said, but she hardly met his eyes, and she turned away when he kissed her. They were taken to a table at the back of the place. Jocelin upset a bowl of olives, and the meal was as gloomy and chaotic as the burned suppers at home. The children fell asleep on the drive back, and Seton could see that he had failed—failed or been outwitted again. He wondered, for the first time, if he was dealing not with the shadows and mysteries of Jessica's sex but with plain fractiousness.

He tried again, along the same lines; he asked the Thompsons for cocktails one Saturday afternoon. He could tell that they didn't want to come. They were going to the Carmignoles'—everyone was going to the Carmignoles'—and it was a year or more since the Setons had entertained; their house had suffered a kind of social infamy. The Thompsons came only out of friendship, and they came only for one drink. They were an attractive couple, and Jack Thompson seemed to enjoy a tender mastery over his wife that Seton envied. He had told Jessica the Thompsons were coming. She had said nothing. She was not in the living room when they arrived, but she appeared a few minutes later, carrying a laundry basket full of wash, and when Seton asked her if she wouldn't have a drink, she said that she didn't have time. The Thompsons could see that he was in trouble, but they could not stay to help him—they would be late at the Carmignoles'. But when Lucy Thompson had got into the car, Jack came back to the door and spoke to Seton so forcefully —so clearly out of friendship and sympathy—that Seton hung on his words. He said that he could see what was going on, and that Seton should have a hobby—a specific hobby: he should take piano lessons. There was a lady named Miss Deming and he should see her. She would help. Then he waved goodbye and went down to his car. This advice did not seem in any way strange to Seton. He was desperate and tired, and where was the sense in his life? When he returned to the living room, Phyllis was attacking the chair again with the beer-can opener. Her excuse was that she had lost a quarter in the upholstery. Jocelin and Millicent were crying. Jessica had begun to burn the evening meal.

They had burned veal on Sunday, burned meat loaf on Monday, and on Tuesday the meat was so burned that Seton couldn't guess what it was. He thought of Miss Deming, and decided she might be a jolly trollop who consoled the men of the neighborhood under the guise of giving music lessons. But when he telephoned, her voice was the voice of a crone. He said that Jack Thompson had given him her name, and she said for him to come the next evening at seven o'clock. As he left his house after supper on Wednesday, he thought that there was at least some therapy in getting out of the place and absorbing himself in something besides his domestic and business worries. Miss Deming lived on Bellevue Avenue, on the other side of town. The house numbers were difficult to see, and Seton parked his car at the curb and walked, looking for the number of her house.

It was an evening in the fall. Bellevue Avenue was one of those back streets of frame houses that are irreproachable in their demeanor, their effect, but that are ornamented, through some caprice, with little minarets and curtains of wooden beading, like a mistaken or at least a mysterious nod to the faraway mosques and harems of bloody Islam. This paradox gave the place its charm. The street was declining, but it was declining gracefully; its decay was luxuriant, and in the back yards roses bloomed in profusion, and cardinals sang in the fir trees. A few householders were still raking their lawns. Seton had been raised on just such a street, and he was charmed to stumble on this fragment of his past. The

sun was setting—there was a show of red light at the foot
of the street—and at the sight of this he felt a pang in his
stomach as keen as hunger, but it was not hunger, it was
simple aspiration. Oh to lead an illustrious life!

Miss Deming's house had no porch, and may have needed
paint more than the others, although he could not tell for
sure, now that the light had begun to fade. A sign on the door
said, KNOCK AND COME IN. He stepped into a small hallway,
with a staircase and a wooden hatrack. In a farther room he
saw a man as old as himself bent over the piano keys. "You're
early," Miss Deming called out. "Please sit down and wait."

She spoke with such deep resignation, such weariness, that
the tone of her voice seemed to imply to Seton that what he
waited for would be disgusting and painful. He sat down on a
bench, under the hatrack. He was uncomfortable. His hands
sweated, and he felt painfully large for the house, the bench,
the situation. How mysterious was this life, he thought, where
his wife had hidden her charms and he was planning to study
the piano. His discomfort got so intense that he thought for
a moment of fleeing. He could step out of the door, into Bellevue Avenue, and never come back again. A memory of the
confusion at home kept him where he was. Then the thought
of waiting as a mode of eternity attacked him. How much
time one spent waiting in dentists' and doctors' anterooms,
waiting for trains, for planes, waiting in front of telephone
booths and in restaurants. It seemed that he had wasted the
best of his life in waiting, and that by contracting to wait
for piano lessons he might throw away the few vivid years
that were left to him. Again he thought of escaping, but at
that moment the lesson in the other room came to an end.
"You've not been practicing enough," he heard Miss Deming
say crossly. "You have to practice an hour a day, without ex-

ception, or else you'll simply be wasting my time." Her pupil came through the little hall with his coat collar turned up so that Seton couldn't see his face. "Next," she said.

The little room with the upright piano in it was more cluttered than the hall. Miss Deming hardly looked up when he came in. She was a small woman. Her brown hair was streaked with gray, braided, and pinned to her head in a sparse coronet. She sat on an inflated cushion, with her hands folded in her lap, and moved her lips now and then with distaste, as if something galled her. Seton blundered onto the little piano stool. "I've never taken piano lessons," he said. "I once took cornet lessons. I rented a cornet when I was in high school—"

"We'll forget about that," she said. She pointed out middle C and asked him to play a scale. His fingers, in the bright light from the music rack, looked enormous and naked. He struggled with his scale. Once or twice, she rapped his knuckles with a pencil; once or twice, she manipulated his fingers with hers, and he had a vision of her life as a nightmare of clean hands, dirty hands, hairy hands, limp and muscular hands, and he decided that this might account for her feeling of distaste. Halfway through the lesson, Seton dropped his hands into his lap. His irresolution only made her impatient, and she placed his hands back on the keys. He wanted to smoke, but on the wall above the piano there was a large sign that forbade this. His shirt was wet when the lesson ended.

"Please bring the exact change when you come again. Put the money in the vase on the desk," she said. "Next." Seton and the next pupil passed each other in the doorway, but the stranger averted his face.

The end of the ordeal elated Seton, and as he stepped out

into the darkness of Bellevue Avenue he had a pleasant and silly image of himself as a pianist. He wondered if these simple pleasures were what Jack Thompson had meant. The children were in bed when he got home, and he sat down to practice. Miss Deming had given him a two-handed finger drill with a little melody, and he went over this again and again for an hour. He practiced every day, including Sunday, and sincerely hoped when he went for his second lesson that she would compliment him by giving him something more difficult, but she spent the hour criticizing his phrasing and fingering, and told him to practice the drill for another week. He thought that at least after his third lesson he would have a change, but he went home with the same drill.

Jessica neither encouraged him nor complained. She seemed mystified by this turn of events. The music got on her nerves, and he could see where it would. The simple drill, with its melody, impressed itself even onto the memories of his daughters. It seemed to become a part of all their lives, as unwelcome as an infection, and as pestilential. It drifted through Seton's mind all during the business day, and at any sudden turn of feeling—pain or surprise—the melody would swell and come to the front of his consciousness. Seton had never known that this drudgery, this harrying of the mind was a part of mastering the piano. Now in the evening after supper when he sat down to practice, Jessica hastily left the room and went upstairs. She seemed intimidated by the music, or perhaps afraid. His own relationship to the drill was oppressive and unclear. Taking a late train one evening and walking up from the station past the Thompsons', he heard the same pestilential drill coming through the walls of their house. Jack must be practicing. There was nothing very strange about this, but when he passed the Carmignoles' and heard the drill again, he wondered if it was not his own memory that made it ring in his ears. The night was dark, and with his sense of reality thus shaken, he stood on his own doorstep thinking that the world changed more swiftly than one could perceive—died and renewed itself—and that he moved through the events of his life with no more comprehension than a naked swimmer.

Jessica had not burned the meat that night. She had kept a decent supper for him in the oven, and she served it to him with a timidity that made him wonder if she was not about to return to him as his wife. After supper, he read to the children and then rolled back his shirtsleeves and sat down at the piano. As Jessica was preparing to leave the room, she turned and spoke to him. Her manner was pleading, and this made her eyes seem larger and darker, and deepened her natural pallor. "I don't like to interfere," she said softly, "and I know I don't know anything about music, but I wonder if you couldn't ask her—your teacher—if she couldn't give you something else to practice. That exercise is on my mind so. I hear it all day. If she could give you a new piece—"

"I know what you mean," he said. "I'll ask her."

By his fifth lesson, the days had grown much shorter and there was no longer any fiery sunset at the foot of Bellevue Avenue to remind him of his high hopes, his longings. He knocked, and stepped into the little house, and noticed at once the smell of cigarette smoke. He took off his hat and coat and went into the living room, but Miss Deming was not on her rubber cushion. He called her, and she answered from the kitchen and opened the door onto a scene that astonished him.

Two young men sat at the kitchen table, smoking and drinking beer. Their dark hair gleamed with oil and was swept back in wings. They wore motorcycle boots and red hunting shirts, and their manners seemed developed, to a fine point, for the expression of lawless youth. "We'll be waiting for you, lover," one of them said loudly as she closed the door after her, and as she came toward Seton he saw a look of pleasure on her face—of lightness and self-esteem—fade, and the return of her habitually galled look.

"My boys," she said, and sighed.

"Are they neighbors?" Seton asked.

"Oh, no. They come from New York. They come up and spend the night sometimes. I help them when I can, poor things. They're like sons to me."

"It must be nice for them," Seton said.

"Please commence," she said. All the feeling had left her voice.

"My wife wanted to know if I couldn't have something different—a new piece."

"They always do," she said wearily.

"Something a little less repetitious," Seton said.

"None of the gentlemen who come here have ever complained about my methods. If you're not satisfied, you don't have to come. Of course, Mr. Purvis went too far. Mrs. Purvis is still in the sanatorium, but I don't think the fault is mine. You want to bring her to her knees, don't you? Isn't that what you're here for? Please commence."

Seton began to play, but with more than his usual clumsiness. The unholy old woman's remarks had stunned him. What had he got into? Was he guilty? Had his instinct to flee when he first entered the house been the one he should have followed? Had he, by condoning the stuffiness of the place, committed himself to some kind of obscenity, some kind of witchcraft? Had he agreed to hold over a lovely woman the subtle threat of madness? The old crone spoke softly now and, he thought, wickedly. "Play the melody lightly, lightly, lightly," she said. "That is how it will do its work."

He went on playing, borne along on an unthinking devotion to consecutiveness, for if he protested, as he knew he should, he would only authenticate the nightmare. His head and his fingers worked with perfect independence of his feelings, and while one part of him was full of shock, alarm, and self-reproach, his fingers went on producing the insidious melody. From the kitchen he could hear deep laughter, the pouring of beer, the shuffle of motorcycle boots. Perhaps because she wanted to rejoin her friends—her boys—she cut the lesson short, and Seton's relief was euphoric.

He had to ask himself again and again if she had really said what he thought he heard her say, and it seemed so improbable that he wanted to stop and talk with Jack Thompson about it, until he realized that he could not mention what had happened; he would not be able to put it into words. This darkness where men and women struggled pitilessly for supremacy and withered crones practiced witchcraft was not the world where he made his life. The old lady seemed to inhabit some barrier reef of consciousness, some gray moment after waking that would be demolished by the light of day.

Jessica was in the living room when he got home, and as he

put his music on the rack he saw a look of dread in her face. "Did she give you a piece?" she asked. "Did she give you something besides that drill?"

"Not this time," he said. "I guess I'm not ready. Perhaps next time."

"Are you going to practice now?"

"I might."

"Oh, not tonight, darling! Please not tonight! Please, please, *please* not tonight, my love!" and she was on her knees.

The restoration of Seton's happiness—and it returned to them both with a rush—left him oddly self-righteous about how it had come about, and when he thought of Miss Deming he thought of her with contempt and disgust. Caught up in a whirl of palatable suppers and lovemaking, he didn't go near the piano. He washed his hands of her methods. He had chosen to forget the whole thing. But when Wednesday night came around again, he got up to go there at the usual time and say goodbye. He could have telephoned her. Jessica was uneasy about his going back, but he explained that it was merely to end the arrangement, and kissed her, and went out.

It was a dark night. The Turkish shapes of Bellevue Avenue were dimly lighted. Someone was burning leaves. He knocked on Miss Deming's door and stepped into the little hall. The house was dark. The only light came through the windows from the street. "Miss Deming," he called. "Miss Deming?" He called her name three times. The chair beside the piano bench was empty, but he could feel the old lady's touch on everything in the place. She was not there—that is, she did not answer his voice—but she seemed to be standing in the door to the kitchen, standing on the stairs, standing in the dark at the end of the hall; and a light sound he heard from upstairs seemed to be her footfall.

He went home, and he hadn't been there half an hour when the police came and asked him to come with them. He went outside—he didn't want the children to hear—and he made the natural mistake of protesting, since, after all, was he not a most law-abiding man? Had he not always paid for his morning paper, obeyed the traffic lights, bathed daily, prayed weekly, kept his tax affairs in order, and paid his bills on the tenth of the month? There was not, in the broad landscape of his past, a trace, a hint of illegality. What did the police want with him? They wouldn't say, but they insisted that he come with them, and finally he got into the patrol car with them and drove to the other side of town, across some railroad tracks, to a dead-end place, a dump, where there were some other policemen. It was a scene for violence—bare, ugly, hidden away from any house, and with no one to hear her cries for help. She lay on the crossroads, like a witch. Her neck was broken, and her clothes were still disordered from her struggle with the great powers of death. They asked if he knew her, and he said yes. Had he ever seen any young men around her house, they asked, and he said no. His name and address had been found in a notebook on her desk, and he explained that she had been his piano teacher. They were satisfied with this explanation, and they let him go.

The Seaside Houses

EACH YEAR, WE RENT A HOUSE AT THE EDGE OF THE SEA and drive there in the first of the summer—with the dog and cat, the children, and the cook—arriving at a strange place a little before dark. The journey to the sea has its ceremonious excitements, it has gone on for so many years now, and there is the sense that we are, as in our dreams we have always known ourselves to be, migrants and wanderers—travelers, at least, with a traveler's acuteness of feeling. I never investigate the houses that we rent, and so the wooden castle with a tower, the pile, the Staffordshire cottage covered with roses, and the Southern mansion all loom up in the last of the sea light with the enormous appeal of the unknown. You get the sea-rusted keys from the house next door. You unfasten the lock and step into a dark or a light hallway, about to begin a vacation—a month that promises to have no worries of any kind. But as strong as or stronger than this pleasant sense of beginnings is the sense of having stepped into the midst of someone else's life. All my dealings are with agents, and I have never known the people from whom we have rented, but their ability to leave behind them a sense of physical and emotional presences is amazing. Our affairs are certainly not written in air and water, but they do seem to be chronicled in scuffed baseboards, odors, and tastes in furniture and paintings, and the climates we step into in these rented places are as marked as the changes of weather on the beach. Sometimes there is in the long hallway a benignness, a purity and clearness of feeling to which we all respond. Someone was enormously happy here, and we rent their happiness as we rent their beach and their catboat. Sometimes the climate of the place seems mysterious, and remains a mystery until we leave in August. Who, we wonder, is the lady in the portrait in the upstairs hallway? Whose was the Aqualung, the set of Virginia Woolf? Who hid the copy of *Fanny Hill* in the china closet, who played the zither, who slept in the cradle, and who was the woman who painted red enamel on the nails of the claw-footed bathtub? What was this moment in her life?

The dog and the children run down to the beach, and we bring in our things, wandering, it seems, through the dense histories of strangers. Who owned the *Lederhosen,* who spilled ink (or blood) on the carpet, who broke the pantry window? And what do you make of a bedroom bookshelf stocked with *Married Happiness, An Illustrated Guide to Sexual Happiness in Marriage, The Right to Sexual Felicity,* and *A Guide to Sexual Happiness for Married Couples?* But outside the windows we hear the percussive noise of the sea; it shakes the bluff where the house stands, and sends its rhythm up through the plaster and timbers of the place, and in the end we all go down to the beach—it is what we came for, after all—and the rented house on the bluff, burning now with our lights, is one of those images that have preserved their urgency and their fitness. Fishing in the spring woods, you step on a clump of wild mint and the fragrance released is like the essence of that day. Walking on the Palatine, bored with antiquities and life in general, you see an owl fly out of the ruins of the palace of Septimius Severus and suddenly that day, that raffish and noisy city, all make sense. Lying in bed, you draw on your cigarette and the red glow lights an arm, a breast, and a thigh around which the world seems to revolve. These images are like the embers of our best feelings, and, standing on the beach, for that first hour, it seems as if we could build them into a fire. After dark we shake up a drink, send the children to bed, and make love in a strange room that smells of someone else's soap— all measures taken to exorcise the owners and secure our possession of the place. But in the middle of the night the terrace door flies open with a crash, although there seems to be no wind, and my wife says, half asleep, "Oh, why have they come back? Why have they come back? What have they lost?"

Broadmere is the rented house I remember most clearly, and we got there at the usual time of day. It was a large white house, and it stood on a bluff facing south, which was the open sea on that coast. I got the key from a Southern lady in a house across the garden, and opened the door onto a hallway with a curved staircase. The Greenwoods, the owners, seemed to have left that day, seemed in fact to have left a minute earlier. There were flowers in the vases, cigarette butts in the ashtrays, and a dirty glass on the table. We brought in the suitcases and sent the children down to the beach, and I stood in the living room waiting for my wife to join me. The stir, the discord of the Greenwoods' sudden departure still seemed to be in the air. I felt that they had gone hastily and unwillingly, and that they had not wanted to rent their summer house. The room had a bay window looking out to sea, but in the twilight the place seemed drab, and I found it depressing. I turned on a lamp, but the bulb was dim and I thought that Mr. Greenwood had been a parsimonious and mean man. Whatever he had been, I seemed to feel his presence with uncommon force. On the bookshelf there was a small sailing trophy that he had won ten years before. The books were mostly Literary Guild selections. I took a biography of Queen Victoria off the shelf, but the binding was stiff, and I think no one had read it. Hidden behind the book was an empty whiskey bottle. The furniture seemed substantial and in good taste, but I was not happy or at ease in the room. There was an upright piano in the corner, and I played some scales to see if it was in tune (it wasn't) and opened the piano bench to look for music. There was some sheet music, and two more empty whiskey bottles. Why hadn't he taken out his empties like the rest of us? Had he been a secret drinker? Would this account for the drabness of the room? Had he learned to take the top off the bottle without making a sound, and mastered the more difficult trick of canting the glass and the bottle so that the whiskey wouldn't splash? My wife came in, carrying an empty suitcase, which I took up to the attic. This part of the house was neat and clean. All the tools and the paints were labeled and in their places, and all this neatness, unlike the living room, conveyed an atmosphere of earnestness and probity. He must have spent a good deal of time in the attic, I thought.

It was getting dark, and I joined my wife and children on the beach.

The sea was running high and the long white line of the surf reached, like an artery, down the shore for as far as we could see. We stood, my wife and I, with our arms loosely around one another—for don't we all come down to the sea as lovers, the pretty woman in her pregnancy bathing suit with a fair husband, the old couples who bathe their gnarled legs, and the bucks and the girls, looking out to the ocean and its fumes for some riggish and exalted promise of romance? When it was dark and time to go to bed, I told my youngest son a story. He slept in a pleasant room that faced the east, where there was a lighthouse on a point, and the beam swept in through the window. Then I noticed something on the corner baseboard—a thread or a spider, I thought —and knelt down to see what it was. Someone had written there, in a small hand, "My father is a rat. I repeat. My father is a rat." I kissed my son good night and we all went to sleep.

Sunday was a lovely day, and I woke in very high spirits, but, walking around the place before breakfast, I came on another cache of whiskey bottles hidden behind a yew tree, and I felt a return of that drabness—it was nearly like despair —that I had first experienced in the living room. I was worried and curious about Mr. Greenwood. His troubles seemed inescapable. I thought of going into the village and asking about him, but this kind of curiosity seems to me indecent. Later in the day, I found his photograph in a shirt drawer. The glass covering the picture was broken. He was dressed in the uniform of an Air Force major, and had a long and a romantic face. I was pleased with his handsomeness, as I had been pleased with his sailing trophy, but these two possessions were not quite enough to cure the house of its drabness. I did not like the place, and this seemed to affect my temper. Later I tried to teach my oldest son how to surf-cast with a drail, but he kept fouling his line and getting sand in the reel, and we had a quarrel. After lunch we drove to the boatyard where the sailboat that went with the house was stored. When I asked about the boat, the proprietor laughed. It had not been in the water for five years and was falling to pieces. This was a grave disappointment, but I did not think angrily of Mr. Greenwood as a liar, which he was; I thought of him sympathetically as a man forced into those embarrassing expedients that go with a rapidly diminishing income. That night in the living room, reading one of his books, I noticed that the sofa cushions seemed unyielding. Reaching under them, I found three copies of a magazine dealing with sunbathing. They were illustrated with many pictures of men and women wearing nothing but their shoes. I put the magazines into the fireplace and lighted them with a match, but the paper was coated and they burned slowly. Why should I be made so angry, I wondered; why should I seem so absorbed in this image of a lonely and drunken man? In the upstairs hallway there was a bad smell, left perhaps by an unhousebroken cat or a stopped drain, but it seemed to me like the distillate, the essence, of a bitter quarrel. I slept poorly.

On Monday it rained. The children baked cookies in the morning. I walked on the beach. In the afternoon we visited the local museum, where there was one stuffed peacock, one spiked German helmet, an assortment of shrapnel, a collection of butterflies, and some old photographs. You could hear the rain on the museum roof. On Monday night I had a strange dream. I dreamed I was sailing for Naples on the *Cristoforo Colombo* and sharing a tourist cabin with an old man. The old man never appeared, but his belongings were heaped on the lower berth. There was a greasy fedora, a battered umbrella, a paper-back novel, and a bottle of laxative pills. I wanted a drink. I am not an alcoholic, but in my dream I experienced all the physical and emotional torments of a man who is. I went up to the bar. The bar was closed. The bartender was there, locking up the cash register, and all the bottles were draped in cheesecloth. I begged him to open the bar, but he said he had spent the last ten hours cleaning staterooms and that he was going to bed. I asked if he would sell me a bottle, and he said no. Then—he was an Italian—I explained slyly that the bottle was not for me but for my little daughter. His attitude changed at once. If it was for my little daughter, he would be happy to give me a bottle, but it must be a beautiful bottle, and after searching around the bar he came up with a swan-shaped bottle, full of liqueur. I told him my daughter wouldn't like this at all, that what she wanted was gin, and he finally produced a bottle of gin and charged me ten thousand lire. When I woke, it seemed that I had dreamed one of Mr. Greenwood's dreams.

We had our first caller on Wednesday. This was Mrs. Whiteside, the Southern lady from whom we got the key. She rang our bell at five and presented us with a box of strawberries. Her daughter, Mary-Lee, a girl of about twelve, was with her. Mrs. Whiteside was formidably decorous, but Mary-Lee had gone in heavily for makeup. Her eyebrows were plucked, her eyelids were painted, and the rest of her face was highly colored. I suppose she didn't have anything else to do. I asked Mrs. Whiteside in enthusiastically, because I wanted to cross-question her about the Greenwoods. "Isn't it a beautiful staircase?" she asked when she stepped into the hall. "They had it built for their daughter's wedding. Dolores was only four at the time, but they liked to imagine that she would stand by the window in her white dress and throw her flowers down to her attendants." I bowed Mrs. Whiteside into the living room and gave her a glass of sherry. "We're pleased to have you here, Mr. Ogden," she said. "It's so nice to have children running on the beach again. But it's only fair to say that we all miss the Greenwoods. They were charming people, and they've never rented before. This is their first summer away from the beach. Oh, he loved Broadmere. It was his pride and joy. I can't imagine what he'll do without it." If the Greenwoods were so charming, I wondered who had been the secret drinker. "What does Mr. Greenwood do?" I asked, trying to finesse the directness of my question by crossing the room and filling her glass again. "He's in synthetic yarns," she said. "Although I believe he's on the lookout for something more interesting." This seemed to be a hint, a step perhaps in the right direction. "You mean he's looking for a job?" I asked quickly. "I really can't say," she replied.

She was one of those old women who you might say were as tranquil as the waters under a bridge, but she seemed to me monolithic, to possess some of the community's biting teeth, and perhaps to secrete some of its venom. She seemed by her various and painful disappointments (Mr. Whiteside had passed away, and there was very little money) to have been pushed up out of the stream of life to sit on its banks in unremittent lugubriousness, watching the rest of us speed down to sea. What I mean to say is that I thought I detected beneath her melodious voice a vein of corrosive bitterness. In all, she drank five glasses of sherry.

She was about to go. She sighed and started to get up. "Well, I'm so glad of this chance to welcome you," she said. "It's so nice to have children running on the beach again, and while the Greenwoods were charming, they had their difficulties. I say that I miss them, but I can't say that I miss hearing them quarrel, and they quarreled every single night last summer. Oh, the things he used to say! They were what I suppose you would call incompatible." She rolled her eyes in the direction of Mary-Lee to suggest that she could have told us much more. "I like to work in my garden sometimes after the heat of the day, but when they were quarreling I couldn't step out of the house, and I sometimes had to close the doors and windows. I don't suppose I should tell you all of this, but the truth will out, won't it?" She got to her feet and went into the hall. "As I say, they had the staircase built for the marriage of their daughter, but poor Dolores was married in the Municipal Building, eight months pregnant by a garage mechanic. It's nice to have you here. Come along, Mary-Lee."

I had, in a sense, what I wanted. She had authenticated the drabness of the house. But why should I be so moved, as I was, by the poor man's wish to see his daughter happily married? It seemed to me that I could see them standing in the hallway when the staircase was completed. Dolores would be playing on the floor. They would have their arms around each other; they would be smiling up at the arched window and its vision of cheer, propriety, and enduring happiness. But where had they all gone, and why had this simple wish ended in disaster?

In the morning it rained again, and the cook suddenly announced that her sister in New York was dying and that she had to go home. She had not received any letters or telephone calls that I knew of, but I drove her to the airport and let her go. I returned reluctantly to the house. I had got to hate the place. I found a plastic chess set and tried to teach my son to play chess, but this ended in a quarrel. The other children lay in bed, reading comics. I was short-tempered with everyone, and decided that for their own good I should return to New York for a day or two. I lied to my wife about some urgent business, and she took me to the plane the next morning. It felt good to be airborne and away from the drabness of Broadmere. It was hot and sunny in New York —it felt and smelled like midsummer. I stayed at the office until late, and stopped at a bar near Grand Central Station. I had been there a few minutes when Greenwood came in. His romantic looks were ruined, but I recognized him at once from the photograph in the shirt drawer. He ordered a Martini and a glass of water, and drank off the water, as if that was what he had come for.

You could see at a glance that he was one of that legion of wage-earning ghosts who haunt midtown Manhattan, dreaming of a new job in Madrid, Dublin, or Cleveland. His hair was slicked down. His face had the striking ruddiness of a baseball-park or race-track burn, although you could see by the way his hands shook that the flush was alcoholic. The bartender knew him, and they chatted for a while, but then the bartender went over to the cash register to add up his slips and Mr. Greenwood was left alone. He felt this. You could see it in his face. He felt that he had been left alone. It was late, all the express trains would have pulled out, and the rest of them were drifting in—the ghosts, I mean. God knows where they come from or where they go, this host of prosperous and well-dressed hangers-on who, in spite of the atmosphere of a fraternity they generate, would not think of speaking to one another. They all have a bottle hidden behind the Literary Guild selections and another in the piano bench. I thought of introducing myself to Greenwood, and then thought better of it. I had taken his beloved house away from him, and he was bound to be unfriendly. I couldn't guess the incidents in his autobiography, but I could guess its atmosphere and drift. Daddy would have died or absconded when he was young. The absence of a male parent is not so hard to discern among the marks life leaves on our faces. He would have been raised by his mother and his aunt, have gone to the state university and have majored (my guess) in general merchandising. He would have been in charge of PX supplies during the war. Nothing had worked out after the war. He had lost his daughter, his house, the love of his wife, and his interest in business, but none of these losses would account for his pain and bewilderment. The real cause would remain concealed from him, concealed from me, concealed from us all. It is what makes the railroad-station bars at that hour seem so mysterious. "Stupid," he said to the bartender. "Oh, Stupid. Do you think you could find the time to sweeten my drink?"

It was the first note of ugliness, but there would be nothing much but ugliness afterward. He would get very mean. Thin, fat, choleric or merry, young or old, all the ghosts do. In the end, they all drift home to accuse the doorman of incivility, to rail at their wives for extravagance, to lecture their bewildered children on ingratitude, and then to fall asleep on the guest-room bed with all their clothes on. But it wasn't this image that troubled me but the image of him standing in the new hallway, imagining that he saw his daughter at the head of the stairs in her wedding dress. We had not spoken, I didn't know him, his losses were not mine, and yet I felt them so strongly that I didn't want to spend the night alone, and so I spent it with a sloppy woman who works in our office. In the morning, I took a plane back to the sea, where it was still raining and where I found my wife washing pots in the kitchen sink. I had a hangover and felt painfully depraved, guilty, and unclean. I thought I might feel better if I went for a swim, and I asked my wife for my bathing trunks.

"They're around here somewhere," she said crossly. "They're kicking around underfoot somewhere. You left them wet on the bedroom rug and I hung them up in the shower."

"They're not in the shower," I said.

"Well, they're around here somewhere," she said. "Have you looked on the dining-room table?"

"Now, listen," I said. "I don't see why you have to speak of my bathing trunks as if they had been wandering around the house, drinking whiskey, breaking wind, and telling dirty stories to mixed company. I'm just asking for an *innocent* pair of bathing trunks." Then I sneezed, and I waited for her to bless me as she always did but she said nothing. "And another thing I can't find," I said, "is my handkerchiefs."

"Blow your nose on Kleenex," she said.

"I don't want to blow my nose on Kleenex," I said. I must have raised my voice, because I could hear Mrs. Whiteside calling Mary-Lee indoors and shutting a window.

"Oh, God, you bore me this morning," my wife said.

"I've been bored for the last six years," I said.

I took a cab to the airport and an afternoon plane back to the city. We had been married twelve years and had been lovers for two years before our marriage, making a total of fourteen years in all that we had been together, and I never saw her again.

This is being written in another seaside house with another wife. I sit in a chair of no discernible period or inspiration. Its cushions have a musty smell. The ashtray was filched from the Excelsior in Rome. My whiskey glass once held jelly. The table I'm writing on has a bum leg. The lamp is dim. Magda, my wife, is dyeing her hair. She dyes it orange, and this has to be done once a week. It is foggy, we are near a channel marked with buoys, and I can hear as many bells as I would hear in any pious village on a Sunday morning. There are high bells, low bells, and bells that seem to ring from under the sea. When Magda asks me to get her glasses, I step quietly onto the porch. The lights from the cottage, shining into the fog, give an illusion of substance, and it seems as if I might stumble on a beam of light. The shore is curved, and I can see the lights of other haunted cottages where people are building up an accrual of happiness or misery that will be left for the August tenants or the people who come next year. Are we truly this close to one another? Must we impose our burdens on strangers? And is our sense of the universality of suffering so inescapable? "My glasses, my glasses!" Magda shouts. "How many times do I have to ask you to bring them for me?" I get her her glasses, and when she is finished with her hair we go to bed. In the middle of the night, the porch door flies open, but my first, my gentle wife is not there to ask, "Why have they come back? What have they lost?"

Just One More Time

THERE IS NO SENSE IN LOOKING FOR TROUBLE, BUT IN ANY big, true picture of the city where we all live there is surely room for one more word on the diehards, the hangers-on, the people who never got along and who never gave up, the insatiables that we have all known at one time or another. I mean the shoestring aristocrats of the upper East Side— the elegant, charming, and shabby men who work for brokerage houses, and their high-flown wives, with their thrift-shop minks and their ash-can fur pieces, their alligator shoes and their snotty ways with doormen and with the cashiers in supermarkets, their gold jewelry and their dregs of Je Reviens and Chanel. I'm thinking of the Beers now—Alfreda and Bob —who lived in the East Side apartment house that Bob's father used to own, surrounded by sailing trophies, autographed photographs of President Hoover, Spanish furniture, and other relics of the golden age. It wasn't much of a place, really—large and dark—but it was more than they could afford; you could tell by the faces of the doormen and the elevator operators when you told them where you were going. I suppose they were always two or three months behind with

214

the rent and had nothing to spare for tips. Of course, Alfreda had been to school in Fiesole. Her father, like Bob's had lost millions and millions and millions of dollars. All her memories were thickly inlaid with patines of bright gold: yesteryear's high bridge stakes, and how difficult it was to get the Daimler started on a rainy day, and picnics on the Brandywine with the du Pont girls.

She was a good-looking woman—long-faced and with that New England fairness that seems to state a tenuous racial claim to privilege. She looked imperturbable. When they were on their uppers, she worked—first at the Steuben glass store, on Fifth Avenue, and then she went to Jensen's, where she got into trouble by insisting on her right to smoke. She went from there to Bonwit's, and from Bonwit's to Bendel's. Schwarz's took her on one Christmas, and she was on the street-floor glove counter at Saks the next Easter. She had a couple of children between jobs and she used to leave them in the care of an old Scotchwoman—an old family retainer from the good days—who seemed just as unable as the Beers to make an advantageous adjustment to change.

They were the kind of people that you met continually at railroad stations and cocktail parties. I mean Sunday-night railroad stations; weekend and season's-end places like the junction at Hyannis or Flemington; places like the station at Lake George, or Aiken and Greenville in the early spring; places like Westhampton, the Nantucket steamer, Stonington, and Bar Harbor; or, to go farther afield, places like Paddington Station, Rome, and the Antwerp night boat. "Hello! Hello!" they called across the crowd of travelers, and there he would be, in his white raincoat, with his stick and his Homburg, and there she was, in her mink or her ash-can fur piece. And in some ways the cocktail parties where your paths crossed were not so different, after all, from the depots, junctions, and boat trains where you met. They were the kind of party where the company is never very numerous and the liquor is never very good—parties where, as you drink and talk, you feel a palpable lassitude overtaking any natural social ardor, as if the ties of family, society, school, and place that held the group together were dissolving like the ice in your drink. But the atmosphere is not so much one of social dissolution as of social change, realignment— in effect, the atmosphere of travel. The guests seem to be gathered in a boat shed or at a railroad junction, waiting for the boat or the train to depart. Past the maid who takes the wraps, past the foyer and the fireproof door, there seems to lie a stretch of dark water, stormy water sometimes—the cry of the wind, the creak of iron sign hinges and the lights, the deckhand voices, and the soulful whistling of an approaching Channel boat.

One reason you always saw the Beers at cocktail parties and railroad stations was that they were always looking for somebody. They weren't looking for somebody like you or me—they were looking for the Marchioness of Bath—but any port in a storm. The way they used to come in to a party and stare around them is understandable—we all do it—but the way they used to peer at their fellow travelers on a station platform was something else. In any place where those two had to wait fifteen minutes or longer for a public conveyance they would turn the crowd inside out, peering under hat-brims and behind newspapers for somebody they might happen to know.

I'm speaking of the thirties and the forties now, the years before and after the Big War—years when the Beers' financial problems must have been complicated by the fact that their children were old enough to go to expensive schools. They did some unsavory things; they kited checks, and, borrowing someone's car for a weekend, they ran it into a ditch and walked away, washing their hands of the whole thing. These tricks brought some precariousness to their social as well as their economic status, but they continued to operate on a margin of charm and expectation—there was Aunt Margaret in Philadelphia and Aunt Laura in Boston—and, to tell the truth, they were charming. People were always glad to see them, for, if they were the pathetic grasshoppers of some gorgeous economic summer, they somehow had it in their power to remind one of good things—good places, games, food, and company—and the ardor with which they looked for friends on railroad platforms could perhaps be accounted for by the fact that they were only looking for a world that they understood.

Then Aunt Margaret died, and this is how I discovered that interesting fact. It was in the spring, and my boss and his wife were sailing for England, and I went down to the boat one morning with a box of cigars and a historical romance. The ship was new, as I recall, with lots of drifters looking at the sets of Edna Ferber under lock and key in the library and admiring the dry swimming pools and the dry bars. The passageways were crowded, and every cabin in first class was full of flowers and of well-wishers drinking champagne at eleven o'clock on a gloomy morning, with the rich green soup of New York Harbor sending its tragic smell up to the clouds. I gave my boss and his wife their presents, and then, looking for the main deck, passed a cabin or suite where I heard Alfreda's boarding-school laugh. The place was jammed, and a waiter was pouring champagne, and when I had greeted my friends, Alfreda took me aside. "Aunt Margaret has departed this life," she said, "and we're *loaded* again. . . ." I had some champagne, and then the all-ashore whistle blew—vehement, deafening, the hoarse summons of life itself, and somehow, like the smell of harbor water, tragic, too; for, watching the party break up, I wondered how long Aunt Margaret's fortune would last those two. Their debts were enormous, and their habits were foolish, and even a hundred thousand wouldn't take them far.

This idea seems to have stayed at the back of my mind, for at a heavyweight fight at Yankee Stadium that fall I thought I saw Bob wandering around with a tray of binoculars to rent. I called his name—I shouted—and it wasn't he, but the resemblance was so striking that I felt as if I *had* seen him, or had at least seen the scope of the vivid social and economic contrasts in store for such a couple.

I wish I could say that, leaving the theatre one snowy evening, I saw Alfreda selling pencils on Forty-sixth Street and that she would return to some basement on the West Side where Bob lay dying on a pallet, but this would only reflect on the poverty of my imagination.

In saying that the Beers were the kind of people you met at railroad stations and cocktail parties, I overlooked the beaches. They were *very* aquatic. You know how it is. In the summer months, the northeastern coast up from Long Island and deep into Maine, including all the sea islands, seems to be transformed into a vast social clearinghouse, and as you sit on the sand listening to the heavy furniture of the North

Atlantic, figures from your social past appear in the surf, as thick as raisins in a cake. A wave takes form, accelerates its ride over the shallows, boils, and breaks, revealing Consuelo Roosevelt and Mr. and Mrs. Dundas Vanderbilt, with the children of both marriages. Then a wave comes in from the right like a cavalry charge, bearing landward on the rubber raft Lathrope Macy with Emerson Crane's second wife, and the Bishop of Pittsburgh in an inner tube. Then a wave breaks at your feet with the noise of a slammed trunk lid and there are the Beers. "How nice to see you, how very *nice* to see you . . ."

So the summer and the sea will be the setting for their last appearance—their last appearance for our purposes here, at any rate. We are in a small town in Maine—let's say—and decide to take the family for a sail and a picnic. The man at the inn tells us where there is a boat livery, and we pack our sandwiches and follow his directions to a wharf. We find an old man in a shack with a catboat to rent, and we make a deposit and sign a dirty paper, noticing that the old man, at ten in the morning, is drunk. He rows us out to the mooring in a skiff, and we say goodbye, and then, seeing how dilapidated his catboat is, we call after him, but he has already headed for the mainland and is out of hearing.

The floor boards are floating, the rudder pin is bent, and one of the bolts in the rudder has rusted away. The blocks are broken, and when we pump her dry and hoist the sail, it is rotted and torn. We get under way at last—urged by the children—and sail out to an island and eat our picnic. Then we start home. But now the wind has freshened; it has backed around to the southwest; and when we have left the island our port stay snaps, and the wire flies upward and coils itself around the mast. We take down the sail and repair the stay with rope. Then we see that we are on an ebb tide and traveling rapidly out to sea. With the repaired stay we sail for ten minutes before the starboard stay gives. Now we are in trouble. We think of the old man in the shack, who holds the only knowledge of our whereabouts in his drunken head. We try to paddle with the floor boards, but we can make no headway against the sweep of the tide. Who will save us? The Beers!

They come over the horizon at dusk in one of those bulky cabin cruisers, with a banquette on the bridge and shaded lamps and bowls of roses in the cabin. A hired hand is at the helm, and Bob throws us a line. This is more than a chance reunion of old friends—our lives have been saved. We are nearly delirious. The hired hand is settled in the catboat, and ten minutes after we have been snatched from the jaws of death we are drinking Martinis on the bridge. They will take us back to their house, they say. We can spend the night there. And while the background and the appointments are not so different, their relationship to them has been revolutionized. It is *their* house, *their* boat. We wonder how—we gape—and Bob is civil enough to give us an explanation, in a low voice, a mumble, nearly, as if the facts were parenthetical. "We took most of Aunt Margaret's money and all of Aunt Laura's and a little something Uncle Ralph left us and invested it all in the market, you know, and it's more than tripled in the last two years. I've bought back everything Dad lost—everything I wanted, that is. That's my schooner over there. Of course, the house is new. Those are our lights." The afternoon and the ocean, which seemed so menacing in the catboat, now spread out around us with a miraculous tranquillity, and we settle back to enjoy our company, for the Beers are charming—they always were—and now they appear to be smart, for what else was it but smart of them to know that summertime would come again?

Marito in Città

꿏

Some years ago there was a popular song in Italy called "Marito in Città." The air was as simple and catching as a street song. The words went, *"La moglie ce ne va, marito poverino, solo in cittadina,"* and dealt with the plight of a man alone, in the lighthearted and farcical manner that seems traditional, as if to be alone were an essentially comic situation such as getting tangled up in a trout line. Mr. Estabrook had heard the song while traveling in Europe with his wife (fourteen days; ten cities) and some capricious tissue of his memory had taken an indelible impression of the words and the music. He had not forgotten it; indeed, it seemed that he could not forget it, although it was in conflict with his regard for the possibilities of aloneness.

The scene, the moment when his wife and four children left for the mountains, had the charm, the air of ordination, and the deceptive simplicity of an old-fashioned magazine cover. One could have guessed at it all—the summer morning, the station wagon, the bags, the clear-eyed children, the filled change rack for toll stations, some ceremonious observation of a change in the season, another ring in the planet's age. He shook hands with his sons and kissed his wife and his daughters and watched the car move along the driveway with a feeling that this instant was momentous, that had he been given the power to scrutinize the forces that were involved he would have arrived at something like a revelation. The women and children of Rome, Paris, London, and New York were, he knew, on their way to the highlands or the sea. It was a weekday, and so he locked Scamper, the dog, into the kitchen and drove to the station singing, *"Marito in città, la moglie ce ne va,"* et cetera, et cetera.

One knows how it will go, of course; it will never quite transcend the farcical strictures of a street song, but Mr. Estabrook's aspirations were earnest, fresh, and worth observing. He was familiar with the vast and evangelical literature of solitude, and he intended to exploit the weeks of his aloneness. He could clean his telescope and study the stars. He could read. He could practice the Bach two-part variations on the piano. He could—so like an expatriate who claims that the limpidity and sometimes the anguish of his estrangement promises a high degree of self-discovery—learn more about himself. He would observe the migratory habits of birds, the changes in the garden, the clouds in the sky. He had a distinct image of himself, his powers of observation greatly heightened by the adventure of aloneness. When he got home on his first night, he found that Scamper had got out of the kitchen and slept on a sofa in the living room, which he had covered with mud and hair. Scamper was a mongrel, the children's pet. Mr. Estabrook spoke reproachfully to the dog and turned up the sofa cushions. The next problem that he faced was one that is seldom touched on in the literature of solitude—the problem of his rudimentary appetites. This was to sound, in spite of himself, the note of low comedy, *O, marito in città.* He could imagine himself in clean chinos, setting up his telescope in the garden at dusk, but he could not imagine who was going to feed this self-possessed figure.

He fried himself some eggs, but he found that he couldn't eat them. He made an Old-Fashioned cocktail with particular care and drank it. Then he returned to the eggs, but he still found them revolting. He drank another cocktail and approached the eggs from a different direction, but they were still repulsive. He gave the eggs to Scamper and drove out to the state highway, where there was a restaurant. The music, when he entered the place, seemed as loud as parade music, and a waitress was standing on a chair, stringing curtains onto a rod. "I'll be with you in a minute," she said. "Sit down anywheres." He chose a place at one of the forty empty tables. He was not actually disappointed in his situation, he had by design surrounded himself with a large number of men, women, and children, and it was only natural that he should feel then, as he did, not alone but lonely. Considering the physical and spiritual repercussions of this condition, it seemed strange to him that there was only one word for it. He was lonely, and he was in pain. The food was not just bad; it seemed incredible. Here was that total absence of recollection that is the essence of tastelessness. He could eat nothing. He stirred up his stringy pepper steak and ordered some ice cream, to spare the feeling of the waitress. The food reminded him of all those who through clumsiness or bad luck must make their lives alone and eat this fare each night. It was frightening, and he went to a movie.

The long summer dusk still filled the air with a soft light. The wishing star hung above the enormous screen, canted a little toward the audience with a certain air of doom. Faded in the fading light, the figures and animals of a cartoon chased one another across the screen, exploded, danced, sang, pratfell. The fanfare and the credits for the feature he had come to see went on through the last of the twilight, and then, as night fell, a screenplay of incredible assininity began to unfold. His moral indignation at this confluence of hunger, boredom, and loneliness was violent, and he thought sadly of the men who had been obliged to write the movie, and of the hard-working actors who were paid to repeat these crude lines. He could see them at the end of the day, getting out of their convertibles in Beverly Hills, utterly discouraged. Fifteen minutes was all he could stand, and he went home.

Scamper had shifted from the dismantled sofa to a chair, whose light silk covering he had dirtied with hair and mud. "Bad Scamper," Mr. Estabrook said, and then he took those precautions to save the furniture that he was to repeat each night. He upended a footstool on the sofa, upended the silk chairs, put a wastebasket on the love seat in the hallway, and put the upholstered dining-room chairs upside down on the table, as they do in restaurants when the floor is being mopped. With the lights off and everything upside down, the permanence of his house was challenged, and he felt for a moment like a ghost who has come back to see time's ruin.

Lying in bed he thought, quite naturally, of his wife. He had learned, from experience, that it was sensible to make their separations ardent, and on the day but one before they left, he had declared himself; but Mrs. Estabrook was tired. On the next night, he declared himself again. Mrs. Estabrook seemed acquiescent, but what she then did was to go down to the kitchen, put four heavy blankets into the washing machine, blow a fuse, and flood the floor. Standing in the kitchen doorway, utterly unaccommodated, he wondered why she did this. She had merely meant to be elusive! Watching her, a dignified but rather heavy woman, mopping up the kitchen floor, he thought that she had wanted, like any nymph, to run through the bosky—dappled her back, the water flashing at her feet—and being short-winded these days, and there being no bosky, she had been reduced to putting blankets into a washing machine. It had never crossed his mind before that the passion to be elusive was as strong in her sex as the passion to pursue was in his. This glimpse of things moved him; contented him, in a way; but was, as it so happened, the only contentment he had that night.

The image of a cleanly, self-possessed man exploiting his solitude was not easy to come by, but then he had not expected that it would be. On the next night, he practiced the two-part variations until eleven. On the night after that, he got out his telescope. He had been unable to solve the problem of feeding himself, and in the space of a week had lost more than fifteen pounds. His trousers, when he belted them in around his middle, gathered in folds like a shirt. He took three pairs of trousers down to the dry cleaner's in the village. It was past closing time, but the proprietor was still there, a man crushed by life. He had torn Mrs. Hazelton's lace pillowcases and lost Mr. Fitch's silk shirts. His equipment was in hock, the union wanted health insurance, and everything that he ate—even yoghurt—seemed to turn to fire in his esophagus. He spoke despairingly to Mr. Estabrook. "We don't keep a tailor on the premises no more, but there's a woman up on Maple Avenue who does alterations. Mrs.

Zagreb. It's at the corner of Maple Avenue and Clinton Street. There's a sign in the window."

It was a dark night and that time of year when there are many fireflies. Maple Avenue was what it claimed to be, and the dense foliage doubled the darkness on the street. The house on the corner was frame, with a porch. The maples were so thick there that no grass grew on the lawn. There was a sign—ALTERATIONS—in the window. He rang a bell. "Just a minute," someone called. The voice was strong and gay. A woman opened the door with one hand, rubbing a towel in her dark hair with the other. She seemed surprised to see him. "Come in," she said, "come in. I've just washed my hair." There was a small hall, and he followed her through this into a small living room. "I have some trousers that I want taken in," he said. "Do you do that kind of thing?"

"I do everything," she laughed. "But why are you losing weight? Are you on a diet?"

She had put down her towel, but she continued to shake her hair and rough it with her fingers. She moved around the room while she talked, and seemed to fill the room with restlessness—a characteristic that might have annoyed him in someone else but that in her seemed graceful, fascinating, the prompting of some inner urgency.

"I'm not dieting," he said.

"You're not ill?" Her concern was swift and genuine; he might have been her oldest friend.

"Oh, no. It's just that I've been trying to cook for myself."

"Oh, you poor boy," she said. "Do you know your measurements?"

"No."

"Well, we'll have to take them."

Moving, stirring the air and shaking her hair, she crossed the room and got a yellow tape measure from a drawer. In order to measure his waist she had to put her hands under his jacket—a gesture that seemed amorous. When the measure was around his waist, he put his arms around her waist and thrust himself against her. She merely laughed and shook her hair. Then she pushed him away lightly, much more like a promise than a rebuff. "Oh, no," she said, "not tonight, not tonight, my dear." She crossed the room and faced him from there. Her face was tender, and darkened with indecision, but when he came toward her she hung her head, shook it vigorously. "No, no, no," she said. "Not tonight. Please."

"But I can see you again?"

"Of course, but not tonight." She crossed the room and laid her hand against his cheek. "Now, you go," she said, "and I'll call you. You're very nice, but now you go."

He stumbled out of the door, stunned but feeling wonderfully important. He had been in the room three minutes, four at the most, and what had there been between them, this instantaneous recognition of their fitness as lovers? He had been excited when he first saw her—had been excited by her strong, gay voice. Why had they been able to move so effortlessly, so directly toward one another? And where was his sense of good and evil, his passionate desire to be worthy, manly, and, within his vows, chaste? He was a member of the Church of Christ, he was a member of the vestry, a devout and habitual communicant, sincerely sworn to defend the articles of faith. He had already committed a mortal sin. But driving under the maples and through the summer night, he could not, under the most intense examination, find anything in his instincts but goodness and magnanimity and a much enlarged sense of the world. He struggled with some scrambled eggs, practiced the variations, and tried to sleep. "*O, marito in città!*"

It was the memory of Mrs. Zagreb's front that tormented him. Its softness and fragrance seemed to hang in the air while he waited for sleep, it followed into his dreams, and when he woke his face seemed buried in Mrs. Zagreb's front, glistening like marble and tasting to his thirsty lips as various and soft as the airs of a summer night.

In the morning, he took a cold shower, but Mrs. Zagreb's front seemed merely to wait outside the shower curtain. It rested against his cheek as he drove to the train, read over his shoulder as he rode the eight-thirty-three, jiggled along with him through the shuttle and the downtown train, and haunted him through the business day. He thought he was going mad. As soon as he got home, he looked up her number in the *Social Register* that his wife kept by the telephone. This was a mistake, of course, but he found her number in a local directory and called her. "Your trousers are ready," she said. "You can come and get them whenever you want. Now, if you'd like."

She called for him to come in. He found her in the living room, and she handed him his trousers. Then he was shy and wondered if he hadn't invented the night before. Here, with his shyness, was the truth, and all the rest had been imagining. Here was a widowed seamstress handing some trousers to a lonely man, no longer young, in a frame house that needed paint on Maple Avenue. The world was ruled by common sense, legitimate passions, and articles of faith. She shook her head. This then was a mannerism and had nothing to do with washing her hair. She pushed it off her forehead; ran her fingers through the dark curls. "If you have time for a drink," she said, "there's everything in the kitchen."

"I'd love a drink," he said. "Will you have one with me?"

"I'll have a whiskey and soda," she said.

Feeling sad, heavyhearted, important, caught up on those streams of feeling that never surface, he went into the kitchen and made their drinks. When he came back into the room, she was sitting on a sofa, and he joined her there; seemed immersed in her mouth, as if it was a maelstrom; spun around thrice and sped down the length of some stupendous timelessness. The dialogue of sudden love doesn't seem to change much from country to country. We say across the pillow, in any language, "Hullo, hullo, hullo, hullo, hullo," as if we were involved in some interminable and tender transoceanic telephone conversation, and the adulteress, taking the adulterer into her arms, will cry, "Oh, my love, why are you so bitter?" She praised his hair, his neck, the declivity in his back. She smelled faintly of soap—no perfume—and when he said so she said softly, "But I never wear perfume when I'm going to make love." They went side by side up the narrow stairs to her room—the largest room in a small house, but small at that, and sparsely furnished, like a room in a summer cottage, with old furniture that had been painted white and with a worn white rug. Her suppleness, her wiles, seemed to him like a staggering source of purity. He thought he had never known so pure, gallant, courageous, and easy a spirit. So they kept saying "Hullo, hullo, hullo, hullo" until three, when she made him leave.

He walked in his garden at half past three or four. There

was a quarter moon, the air was soft and the light vaporous, the clouds formed like a beach and the stars were strewn among them like shells and moraine. Some flower that blooms in July—phlox or Nicotiana—had scented the air, and the meaning of the vaporous light had not much changed since he was an adolescent; it now, as it had then, seemed to hold out the opportunities of romantic love. But what about the structures of his faith? He had broken a sacred commandment, broken it repeatedly, joyously, and would break it at every opportunity he was given; therefore, he had committed a mortal sin, and must be denied the sacraments of his church. But he could not alter the feeling that Mrs. Zagreb, in her knowledgeableness, represented uncommon purity and virtue. But if these were his genuine feelings, then he must resign from the vestry, the church, improvise his own schemes of good and evil, and look for a life beyond the articles of faith. Had he known other adulterers to take communion? He had. Was his church a social convenience, a sign of deliquescence and hypocrisy, a means of getting ahead? Were the stirring words said at weddings and funerals no more than customs and no more religious than the custom of taking off one's hat in the elevator at Brooks Brothers when a woman enters the car? Christened, reared, and drilled in church dogma, the thought of giving up his faith was unimaginable. It was his best sense of the miraculousness of life, the receipt of a vigorous and omniscient love, widespread and incandescent as the light of day. Should he ask the suffragan bishop to reassess the ten commandments, to include in their prayers some special reference to the feelings of magnanimity and love that follow sexual engorgements?

He walked in the garden, conscious of the fact that she

had at least given him the illusion of playing an important romantic role, a lead, a thrilling improvement over the sundry messengers, porters, and clowns of monogamy, and there was no doubt about the fact that her praise had turned his head. Was her excitement over the declivity in his back cunning, sly, a pitiless exploitation of the enormous and deep-buried vanity in men? The sky had begun to lighten, and undressing for bed he looked at himself in the mirror. Yes, her praise had all been lies. His abdomen had a dismal sag. Or had it? He held it in, distended it, examined it full face and profile, and went to bed.

The next day was Saturday, and he made a schedule for himself. Cut the lawns, clip the hedges, split some firewood, and paint the storm windows. He worked contentedly until five, when he took a shower and made a drink. His plan was to scramble some eggs and, since the sky was clear, set up his telescope, but when he had finished his drink he went humbly to the telephone and called Mrs. Zagreb. He called her at intervals of fifteen minutes until after dark, and then he got into his car and drove over to Maple Avenue. A light was burning in her bedroom. The rest of the house was dark. A large car with a state seal beside the license plate was parked under the maples, and a chauffeur was asleep in the front seat.

He had been asked to take the collection at Holy Communion, and so he did, but, when he got to his knees to make his general confession, he could not admit that what he had done was an offense to divine majesty; the burden of his sins was not intolerable; the memory of them was anything but grievous. He improvised a heretical thanksgiving for the constancy and intelligence of his wife, the clear eyes of his children, and the suppleness of his mistress. He did not take communion, and when the priest fired a questioning look in his direction, he was tempted to say clearly, "I am unashamedly involved in an adultery." He read the papers until eleven, when he called Mrs. Zagreb and she said he could come whenever he wanted. He was there in ten minutes, and made her bones crack as soon as he entered the house. "I came by last night," he said.

"I thought you might," she said. "I know a lot of men. Do you mind?"

"Not at all," he said.

"Someday," she said, "I'm going to take a piece of paper and write on it everything that I know about men. And then I'll put it into the fireplace and burn it."

"You don't have a fireplace," he said.

"That's so," she said, but they said nothing much else for the rest of the afternoon and half the night but "Hullo, hullo, hullo, hullo."

When he came home the next evening, there was a letter from his wife on the hall table. He seemed to see directly through the envelope into its contents. In it she would explain intelligently and dispassionately that her old lover, Olney Pratt, had returned from Saudi Arabia and asked her to marry him. She wanted her freedom, and she hoped he would understand. She and Olney had never ceased loving one another, and they would be dishonest to their innermost selves if they denied this love another day. She was sure they could reach an agreement on the custody of the children. He had been a good provider and a patient man, but she did not wish ever to see him again.

He held the letter in his hand thinking that his wife's hand-writing expressed her femininity, her intelligence, her depth; it was the hand of a woman asking for freedom. He tore the letter open, fully prepared to read about Olney Pratt, but he read instead: "Dear Lover-bear, the nights are *terribly* cold, and I *miss* . . ." On and on it went for two pages. He was still reading when the doorbell rang. It was Doris Hamilton, a neighbor. "I know you don't answer the telephone, and I know you don't like to dine out," she said, "but I'm determined that you should have at least one good dinner this month, and I've come to shanghai you."

"Well," he said.

"Now you march upstairs and take a shower, and I'll make myself a drink," she said. "We're going to have hot boiled lobster. Aunt Molly sent down a bushel this morning, and you'll have to help us eat them. Eddie has to go to the doctor after dinner, and you can go home whenever you like."

He went upstairs and did as he was told. When he had changed and come down, she was in the living room with a drink, and they drove over to her house in separate cars. They dined by candlelight off a table in the garden, and, washed and in a clean duck suit, he found himself contented with the role he had so recently and so passionately abdicated. It was not a romantic lead, but it had some subtle prominence. After dinner, Eddie excused himself and went off to see his psychiatrist, as he did three nights each week. "I don't suppose you've seen anyone," Doris said. "I don't suppose you know the gossip."

"I really haven't seen anyone."

"I know. I've heard you practicing the piano. Well, Lois Spinner is suing Frank, and suing the buttons off him."

"Why?"

"Well, he's been carrying on with this disgusting slut, a perfectly disgusting woman. His older son, Ralph—he's a marvelous boy—saw them together in a restaurant. They were *feeding* each other. None of his children want to see him again."

"Men have had mistresses before," he said tentatively.

"Adultery is a mortal sin," she said gaily, "and was punished in many societies with death."

"Do you feel this strongly about divorce?"

"Oh, he had no intention of marrying the pig. He simply thought he could play his dirty games, humiliate, disgrace, and wound his family and return to their affections when he got bored. The divorce was not his idea. He's begged Lois not to divorce him. I believe he's threatened to kill himself."

"I've known men," he said, "to divide their attentions between a mistress and a wife."

"I daresay you've never known it to be done successfully," she said.

The fell truth in this had never quite appeared to him. "Adultery is a commonplace," he said. "It is the subject of most of our literature, most of our plays, our movies. Popular songs are written about it."

"You wouldn't want to confuse your life with a French farce, would you?"

The authority with which she spoke astonished him. Here was the irresistibility of the lawful world, the varsity team, the best club. Suddenly, the image of Mrs. Zagreb's bedroom, whose bleakness had seemed to him so poignant, returned to him in an unsavory light. He remembered that the window curtains were torn and that those hands that had so praised him were coarse and stubby. The promiscuity that he had thought to be the wellspring of her pureness now seemed to be an incurable illness. The kindnesses she had showed him seemed perverse and disgusting. She had groveled before his nakedness. Sitting in the summer night, in his clean clothes, he thought of Mrs. Estabrook, serene and refreshed, leading her four intelligent and handsome children across some gallery in his head. Adultery was the raw material of farce, popular music, madness, and self-destruction.

"It was terribly nice of you to have had me," he said. "And now I think I'll run along. I'll practice the piano before I go to bed."

"I'll listen," said Doris. "I can hear it quite clearly across the garden."

The telephone was ringing when he came in. "I'm alone," said Mrs. Zagreb, "and I thought you might like a drink." He was there in a few minutes, went once more to the bottom of the sea, into that stupendous timelessness, secured against the pain of living. But, when it was time to go, he said that he could not see her again. "That's perfectly all right," she said. And then, "Did anyone ever fall in love with you?"

"Yes," he said, "once. It was a couple of years ago. I had to go out to Indianapolis to set up a training schedule, and I had to stay with these people—it was part of the job—and there was this terribly nice woman, and every time she saw me she'd start crying. She cried at breakfast. She cried all through cocktails and dinner. It was awful. I had to move to a hotel, and naturally, I couldn't ever tell anyone."

"Good night," she said, "good night and goodbye."

"Good night, my love," he said, "good night and goodbye."

His wife called the next night while he was setting up the telescope. Oh, what excitement! They were driving down the next day. His daughter was going to announce her engagement to Frank Emmet. They wanted to be married before Christmas. Photographs had to be taken, announcements sent to the papers, a tent must be rented, wine ordered, et cetera. And his son had won the sailboat races on Monday, Tuesday, and Wednesday. "Good night, my darling," his wife said, and he fell into a chair, profoundly gratified at this requital of so many of his aspirations. He loved his daughter, he liked Frank Emmet, he even liked Frank Emmet's parents, who were rich, and the thought of his beloved son at the tiller, bringing his boat down the last tack toward the committee launch, filled him with great cheer. And Mrs. Zagreb? She wouldn't know how to sail. She would get tangled up in the mainsheet, vomit to windward, and pass out in the cabin once they were past the point. She wouldn't know how to play tennis. Why, she wouldn't even know how to ski! Then, watched by Scamper, he dismantled the living room. In the hallway, he put a wastebasket on the love seat. In the dining room, he upended the chairs on the table and turned out the lights. Walking through the dismantled house, he felt again the chill and bewilderment of someone who has come back to see time's ruin. Then he went up to bed, singing, *"Marito in città, la moglie ce ne va, o, povero marito!"*

A Vision of the World

THIS IS BEING WRITTEN IN ANOTHER SEASIDE COTTAGE ON
another coast. Gin and whiskey have bitten rings in the table
where I sit. The light is dim. On the wall there is a colored
lithograph of a kitten wearing a flowered hat, a silk dress,
and white gloves. The air is musty, but I think it is a pleasant smell—heartening and carnal, like bilge water or the land
wind. The tide is high, and the sea below the bluff slams its
bulkheads, its doors, and shakes its chains with such power
that it makes the lamp on my table jump. I am here alone
to rest up from a chain of events that began one Saturday afternoon when I was spading up my garden. A foot or two below
the surface I found a small round can that might have contained shoe polish. I pried the can open with a knife. Inside
I found a piece of oilcloth, and within this a note on lined
paper. It read, "I, Nils Jugstrum, promise myself that if I am
not a member of the Gory Brook Country Club by the time
I am twenty-five years old I will hang myself." I knew that
twenty years ago the neighborhood where I live had been

farmland, and I guessed that some farmer's boy, gazing off to the green fairways of Gory Brook, had made this vow and buried it in the ground. I was moved, as I always am, by these broken lines of communication in which we express our most acute feelings. The note seemed, like some impulse of romantic love, to let me deeper into the afternoon.

The sky was blue. It seemed like music. I had just cut the grass, and the smell of it was in the air. This reminded me of those overtures and promises of love we know when we are young. At the end of a foot race you throw yourself onto the grass by the cinder track, gasping for breath, and the ardor with which you embrace the schoolhouse lawn is a promise you will follow all the days of your life. Thinking then of peaceable things, I noticed that the black ants had conquered the red ants and were taking the corpses off the field. A robin flew by, pursued by two jays. The cat was in the currant hedge, scouting a sparrow. A pair of orioles passed, pecking each other, and then I saw, a foot or so from where I stood, a copperhead working itself out of the last length of its dark winter skin. What I experienced was not fright or dread; it was shock at my unpreparedness for this branch of death. Here was lethal venom, as much a part of the earth as the running water in the brook, but I seemed to have no space for it in my considerations. I went back to the house to get the shotgun, but I had the misfortune then to meet up with the older of my two dogs, a gun-shy bitch. At the sight of the gun she began to bark and whimper, torn unmercifully by her instincts and anxieties. Her barking brought the second dog, a natural hunter, bounding down the stairs, ready to retrieve a rabbit or a bird, and, followed by two dogs, one barking in joy and the other in horror, I returned to the garden in time to see the viper disappear into a stone wall.

After this I drove into the village and bought some grass seed and then went out to the supermarket on Route 27, to get some brioches my wife had ordered. I think you may need a camera these days to record a supermarket on a Saturday afternoon. Our language is traditional, the accrual of centuries of intercourse. Except for the shapes of the pastry, there was nothing traditional to be seen at the bakery counter where I waited. We were six or seven, delayed by an old man with a long list, a scroll of groceries. Looking over his shoulder I read,

> 6 eggs
> hors d'oeuvres

He saw me reading his document and held it against his chest like a prudent card player. Then suddenly the piped-in music changed from a love song to a cha-cha, and the woman beside me began to move her shoulders shyly and to execute a few steps. "Would you like to dance, Madam?" I asked. She was very plain, but when I held out my arms she stepped into them, and we danced for a minute or two. You could see that she loved to dance, but with a face like that she couldn't have had many chances. She then blushed a deep red, stepped out of my arms, and went over to the glass case, where she studied the Boston cream pies. I felt that we had made a step in the right direction, and when I got my brioches and drove home I was elated. A policeman stopped me at the corner of Alewives' Lane, to let a parade go by. First to come was a young girl in boots and shorts that emphasized the fineness of her thighs. She had an enormous nose, wore a busby, and pumped an aluminum baton. She was followed by another girl, with finer and more ample thighs, who marched with her pelvis so far in advance of the rest of her that her spine was strangely curved. She wore bifocals and seemed terribly bored by this forwardness of her pelvis. A band of boys, with here and there a gray-haired ringer, brought up the rear, playing "The Caissons Go Rolling Along." They carried no banners, they had no discernible purpose or destination, and it all seemed to me terribly funny. I laughed all the way home.

But my wife was sad.

"What's the matter, darling?" I asked.

"I just have this terrible feeling that I'm a character in a television situation comedy," she said. "I mean I'm nice looking, I'm well-dressed, I have humorous and attractive children, but I have this terrible feeling that I'm in black-and-white and that I can be turned off by anybody. I just have this terrible feeling that I can be turned *off*." My wife is often sad because her sadness is not a sad sadness, sorry because her sorrow is not a crushing sorrow. She grieves because her grief is not an acute grief, and when I tell her that this sorrow over the inadequacies of her sorrow may be a new hue in the spectrum of human pain, she is not consoled. Oh, I sometimes think of leaving her. I could conceivably make a life without her and the children, I could get along without the companionship of my friends, but I could not bring myself to leave my lawns and gardens, I could not part from the porch screens that I have repaired and painted, I cannot divorce myself from the serpentine brick walk I have laid between the side door and the rose garden; and so, while my chains are forged of turf and house paint, they will still bind me until I die. But I was grateful to my wife then for what she had said, for stating that the externals of her life had the quality of a dream. The uninhibited energies of the imagination had created the supermarket, the viper, and the note in the shoe-polish can. Compared to these, my wildest reveries had the literalness of double-entry bookkeeping. It pleased me to think that our external life has the quality of a dream and that in our dreams we find the virtues of conservatism. I then went into the house, where I found the cleaning woman smoking a stolen Egyptian cigarette and piecing together the torn letters in the wastebasket.

We went to Gory Brook that night for dinner. I checked the list of members, looking for Nils Jugstrum, but he wasn't there, and I wondered if he had hanged himself. And for what? It was the usual. Gracie Masters, the only daughter of a millionaire funeral director, was dancing with Pinky Townsend. Pinky was out on fifty-thousand-dollars' bail for stock-market manipulation. When bail was set, he took the fifty thousand out of his wallet. I danced a set with Millie Surcliffe. The music was "Rain," "Moonlight on the Ganges," "When the Red Red Robin Comes Bob Bob Bobbin' Along," "Five Foot Two, Eyes of Blue," "Carolina in the Morning," and "The Sheik of Araby." We seemed to be dancing on the grave of social coherence. But while the scene was plainly revolutionary, where was the new day, the world to come? The next set was "Lena from Palesteena," "I'm Forever Blowing Bubbles," "Louisville Lou," "Smiles," and "The Red Red Robin" again. That last one really gets us jumping, but when the band blew the spit out of their instruments I saw them shaking their heads in deep moral disapproval of our antics. Millie went back to her table, and I stood by

the door, wondering why my heart should heave when I
see people leave a dance floor at the end of a set—heave as it
heaves when I see a crowd pack up and leave a beach as the
shadow of the cliff falls over the water and the sand, heave
as if I saw in these gentle departures the energies and the
thoughtlessness of life itself.

Time, I thought, strips us rudely of the privileges of the
bystander, and in the end that couple chatting loudly in
bad French in the lobby of the Grande Bretagne (Athens)
turns out to be us. Someone else has got our post behind
the potted palms, our quiet corner in the bar, and, exposed,
perforce we cast around for other avenues of observation.
What I wanted to identify then was not a chain of facts but
an essence—something like that indecipherable collision of
contingencies that can produce exaltation or despair. What
I wanted to do was to grant my dreams, in so incoherent a
world, their legitimacy. None of this made me moody, and
I danced, drank, and told stories at the bar until about one,
when we went home. I turned on the television set to
a commercial that, like so much else I had seen that day,
seemed terribly funny. A young woman with a boarding-
school accent was asking, "Do you offend with wet-fur-coat
odor? A fifty-thousand-dollar sable cape caught in a thunder-
shower can smell worse than an old hound dog who's been
chasing a fox through a swamp. *Nothing* smells worse than
wet mink. Even a light mist can make lamb, opossum, civet,
baum marten, and other less costly and serviceable furs as
malodorous as a badly ventilated lion house in a zoo. Safeguard yourself from embarrassment and anxiety by light
applications of Elixircol before you wear your furs. . . ."
She belonged to the dream world, and I told her so before

I turned her off. I fell asleep in the moonlight and dreamed of an island.

I was with some other men, and seemed to have reached the place on a sailing boat. I was sunburned, I remember, and, touching my jaw, I felt a three- or four-day stubble. The island was in the Pacific. There was a smell of rancid cooking oil in the air—a sign of the China coast. It was in the middle of the afternoon when we landed, and we seemed to have nothing much to do. We wandered through the streets. The place either had been occupied by the Army or had served as a military way station, because many of the signs in the windows were written in an approximation of English. "Crews Cutz," I read on a sign in an Oriental barber-shop. Many of the stores had displays of imitation American whiskey. Whiskey was spelled "Whikky." Because we had nothing better to do, we went into a local museum. There were bows, primitive fish hooks, masks, and drums. From the museum we went to a restaurant and ordered a meal. I had a struggle with the local language, but what surprised me was that it seemed to be an informed struggle. I seemed to have studied the language before coming ashore. I distinctly remembered putting together a sentence when the waiter came up to the table. *"Porpozec ciebie nie prosze dorzanin albo zyolpocz ciwego,"* I said. The waiter smiled and complimented me, and, when I woke from the dream, the fact of the language made the island in the sun, its population, and its museum real, vivid, and enduring. I thought with longing of the quiet and friendly natives and the easy pace of their lives.

Sunday passed swiftly and pleasantly in a round of cock-tail parties, but that night I had another dream. I dreamed that I was standing at the bedroom window of the cottage in

Nantucket that we sometimes rent. I was looking south along the fine curve of the beach. I have seen finer, whiter, and more splendid beaches, but when I look at the yellow of the sand and the arc of the curve, I always have the feeling that if I look at the cove long enough it will reveal something to me. The sky was cloudy. The water was gray. It was Sunday —although I couldn't have said how I knew this. It was late, and from the inn I could hear that most pleasant sound of dishes being handled, while families would be eating their Sunday-night suppers in the old matchboard dining room. Then I saw a single figure coming down the beach. It seemed to be a priest or a bishop. He carried a crozier, and wore the mitre, cope, soutane, chasuble, and alb for high votive Mass. His vestments were heavily worked with gold, and now and then they were lifted by the sea wind. His face was clean-shaven. I could not make out his features in the fading light. He saw me at my window, raised his hand, and called. *"Por-pozec, ciebie nie prosze dorzanin albo zyolpocz ciwego."* Then he hurried along the sand, striking his crozier down like a walking stick, his stride impeded by the voluminousness of his vestments. He passed the window where I stood and disappeared where the curve of the bluff overtakes the curve of the shore.

I worked on Monday, and on Tuesday morning woke at about four from a dream in which I had been playing touch football. I was on the winning team. The score was six to eighteen. It was a scrub Sunday-afternoon game on somebody's lawn. Our wives and daughters watched from the edge of the grass, where there were chairs and tables and things to drink. The winning play was a long end run, and when the touchdown had been scored a big blonde named Helen Farmer got up and organized the women into a cheering section. "Rah, rah, rah," they said. *"Porpozec ciebie nie prosze dorzanin albo zyolpocz ciwego. Rah, rah, rah."*

I found none of this disconcerting. It was what I had wanted, in a way. Isn't the unconquerable force in man the love of discovery? The repetition of this sentence had the the excitement of discovery for me. The fact that I had been on the winning team made me feel happy, and I went cheerfully down to breakfast, but our kitchen, alas, is a part of dreamland. With its pink, washable walls, chilling lights, built-in television (where prayers were being said), and artificial potted plants, it made me nostalgic for my dream, and when my wife passed me the stylus and Magic Tablet on which we write our breakfast orders, I wrote, *"Porpozec ciebie nie prosze dorzanin albo zyolpocz ciwego."* She laughed and asked me what I meant. When I repeated the sentence— it seemed, indeed, to be the only thing I wanted to say—she began to cry, and I saw in the bitterness of her tears that I had better take a rest. Dr. Howland came over to give me a sedative, and I took a plane to Florida that afternoon.

Now it is late. I drink a glass of milk and take a sleeping pill. I dream that I see a pretty woman kneeling in a field of wheat. Her light-brown hair is full and so are the skirts of her dress. Her clothing seems old-fashioned—it seems before my time—and I wonder how I can know and feel so tenderly toward a stranger who is dressed in clothing that my grandmother might have worn. And yet she seems real— more real than the Tamiami Trail four miles to the east, with its Smorgorama and Giganticburger stands, more real than the back streets of Sarasota. I do not ask her who she is. I know what she will say. But then she smiles and starts to speak before I can turn away. *"Porpozec ciebie . . ."* she begins. Then either I awake in despair or am waked by the sound of rain on the palms. I think of some farmer who, hearing the noise of rain, will stretch his lame bones and smile, feeling that the rain is falling into his lettuce and his cabbages, his hay and his oats, his parsnips and his corn. I think of some plumber who, waked by the rain, will smile at a vision of the world in which all the drains are miraculously cleansed and free. Right-angle drains, crooked drains, root-choked and rusty drains all gurgle and discharge their waters into the sea. I think that the rain will wake some old lady, who will wonder if she has left her copy of *Dombey and Son* in the garden. Her shawl? Did she cover the chairs? And I know that the sound of the rain will wake some lovers, and that its sound will seem to be a part of that force that has thrust them into one another's arms. Then I sit up in bed and exclaim aloud to myself, "Valor! Love! Virtue! Compassion! Splendor! Kindness! Wisdom! Beauty!" The words seem to have the colors of the earth, and as I recite them I feel my hopefulness mount until I am contented and at peace with the night.

The Ocean

⋘⚬⚬⚬⋙

    I AM KEEPING THIS JOURNAL BECAUSE I BELIEVE MYSELF to be in some danger and because I have no other way of recording my fears. I cannot report them to the police, as you will see, and I cannot confide in my friends. The losses I have recently suffered in self-esteem, reasonableness, and charity are conspicuous, but there is always some painful ambiguity about who is to blame. I might be to blame myself. Let me give you an example. Last night I sat down to dinner with Cora, my wife, at half past six. Our only daughter has left home, and we eat, these days, in the kitchen, off a table ornamented with a goldfish bowl. The meal was cold ham, salad, and potatoes. When I took a mouthful of salad I had to spit it out. "Ah yes," my wife said. "I was afraid that would happen. You left your lighter fluid in the pantry, and I mistook it for vinegar."

    As I say, who was to blame? I have always been careful about putting things in their places, and had she meant to poison me she wouldn't have done anything so clumsy as to put lighter fluid in the salad dressing. If I had not left the fluid in the pantry, the incident wouldn't have taken place. But let me go on for a minute. During dinner a thunderstorm came up. The sky got black. Suddenly there was a soaking rain. As soon as dinner was over, Cora dressed herself in a raincoat and a green shower cap and went out to water the lawn. I watched her from the window. She seemed oblivious of the ragged walls of rain in which she stood, and she watered the lawn carefully, lingering over the burnt spots. I was afraid that she would compromise herself in the eyes of our neighbors. The woman in the house next door would telephone the woman on the corner to say that Cora Fry was watering her lawn in a downpour. My wish that she not be ridiculed by gossip took me to her side, although as I approached her, under my umbrella, I realized that I lacked the tact to get through this gracefully. What should I say? Should I say that a friend was on the telephone? She has no friends. "Come in, dear," I said. "You might get struck."

"Oh, I doubt that very much," she said in her most musical voice. She speaks these days in the octave above middle C.

"Won't you wait until the rain is over?" I asked.

"It won't last long," she said sweetly. "Thunderstorms *never* do."

Under my umbrella, I returned to the house and poured myself a drink. She was right. A minute later the storm blew off, and she went on watering the grass. She had some rightness on her side in both of these incidents, but this does not change my feeling that I am in some danger.

Oh world, world, world, wondrous and bewildering, when did my troubles begin? This is being written in my house in Bullet Park. The time is 10 A.M. The day is Tuesday. You might well ask what I am doing in Bullet Park on a weekday morning. The only other men around are three clergymen, two invalids, and an old codger on Turner Street who has lost his marbles. The neighborhood has the serenity, the stillness of a terrain where all sexual tensions have been suspended—excluding mine, of course, and those of the three clergymen. What is my business? What do I do? Why didn't I catch the train? I am forty-six years old, hale, well dressed, and have a more thorough knowledge of the manufacture and merchandising of Dynaflex than any other man in the entire field. One of my difficulties is my youthful looks. I have a thirty-inch waistline and jet-black hair, and when I tell people that I used to be vice-president in charge of merchandising and executive assistant to the president of Dynaflex—when I tell this to strangers in bars and on trains— they never believe me, because I look so young.

Mr. Estabrook, the president of Dynaflex and in some ways my protector, was an enthusiastic gardener. While admiring his flowers one afternoon, he was stung by a bumblebee, and he died before they could get him to the hospital. I could have had the presidency, but I wanted to stay in merchandising and manufacture. Then the directors—including myself, of course—voted a merger with Milltonium Ltd., putting Eric Penumbra, Milltonium's chief, at the helm. I voted for the merger with some misgivings, but I concealed these and did the most important part of the groundwork for this change. It was my job to bring in the approval of conservative and reluctant stockholders, and one by one I brought them around. The fact that I had worked for Dynaflex since I had left college, that I had never worked for anyone else, inspired their trust. A few days after the merger was a fact, Penumbra called me into his office. "Well," he said, "you've had it."

"Yes, I have," I said. I thought he was complimenting me on having brought in the approvals. I had traveled all over the United States and made two trips to Europe. No one else could have done it.

"You've had it," Penumbra said harshly. "How long will it take you to get out of here?"

"I don't understand," I said.

"How the hell long will it take you to get out of here!" he shouted. "You're obsolete. We can't afford people like you in the shop. I'm asking how long it will take you to get out of here."

"It will take about an hour," I said.

"Well, I'll give you to the end of the week," he said. "If you want to send your secretary up, I'll fire her. You're really lucky. With your pension, severance pay, and the stock you own, you'll have damned near as much money as I take home, without having to lift a finger." Then he left his desk and came to where I stood. He put an arm around my shoulders. He gave me a hug. "Don't worry," Penumbra said. "Obsolescence is something we all have to face. I hope I'll be as calm about it as you when my time comes."

"I certainly hope you will," I said, and I left the office.

I went to the men's room. I locked myself up in a cubicle and wept. I wept at Penumbra's dishonesty, wept for the destinies of Dynaflex, wept for the fate of my secretary—an intelligent spinster, who writes short stories in her spare time—wept bitterly for my own naïveté, for my own lack of guile, wept that I should be overwhelmed by the plain facts of life. At the end of a half hour I dried my tears and washed my face. I took everything out of my office that was personal, took a train home, and broke the news to Cora. I was angry, of course, and she seemed frightened. She began to cry. She retired to her dressing table, which has served as a wailing wall for all the years of our marriage.

"But there's nothing to cry about," I said. "I mean we've got plenty of money. We've got loads of money. We can go to Japan. We can go to India. We can see the English cathedrals." She went on crying, and after dinner I called our daughter Flora, who lives in New York. "I'm sorry, Daddy," she said, when I told her the news. "I'm very sorry, I know how you must feel, and I'd like to see you later but not right now. Remember your promise—you promised to leave me alone."

The next character to enter the scene is my mother-in-law, whose name is Minnie. Minnie is a harsh-voiced blonde of about seventy, with four scars on the side of her face, from cosmetic surgery. You may have seen Minnie rattling around Neiman-Marcus or the lobby of practically any Grand Hotel. Minnie uses the word "fashionable" with great versatility. Of her husband's suicide in 1932 Minnie says, "Jumping out of windows was quite *fashionable*." When her only son was fired out of secondary school for improper conduct and went to live in Paris with an older man, Minnie said, "I know it's revolting, but it seems to be *terribly* fashionable." Of her own outrageous plumage she says, "It's hideously uncomfortable but it's divinely *fashionable*." Minnie is cruel and idle, and Cora, who is her only daughter, hates her. Cora has drafted her nature along lines that are the opposite of Minnie's. She is loving, serious-minded, sober, and kind. I think that in order to safeguard her virtues—her hopefulness, really—Cora has been forced to evolve a fantasy in which her mother is not Minnie at all but is instead some sage and gracious lady, working at an embroidery hoop. Everybody knows how persuasive and treacherous fantasies can be.

I spent the day after I was cashiered by Penumbra hanging around the house. With the offices of Dynaflex shut to me, I was surprised to find that I had almost no place else to go. My club is a college adjunct where they serve a cafeteria lunch, and it is not much of a sanctuary. I have always wanted to read good books, and this seemed to be my chance. I took a copy of Chaucer into the garden and read half a page, but it was hard work for a businessman. I spent the rest of the morning hoeing the lettuce, which made the gardener cross. Lunch with Cora was for some reason strained. After lunch Cora took a nap. So did the maid, I discovered, when I stepped into the kitchen to get a glass of water. She was sound asleep with her head on the table. The stillness of the house at that hour gave me a most peculiar feeling. But the world with all its diversions and entertainments was available to me, and I called New York and booked some theatre tickets for that evening. Cora doesn't much enjoy the theatre, but she came with me. After the theatre we went to the St. Regis to get some supper. When we entered the place, the band was knocking out the last number of a set—all horns up, flags flying, and the toothy drummer whacking crazily at everything he could reach. In the middle of the dance floor was Minnie, shaking her backside, stamping her feet, and popping her thumbs. She was with a broken-winded gigolo, who kept looking desperately over his shoulder, as if he expected his trainer to throw in the sponge. Minnie's plumage was exceptionally brilliant, her face seemed exceptionally haggard, and a lot of people were laughing at her. As I say, Cora seems to have invented a dignified parent, and these encounters with Minnie are cruel. We turned and went away. Cora said nothing during the long drive home.

Minnie must have been beautiful many years ago. It was from Minnie that Cora got her large eyes and her fine nose. Minnie comes to visit us two or three times a year. There is no question about the fact that if she announced her arrivals we would lock up the house and go away. Her ability to make her daughter miserable is consummate and voracious, and so, with some cunning, she makes her arrivals at our house a surprise. I spent the next afternoon trying to read Henry James in the garden. At about five I heard a car stop in front of the house. A little while later it began to rain, and I stepped into the living room and saw Minnie standing by a window. It was quite dark, but no one had bothered to turn on a light. "Why, Minnie," I exclaimed, "how *nice* to see you, what a pleasant surprise. Let me get you a drink . . ." I turned on a lamp and saw that it was Cora.

She turned on me slowly a level and eloquent look of utter misgiving. It might have been a smile had I not known that I had wounded her painfully; had I not felt from her a flow of emotion like the flow of blood from a wound. "Oh, I'm *terribly* sorry, darling," I said. "I'm terribly sorry. I couldn't see." She went out of the room. "It was the dark," I said. "It got so dark all of a sudden, when it began to rain. I'm terribly sorry, but it was just the dark and the rain." I heard her climb the dark stairs and close the door to our room.

When I saw Cora in the morning—and I didn't see her again until morning—I could tell by the pained look on her face that she thought I had wickedly pretended to mistake her for Minnie. I suppose she was as deeply and lastingly hurt as I had been hurt when Penumbra called me obsolete. It was at this point that her voice became an octave higher, and she spoke to me—when she spoke to me at all—in notes that were weary and musical, and her looks were accusing and dark. Now, I might not have noticed any of this had I been absorbed in my work and tired in the evening. To strike a healthy balance between motion and scrutiny was nearly impossible with my opportunities for motion so suddenly curtailed. I went on with my program of serious reading, but more than half my time was spent in observing Cora's sorrows and the disorganized workings of my house. A part-time maid came four times a week, and when I saw her sweeping dust under the rugs and taking cat naps in the kitchen, I got irritable. I said nothing about this, but a vexatious relationship quickly sprang up between us. It was the same with the gardener. If I sat on the terrace to read, he would cut the grass under my chair, and he took a full day, at four dollars an hour, to cut the lawns, although I knew from experience that this could be done in a much shorter time. As for Cora, I saw how empty and friendless her life was. She never went out to lunch. She never played cards. She arranged flowers, went to the hairdresser, gossiped with the maid, and rested. The smallest things began to irritate and offend me, and I was doubly offended by my unreasonable irritability. The sound of Cora's light and innocent footstep as she wandered aimlessly around the house made me cross. I was even offended at her manner of speaking. "I must *try* to arrange the flowers," she would say. "I must *try* to buy a hat. I must *try* to have my hair done. I must *try* to find a yellow pocketbook." Leaving the lunch table she would say, "Now I shall *try* to lie in the sun." But why try? The sun poured from the heavens down onto the terrace, where there was a large assortment of comfortable furniture, and a few minutes after she had stretched herself out in a long chair she was asleep. Rising from her nap she would say, "I must *try* not to get a sunburn," and entering the house she would say, "Now I am going to *try* to take a bath."

I drove down to the station one afternoon to watch the six-thirty-two come in. It was the train I used to return home on. I stopped my car in a long line of cars driven mostly by housewives. I was terribly excited. I was waiting for no one, and the women around me were merely waiting for their husbands, but it seemed to me that we were all waiting for much more. The stage, it seemed, was set. Pete and Harry, the two cab drivers, stood by their cars. With them was the Bruxtons' Airedale, who wanders. Mr. Winters, the station agent, was talking with Louisa Balcolm, the post-mistress, who lives two stops up the line. These, then, were the attendant players, the porters and gossips who would put down the groundwork for the spectacle. I kept an eye on my wristwatch. Then the train pulled in, and a moment later an eruption, a jackpot of humanity, burst through the station doors—so numerous and eager, so like sailors home from the sea, so hurried, so loving, that I laughed with pleasure. There they all were, the short and the tall, the rich and the poor, the sage and the foolish, my enemies and friends, and they all headed out the door with such a light step, so bright an eye, that I knew I must rejoin them. I would simply go back to work. This decision made me feel cheerful and magnanimous, and when I came home my

cheer seemed for a moment to be infectious. Cora spoke for
the first time in days in a voice that was full and warm, but
when I replied, she said, musically, "I was *speaking* to the
goldfish." She was indeed. The beautiful smile that she had
withheld from me was aimed at the goldfish bowl, and I
wondered if she had not left the world, its lights, cities, and
the clash of things, for this sphere of glass and its foolish
castle. Watching her bend lovingly over the goldfish bowl,
I got the distinct impression that she looked longingly into
this other world.

I went to New York in the morning and called the friend
who has always been most complimentary about my work
with Dynaflex. He told me to come to his office at around
noon—I guessed for lunch. "I want to go back to work," I
told him. "I want your help."

"Well, it isn't simple," he said. "It isn't as simple as it
might seem. To begin with, you can't expect much in the way
of sympathy. Everybody in the business knows how generous
Penumbra was to you. Most of us would be happy to change
places. I mean, there's a certain amount of natural envy.
People don't like to help a man who's in a more comfortable
position than they. And another thing is that Penumbra
wants you to stay in retirement. I don't know why this is,
but I know it's a fact, and anybody who took you on would be
in trouble with Milltonium. And, to get on with the unpleasant facts, you're just too damned old. Our president is twenty-
seven. Our biggest competitor has a chief in his early thirties.
So why don't you enjoy yourself? Why don't you take it easy?
Why don't you go around the world?" Then I asked, very
humbly, if I made an investment in his firm—say fifty thou-

sand dollars—could he find me a responsible post. He smiled broadly. It all seemed so easy. "I'll be happy to take your fifty thousand," he said lightly, "but as for finding you anything to do, I'm afraid . . ." Then his secretary came in to say that he was late for lunch.

I stood on a street corner, appearing to wait for the traffic light to change, but I was just waiting. I was staggered. What I wanted to do was to make a sandwich board on which I would list all my grievances. On it I would describe Penumbra's dishonesty, Cora's sorrow, the indignities I had suffered from the maid and gardener, and how cruelly I had been hurled out of the stream of things by a vogue for youth and inexperience. I would hang this sign from my shoulders and march up and down in front of the public library from nine until five, passing out more detailed literature to those who were interested. Throw in a snowstorm, gale winds, and the crash of thunder; I wanted it to be a spectacle.

I then stepped into a side-street restaurant to get a drink and some lunch. It was one of those places where lonely men eat seafood and read the afternoon newspapers and where, in spite of the bath of colored light and distant music, the atmosphere is distinctly contumacious. The headwaiter was a brisk character off the Corso di Roma. He duck-footed, banging down the heels of his Italian shoes, and hunched his shoulders as if his suit jacket bound. He spoke sharply to the bartender, who then whispered to a waiter, "I'll kill him! Someday I'll kill him!" "You and me," whispered the waiter, "we'll kill him together." The hat-check girl joined the whispering. She wanted to kill the manager. The conspirators scattered when the headwaiter returned, but the atmosphere remained mutinous. I drank a cocktail and ordered a salad, and then I overheard the impassioned voice of a man in the booth next to mine. I had nothing better to do than listen. "I go to Minneapolis," he said. "I have to go to Minneapolis, and as soon as I check into the hotel the telephone's ringing. She wants to tell me that the hot-water heater isn't working. There I am in Minneapolis and she's on Long Island and she calls me long distance to say that the hot-water heater isn't working. So then I ask her why doesn't she call the plumber, and then she begins to cry. She cries over long distance for about fifteen minutes, just because I suggest that she might call the plumber. Well, anyhow, in Minneapolis there's this very good jewelry store, and so I bought her a pair of earrings. Sapphires. Eight hundred dollars. I can't afford this kind of thing, but I can't afford not to buy her presents. I mean, I can make eight hundred dollars in ten minutes, but as the tax lawyer says, I don't take away more than a third of what I make, and so a pair of eight-hundred-dollar earrings costs me around two thousand. Anyway, I get the earrings, and I give them to her when I get home, and we go off to a party at the Barnstables'. When we come home, she's lost one of the earrings. She doesn't know where she lost it. She doesn't care. She won't even call the Barnstables to see if it's lying around on the floor. She doesn't want to disturb them. So then I say it's just like throwing money into the fire, and she begins to cry and says that sapphires are cold stones—that they express my inner coldness toward her. She says there wasn't any love in the present—it wasn't a loving present. All I had to do was to step into a jewelry store and buy them, she says. They didn't cost me anything in thoughtfulness and affection. So then I ask her does she expect me to make her some earrings—does she want me to go to night school and learn how to make one of those crummy silver bracelets they make? Hammered. You know. Every little hammer blow a sign of love and affection. Is that what she wants, for Christ's sake? That's another night when I slept in the guest room. . . ."

I went on eating and listening. I waited for the stranger's companion to enter into the conversation, to make some sound of sympathy or assent, but there was none, and I wondered for a moment if he wasn't talking to himself. I craned my neck around the edge of the booth, but he was too far into the corner for me to see. "She has this money of her own," he went on. "I pay the tax on it, and she spends it all on clothes. She's got hundreds and hundreds of dresses and shoes, and three fur coats, and four wigs. *Four.* But if I buy a suit she tells me I'm being wasteful. I have to buy clothes once in a while. I mean, I can't go to the office looking like a bum. If I buy anything, it's very wasteful. Last year, I bought an umbrella, just so I wouldn't get wet. Wasteful. The year before, I bought a light coat. Wasteful. I can't even buy a phonograph record, because I know I'll catch hell for being so wasteful. On my salary—imagine, on my salary, we can't afford to have bacon for breakfast excepting on Sundays. Bacon is wasteful. But you ought to see her telephone bills. She has this friend, this college roommate. I guess they were very close. She lives in Rome. I don't like her. She was married to this very nice fellow, a good friend of mine, and she just ran him into the ground. She just disposed of him. He's a wreck. Well, now she lives in Rome, and Vera keeps calling her on the telephone. Last month my telephone bills to Rome were over eight hundred dollars. So I said, 'Vera,' I said, 'if you want to talk with your girl chum so much, why don't you just get on a plane and fly to Rome? It would be a lot cheaper.' 'I don't want to go to Rome,' she said. 'I hate Rome. It's noisy and dirty.'

"But you know when I think back over my past, and her past, too, it seems to me that this is a situation with a very long taproot. My grandmother was a very emancipated woman, she was very strong on women's rights. When my mother was thirty-two years old, she went to law school and got her degree. She never practiced. She said she went to law school so she'd have more things in common with Dad, but what she actually did was to destroy, really *destroy* the little tenderness that remained between them. She was almost never at home, and when she was she was always studying for her exams. It was always 'Sh-h-h! Your mother's studying law. . . .' My father was a lonely man, but there's an awful lot of lonely men around. They won't say so, of course. Who tells the truth? You meet an old friend on the street. He looks like hell. It's frightening. His face is gray, and his hair's all falling out, and he's got the shakes. So you say, 'Charlie, Charlie, you're looking *great.*' So then he says, shaking all over, 'I never felt better in my life, *never.*' So then you go your way, and he goes his way.

"I can see that it isn't easy for Vera, but what can I do? Honest to God sometimes I'm afraid she'll hurt me—brain me with a hammer while I'm asleep. Not because it's me, but just because I'm a man. Sometimes I think women today are the most miserable creatures in the history of the world. I mean, they're right in the middle of the ocean. For instance, I caught her smooching with Pete Barnstable in the pantry. That was the night she lost the earring, the night when I came back from Minneapolis. So then when I got home, before I noticed the earring was gone, I said what is this, what is this

smooching around with Pete Barnstable? So then she said—
very emancipated—that no woman could be expected to limit
herself to the attentions of one man. So then I said what about
me, did that work for me, too? I mean, if she could smooch
around with Pete Barnstable, didn't it follow that I could take
Mildred Renny out to the parking lot? So then she said I was
turning everything she said into filth. She said I had such a
dirty mind she couldn't talk with me. After that I noticed
she'd lost the earring, and after that we had the scene about
how sapphires are such cold stones, and after that . . ."

His voice dropped to a whisper, and at the same time some
women in the booth on the other side of me began a noisy
and savage attack on a friend they all shared. I was very
anxious to see the face of the man behind me, and I called for
the check, but when I left the booth he was gone, and I would
never know what he looked like.

When I got home, I put the car in the garage and came
into the house by the kitchen door. Cora was at the table,
bending over a dish of cutlets. In one hand she held a can
of lethal pesticide. I couldn't be sure because I'm so near-
sighted, but I think she was sprinkling pesticide on the meat.
She was startled when I came in, and by the time I had my
glasses on she had put the pesticide on the table. Since I had
already made one bad mistake because of my eyesight, I was
reluctant to make another, but there was the pesticide on the
table beside the dish, and that was not where it belonged. It
contained a high percentage of nerve poison. "What in the
world are you doing?" I asked.

"What does it look as if I were doing?" she asked, still
speaking in the octave above middle C.

"It looks as if you were putting pesticide in the cutlets," I said.

"I know you don't grant me much intelligence," she said, "but please grant me enough intelligence to know better than that."

"But what are you doing with the pesticide?" I asked.

"I have been dusting the roses," she said.

I was routed, in a way, routed and frightened. I guessed that meat heavily dosed with pesticide could be fatal. There was a chance that if I ate the cutlets I might die. The extraordinary fact seemed to be that after twenty years of marriage I didn't know Cora well enough to know whether or not she intended to murder me. I would trust a chance delivery man or a cleaning woman, but I did not trust Cora. The prevailing winds seemed not to have blown the smoke of battle off our union. I mixed a Martini and went into the living room. I was not in any danger from which I could not readily escape. I could go to the country club for supper. Why I hesitated to do this seems, in retrospect, to have been because of the blue walls of the room in which I stood. It was a handsome room, its long windows looking out onto a lawn, some trees, and the sky. The orderliness of the room seemed to impose some orderliness on my own conduct—as if by absenting myself from the table I would in some way offend the order of things. If I went to the club for supper I would be yielding to my suspicions and damaging my hopefulness, and I was determined to remain hopeful. The blue walls of the room seemed to be some link in the chain of being that I would offend by driving up to the club and eating an open steak sandwich alone in the bar.

I ate one of the cutlets at dinner. It had a peculiar taste, but by this time I couldn't distinguish between my anxieties and the facts involved. I was terribly sick in the night, but this could have been my imagination. I spent an hour in the bathroom with acute indigestion. Cora seemed to be asleep, but when I returned from the bathroom I did notice that her eyes were open. I was worried, and in the morning I made my own breakfast. The maid cooked lunch, and I doubted that she would poison me. I read some more Henry James in the garden, but as the time for dinner approached I found that I was frightened. I went into the pantry to make a drink. Cora had been preparing dinner, and had gone to some other part of the house. There is a broom closet in the kitchen, and I stepped into it and shut the door. Presently I heard Cora's footsteps as she returned. We keep the pesticides for the roses in a cabinet in the kitchen. I heard her open this cabinet. Then she stepped out into the garden, where I heard her dusting the roses. She then returned to the kitchen, but she did not return the pesticide to the closet. My field of vision through the keyhole was limited. Her back was to me as she spiced the meat, and I couldn't tell if she was using salt and pepper or nerve poison. She then went back to the garden, and I stepped out of the broom closet. The pesticide was not on the table. I went into the living room, and entered the dining room from there when dinner was ready. "Isn't it hot," I asked when I sat down.

"Well," said Cora, "we can't expect to be comfortable, can we, if we hide in broom closets?"

I hung onto my chair, picked at my food, made some small talk, and got through the meal. Now and then she gave me a serene and wicked smile. After dinner I went into the garden. I desperately needed help, and thought then of my daughter. I should explain that Flora graduated from the Villa Mimosa in Florence, and left Smith College in the middle of her freshman year to live in a lower East Side tenement with a sexual freak. I send her an allowance each month and have promised to leave her alone, but, considering the dangerousness of my position, I felt free to break my promise. I felt that if I could see her I could persuade her to come home. I telephoned her then and said that I must see her. She seemed quite friendly and asked me to come to tea.

I had lunch in town the next day, and spent the afternoon at my club, playing cards and drinking whiskey. Flora had given me directions, and I went downtown on the subway for the first time in I don't know how many years. It was all very strange. I've often thought of going to visit my only daughter and her own true love, and now at last I was making this journey. In my reveries the meeting would take place in some club. He would come from a good family. Flora would be happy; she would have the shining face of a young girl first in love. The boy would be serious, but not too serious; intelligent, handsome, and with the winning posture of someone who stands literally at the threshold of a career. I could see the fatuity in these reveries, but had they been so vulgar and idle that I deserved to have them contravened at every point—the scene changed from a club to the city's worst slum and the substitution of a freak with a beard for an earnest young man? I had friends whose daughters married suitable young men from suitable families. Envy struck me in the crowded subway, then petulance. Why had I been singled out for this disaster? I loved my daughter. The power of love I felt for her seemed pure, strong, and natural. Suddenly I felt like crying. Every sort of door had been open for her, she had seen the finest landscapes, she had enjoyed, I thought, the company of those people who were most free to develop their gifts.

It was raining when I left the subway. I followed her directions through a slum to a tenement. I guessed the building to be about eighty years old. Two polished marble columns supported a Romanesque arch. It even had a name. It was called The Eden. I saw the angel with the flaming sword, the naked couple, stooped, their hands over their privates. Masaccio? That was when we went to visit her in Florence. So I entered Eden like an avenging angel, but once under the Romanesque arch I found a corridor as narrow as the companionway in a submarine, and the power of light over my spirits—always considerable—was in this case very depressing, the lights in the hall were so primitive and sorry. Flights of stairs often appear in my dreams, and the stairs I began to climb had a galling look of unreality. I heard Spanish spoken, the roar of water from a toilet, music, and the barking of dogs.

Moved by anger, or perhaps by the drinks I had had at the club, I went up three or four flights at a brisk clip and then found myself suddenly winded; forced to stop short in my climb and engage in a humiliating struggle for breath. It was several minutes before I could continue, and I went the rest of the way slowly. Flora had tacked one of her calling cards to the door. I knocked. "Hi, Daddy," she said brightly, and I kissed her on the brow. Oh, this much of it was good, fresh, and strong. I felt a burst of memory, a recollection of all the happiness we had shared. The door opened onto a kitchen and beyond this was another room. "I want you to meet Peter," she said.

"Hi," said Peter.

"How do you do," I said.

"See what we've made," said Flora. "Isn't it divine? We've just finished it. It was Peter's idea."

What they had made, what they had done was to purchase a skeleton with an armature from a medical supply house and glue butterflies here and there to the polished bone. I recognized some of the specimens from my youth and recognized that I would not at that time have been able to afford them. There was a Catagramme Astarte on the shoulder bone, a Sapphira in one eye socket, and a large cluster of Appia Zarinda at the pubis. "Marvelous," I said, "marvelous," trying to conceal my distaste. Compared to the useful tasks of life, the thought of these two grown people gluing expensive butterflies to the polished bones of some poor stranger made me intensely irritable. I sat in a canvas chair and smiled at Flora. "How are you, my dear?"

"Oh, I'm fine, Daddy," she said. "I'm *fine*."

I kept myself from remarking on either her clothing or her hair. She was dressed all in black, and her hair was straight. The purpose of this costume or uniform escaped me. It was not becoming. It did not appeal to the senses. It seemed to reflect on her self-esteem; it seemed like a costume of mourning or penance, a declaration of her indifference to the silks that I enjoy on women; but what were her reasons for despising finery? His costume was much more bewildering. Was its origin Italian, I wondered. The shoes were effeminate, and the jacket was short, but he looked more like a street boy in nineteenth-century London than someone on the Corso. That would be excepting his hair. He had a beard, a mustache, and long dark curls that reminded me of some minor apostle in a third-rate passion play. His face was not effeminate, but it was delicate, and seemed to me to convey a marked lack of commitment.

"Would you like some coffee, Daddy?" Flora asked.

"No, thank you, dear," I said. "Is there anything to drink?"

"We don't have anything," she said.

"Would Peter be good enough to go out and get me something?" I asked.

"I guess so," Peter said glumly, and I told myself that he was probably not intentionally rude. I gave him a ten-dollar bill and asked him to get me some bourbon.

"I don't think they have bourbon," he said.

"Well, then, Scotch," I said.

"They drink mostly wine in the neighborhood," Peter said.

Then I settled on him a clear, kindly gaze, thinking that I would have him murdered. From what I know of the world there are still assassins to be hired, and I would pay someone to put a knife in his back or push him off a roof. My smile was broad, clear, and genuinely murderous, and the boy slipped into a green coat—another piece of mummery—and went out.

"You don't like him?" Flora asked.

"I despise him," I said.

"But Daddy, you don't *know* him," Flora said.

"My dear, if I knew him any better I would wring his neck."

"He's very kind and sensitive—he's very generous."

"I can see that he's very sensitive," I said.

"He's the kindest person I've ever known," Flora said.

"I'm glad to hear that," I said, "but let's talk about you now, shall we? I didn't come here to talk about Peter."

"But we're living together, Daddy."

"So I've been told. But the reason I came here, Flora, is to find out about you—what your plans are and so forth. I won't disapprove of your plans, whatever they are. I simply want to know what they are. You can't spend the rest of your life gluing butterflies to skeletons. All I want to know is what you plan to do with your life."

"I don't know, Daddy." She raised her face. "Nobody my age knows."

"I'm not taking a consensus of your generation. I am asking you. I am asking you what you would like to make of your life. I am asking you what ideas you have, what dreams you have, what hopes you have for yourself."

"I don't know, Daddy. Nobody my age knows."

"I wish you would eliminate the rest of your generation. I am acquainted with at least fifty girls your age who know precisely what they want to do. They want to be historians, editors, doctors, housewives, and mothers. They want to do something useful."

Peter came back with a bottle of bourbon but he did not return any change. Was this cupidity, I wondered, or absent-mindedness. I said nothing. Flora brought me a glass and some water, and I asked if they would join me in a drink.

"We don't drink much," Peter said.

"Well, I'm glad to hear that," I said. "While you were out, I talked with Flora about her plans. That is, I discovered that she doesn't have any plans, and since she doesn't I'm going to take her back to Bullet Park with me until her thinking is a little more decisive."

"I'm going to stay with Peter," Flora said.

"But supposing Peter had to go away?" I asked. "Suppose

Peter had some interesting offer, such as six months or a year abroad—what would you do then?"

"Oh, Daddy," she asked, "you wouldn't do that, would you?"

"Oh yes I would, I most certainly would," I said. "I would do anything on heaven or earth that I thought might bring you to your senses. Would you like to go abroad, Peter?"

"I don't know," he said. His face could not be said to have brightened, but for a moment his intelligence seemed engaged. "I'd like to go to East Berlin," he said.

"Why?"

"I'd like to go to East Berlin and give my American passport to some great creative person," he said, "some writer or musician, and let him escape to the free world."

"Why," I asked, "don't you paint Peace on your arse and jump off a twelve-story building?"

This was a mistake, a disaster, a catastrophe, and I poured myself some more bourbon. "I'm sorry," I said. "I'm tired. However, my offer still stands. If you want to go to Europe, Peter, I'll be happy to pay your bills."

"Oh, I don't know," Peter said. "I've been. I mean, I've seen most of it."

"Well, keep it in mind," I said. "And as for you, Flora, I want you to come home with me. Come home for a week or two, anyhow. That's all I ask. Ten years from now you will reproach me for not having guided you out of this mess. Ten years from now you'll ask me, 'Daddy, Daddy, oh Daddy, why didn't you teach me not to spend the best years of my life in a slum?' I can't bear the thought of you coming to me ten years from now, to blame me for not having forced you to take my advice."

"I won't go home."

"You can't stay here."

"I can if I want."

"I will stop your allowance."

"I can get a job."

"What kind of a job? You can't type, you can't take short-hand, you don't know the first thing about any sort of business procedure, you can't even run a switchboard."

"I can get a job as a filing clerk."

"Oh my God!" I roared. "Oh my God! After the sailing lessons and the skiing lessons, after the get-togethers and the cotillion, after the year in Florence and the long summers at the sea—after all this it turns out that what you really want is to be a spinster filing clerk with a low civil-service rating, whose principal excitement is to go once or twice a year to a fourth-rate Chinese restaurant with a dozen other spinster filing clerks and get tipsy on two sweet Manhattans."

I fell back into my chair and poured myself some more whiskey. There was a sharp pain in my heart, as if that lumpy organ had weathered every abuse, only to be crippled by misery. The pain was piercing, and I thought I would die— not at that moment, in the canvas chair, but a few days later, perhaps in Bullet Park, or in some comfortable hospital bed. The idea did not alarm me; it was a consolation. I would die, and with those areas of tension that I represented finally removed, my only, only daughter would at last take up her life. My sudden disappearance from the scene would sober her with sorrow and misgiving. My death would mature her. She would go back to Smith, join the glee club, edit the news-paper, befriend girls of her own class, and marry some in-telligent and visionary young man, who seemed, at the moment, to be wearing spectacles, and raise three or four sturdy children. She would be sorry. That was it, and overnight sorrow would show her the inutility of living in a slum with a stray.

"Go home, Daddy," she said. She was crying. "Go home, Daddy, and leave us alone! Please go home, Daddy!"

"I've always tried to understand you," I said. "You used to put four or five records on the player at Bullet Park, and as soon as the music began you'd walk out of the house. I never understood why you did this, but one night I went out of the house to see if I could find you, and, walking down the lawn, with the music coming from all the open windows, I thought I did understand. I mean, I thought you put the records on and left the house because you liked to hear the music pouring out of the windows. I mean, I thought you liked at the end of your walk to come back to a house where music was playing. I was right, wasn't I? I understand that much?"

"Go home, Daddy," she said. "Please go home."

"And it isn't only you, Flora," I said. "I need you. I need you terribly."

"Go home, Daddy," she said, and so I did.

I had some supper in town and came home at around ten. I could hear Cora drawing a bath upstairs, and I took a shower in the bathroom off the kitchen. When I went upstairs, Cora was sitting at her dressing table, brushing her hair. Now, I have neglected to say that Cora is beautiful, and that I love her. She has ash-blond hair, dark brows, full lips, and eyes that are so astonishingly large, volatile, and engaging, so strikingly set, that I sometimes think she might take them off and put them between the pages of a book; leave them on a table. The white is a light blue and the blue itself is of unusual depth. She is a graceful woman, not tall. She smokes continuously and has for most of her life, but she handles her cigarettes with a charming clumsiness, as if this entrenched habit were something she had just picked up. Her arms, legs, front, everything is beautifully proportioned. I love her, and, loving her, I know that love is not a reasonable process. I had not expected or wanted to fall in love when I first saw her at a wedding in the country. Cora was one of the attendants. The wedding was in a garden. A five-piece orchestra in tuxedos was half-hidden in the rhododendrons. From the tent on the hill you could hear the caterer's men icing wine in wash buckets. She was the second to come, and was wearing one of those outlandish costumes that are designed for bridal parties, as if holy matrimony had staked out some unique and mysterious place for itself in sumptuary history. Her dress was blue, as I remember, with things hanging off it, and she wore over her pale hair a broad-brimmed hat that had no crown at all. She wobbled over the lawn in her high-heeled shoes, staring shyly and miserably into a bunch of blue flowers, and when she had reached her position she raised her face and smiled shyly at the guests, and I saw for the first time the complexity and enormousness of her eyes; felt for the first time that she might take them off and put them into a pocket. "Who is she?" I asked aloud. "Who *is* she?" "Sh-h-h," someone said. I was enthralled. My heart and my spirit leaped. I saw absolutely nothing of the rest of the wedding, and when the ceremony was over I raced up the lawn and introduced myself to her. I was not content with anything until she agreed to marry me, a year later.

Now my heart and my spirit leaped as I watched her comb

her hair. A few days ago I had thought that she had retreated into the water of a goldfish bowl. I had suspected her of attempted murder. How could I embrace decently and with the full ardor of my body and mind someone I suspected of murder? Was I embracing despair, was this an obscene passion, had I at that wedding so many years ago seen not beauty at all, but cruelty in her large eyes? I had made her, in my imagination, a goldfish, a murderess, and now when I took her in my arms she was a swan, a flight of stairs, a fountain, the unpatroled, unguarded boundaries to paradise.

But I awoke at three, feeling terribly sad, and feeling rebelliously that I didn't want to study sadness, madness, melancholy, and despair. I wanted to study triumphs, the rediscoveries of love, all that I know in the world to be decent, radiant, and clear. Then the word "love," the impulse to love, welled up in me somewhere above my middle. Love seemed to flow from me in all directions, abundant as water —love for Cora, love for Flora, love for all my friends and neighbors, love for Penumbra. This tremendous flow of vitality could not be contained within its spelling, and I seemed to seize a laundry marker and write "luve" on the wall. I wrote "luve" on the staircase, "luve" on the pantry, "luve" on the oven, the washing machine, and the coffeepot, and when Cora came down in the morning (I would be nowhere around) everywhere she looked she would read "luve," "luve," "luve." Then I saw a green meadow and a sparkling stream. On the ridge there were thatched-roof cottages and a square church tower, so I knew it must be England. I climbed up from the meadow to the streets of the village, looking for the cottage where Cora and Flora would be waiting for me. There seemed to have been some mistake. No one knew their names. I asked at the post office, but the answer here was the same. Then it occurred to me that they would be at the manor house. How stupid I had been! I left the village and walked up a sloping lawn to a Georgian house, where a butler let me in. The squire was entertaining. There were twenty-five or thirty people in the hall, drinking sherry. I took a glass from a tray and looked through the gathering for Flora and my wife, but they were not there. Then I thanked my host and walked down the broad lawn, back to the meadow and the sparkling brook, where I lay on the grass and fell into a sweet sleep.

ABOUT THE AUTHOR

John Cheever was born on the south shore of Boston in 1912, the son of a Massachusetts Yankee and an English emigrant. He received his only formal education at Thayer Academy in South Braintree. His first short story was published when he was sixteen. Since then, he has written over a hundred, most of which have appeared in *The New Yorker;* many of them have won important awards.

Mr. Cheever has published four collections of short stories and two novels prior to the present volume. His first novel, *The Wapshot Chronicle,* received the National Book Award in 1958. His most recent novel, *The Wapshot Scandal,* published early in 1964, was an immediate critical success and became one of the biggest fiction bestsellers of the year.